C0-AVI-784

THE

CHOSEN

FEW

THE
CHOSEN
FEW

Joseph DiLalla
Roy Eaton

A Novel

Tate Publishing *& Enterprises*

The Chosen Few
Copyright © 2008 by Joseph DiLalla and Roy Eaton. All rights reserved.

This title is also available as a Tate Out Loud product. Visit www.tatepublishing.com for more information.

No part of this publication may be reproduced, stored in a retrieval system or transmitted in any way by any means, electronic, mechanical, photocopy, recording or otherwise without the prior permission of the author except as provided by USA copyright law.

This novel is a work of fiction. However, several names, descriptions, entities and incidents included in the story are based on the lives of real people and the existence of real products.

The opinions expressed by the author are not necessarily those of Tate Publishing, LLC.

Published by Tate Publishing & Enterprises, LLC
127 E. Trade Center Terrace | Mustang, Oklahoma 73064 USA
1.888.361.9473 | www.tatepublishing.com

Tate Publishing is committed to excellence in the publishing industry. The company reflects the philosophy established by the founders, based on Psalm 68:11,
"The Lord gave the word and great was the company of those who published it."

Book design copyright © 2008 by Tate Publishing, LLC. All rights reserved.
Cover & interior design by Lynly D. Taylor

Published in the United States of America

ISBN: 978–1–60462–803–6
1. Fiction: Medical   2. Fiction: Suspense

08.07.07

ACKNOWLEDGEMENTS

To Beverly Ann Shipe: thank you for taking time to proof-read and edit our work. Your efforts on our behalf were superb and are truly appreciated.

To David Farrar: thank you for proofreading and editing our work. Your efforts were invaluable and greatly appreciated.

To Julia Wisbach: your contribution in chapter two was worthy and most appreciated.

To JD Byrum, our editor: Thank you for your expertise and patience.

To Lynly Taylor: Thank you for your great cover design and layout. Your efforts on our behalf are greatly appreciated.

DEDICATION

To the millions who have died of cardiovascular
disease and to the millions more who
suffer from this insidious malady.

PREFACE

According to the Centers for Disease Control and Prevention (CDC), nearly one million people die of cardiovascular disease (heart attack or stroke) every year in the United States alone. That is one occurrence every thirty-five seconds.

The CDC estimates that seventy million Americans suffer from the disease, accounting for six million hospitalizations annually.

What if this were avoidable? What if there existed a medication capable of preventing and curing cardiovascular disease, eradicating the disease from the planet?

What social and financial impact would such a wonder drug have on our society? Surely, the financial burden of that number of people being added to the roles of Social Security and Medicare would be tremendous. It would create a budgetary crisis for not only the United States Federal

Government, but indeed, for governments throughout the world.

The impact in the private sector would be no less severe. Cardiac clinics that treat the disease as well as the hospitals that rely on coronary by-pass surgery to remain solvent would suffer, likely resulting in the bankruptcy of many of these institutions.

Pharmaceutical companies, who rely heavily on the profit generated from their cholesterol-lowering statin drugs, would see that revenue disappear, thus causing a sharp drop in their earnings, and in the value of their stock.

Given these factors, would the United States Government and the medical and pharmaceutical industries want this cure brought to market? Or, would corporate greed and governmental pragmatism trump the good of mankind?

H E knew he wasn't a paranoiac, but recent events had caused him to become either paranoid or justly afraid. He could swear the car in his rearview mirror was the same one that followed him to his house in Waterford over the past weekend. It looked the same, a late model non-descript black sedan with tinted windows. When he had pulled into his driveway, the car had driven slowly past his house before speeding up. He remembered thinking it peculiar, and somewhat unnerving, but quickly dismissed the thought. Now, it was back... or was it? He thought he noticed it as he was driving to the hotel after work. How long it had been behind him, he didn't know. He chided himself for his silly suspicions, but the car did appear to be following him. He decided to find out one way or another. He stepped on the gas and pulled away. He watched as the car slowly, but deliberately, closed the gap between them. Next, he slammed on his brakes and made a quick right turn at the next intersection. He looked in his rearview mirror and saw the car go through the intersection. He sighed with relief and then laughed at himself. His fear returned when he glanced in his mirror again and saw the vehicle backing up to make a turn in his direction. Again, he floored it and then slowed enough to fishtail around a corner. He headed to the interstate and flew up the ramp. He sped past and around the light traffic, hoping a cop would pull him over. *Where's a cop when I really need one?* His eyes darted back and forth from the windshield to the rearview mirror. There was no sign of the car. This time he wouldn't relax until he was sure. When he was satisfied he wasn't being tailed, he made his way back to the hotel. Before entering the building, he scanned the parking lot.

He heard the phone ringing as he unlocked the door to his room. He hurried to the phone, but was not in time. He checked to see if the caller had left a message, but found none. He scanned the parking lot one more time before drawing the drapes.

They're on to me. Are they trying to intimidate me? He wondered how far they would go. He knew what he did would eventually draw attention, but he had no other choice. The stakes were too high.

Just then the phone rang a second time. "Hello," he said tentatively.

"You know stealing is a crime. Return what you took and nothing will happen," said the foreboding male voice. "If you don't—" There was a click; then a dial tone.

The call unnerved him. The caller didn't actually

threaten him, but the implication was clear: give it back or else. *What should I do?* He couldn't go to the police because he *had* stolen it, and at this point he didn't know whom to trust. But, he had to take it. Freiz had to be exposed for their endless, avaricious quest for ever-increasing power and wealth. If ever there was a time to put the good of the people ahead of monetary profit, it was now. Pure, unfettered capitalism was just as tyrannical as totalitarianism. No, he had no choice; no matter what the consequences.

CHAPTER ONE

B RETT Bitterman, the Chairman and CEO of Freiz Pharmaceuticals, had just returned from a board of directors meeting. He was going through his messages when one jumped out at him. It was from Seymour Ernst, a research scientist for Expharmica Inc., a competitor of Freiz.

Several years ago when Ernst was passed over for a promotion he felt was rightly his, he had approached Freiz looking for a job. After interviewing him, Bitterman had decided to make him an offer he couldn't refuse and one the disgruntled employee readily accepted. He would stay at Expharmica in his current position, but also work for Freiz as an industrial spy. His charge was to supply Freiz with information on all research and development projects at Expharmica. However, his services had proven to be of little value.

Ernst's contact was Max Trammel, the department head of Security at Freiz, and the only other person who knew of the arrangement with Ernst. Bitterman wondered why Ernst had come to him instead of Trammel. When he instructed his secretary to put out a call for Trammel, he was told that he was home with the flu and wouldn't return until the following Monday. That explained why Ernst didn't go to Trammel, but what was so important that he couldn't wait for his return?

Bitterman told his secretary to hold his calls before sequestering himself in the privacy of his inner office where he then dialed Ernst's cell from his own.

"I received your message. I trust you needed to contact me directly because what you have is of significant importance."

"It is not only significant, it is vital. When can we meet?"

"How soon can you get here?"

"I can be there by one o'clock tomorrow afternoon."

"Very well then, I know the spot," he said referring to the College Diner in New London. After hanging up, Bitterman cleared his calendar for the following afternoon.

Bitterman sat in the rear of the diner, at a wooden booth whose plushly padded high back was covered in red leather held together by a border of decorative brass upholstery tacks. This location seemed to provide the most privacy. The diner, which had a large rectangular bar adjacent to a dozen or so tables in its center and a half dozen booths on either side, was much larger than most because it catered to the locals as well as the Coast Guard cadets and Connecticut College students who were within walking distance. The clock read 1:20 p.m. Ernst was twenty minutes late and Bitterman was getting annoyed. He was the CEO of the largest pharmaceutical company on the planet, and here he sat waiting in a diner for a second-rate scientist from a third-rate drug company. He would wait until one-thirty and no longer; his time was too valuable.

Bitterman was about to leave when he spotted Ernst standing at the entrance with a briefcase dangling from one arm. He was panning the diner looking for Bitterman. A wave from Bitterman caught his attention. Ernst slid into the booth opposite his employer and laid the briefcase next to him.

Ernst apologized for being late, blaming it on a traffic tie-up on I-95. After ordering coffee, Bitterman said curtly, "What do you have for me?"

Ernst wasn't put off by the cold welcome; after all, he knew his place. He was nothing more than a mercenary, a hired gun.

"Expharmica has made a startling discovery, one that could ultimately have a serious, negative impact on Freiz. The push is on at Expharmica. They are investing a vast amount of resources into this project, and have substantially increased their research staff who are working on it twenty-four-seven. Time is of the essence, and that is why I felt compelled to contact you directly."

"I understand, please go on."

"A research team from Expharmica stumbled upon an

anomaly in a small mountain village in Sicily. They were there researching the Mediterranean Diet and its effects on the cardiovascular system. A study of one family turned conventional wisdom upside down. The family's history showed no cases of cardiovascular disease as far back as the late seventeenth century. That in itself is not so unusual, but here's the kicker: all those tested had very high levels of cholesterol, but no incidents of cardiovascular disease even though their diets were relatively high in saturated fats. The researchers were further baffled when they found their subjects' HDL levels low and their LDL levels quite high. They were totally perplexed. How could a group of people with such bad cholesterol numbers be so healthy?"

"Good question. Go on, I'm interested in the answer myself."

"The team discovered that even though the family had low levels of the good cholesterol, the high density lipoproteins that they did have worked very efficiently in keeping their arteries clean."

Bitterman immediately understood the ramifications for Freiz Pharmaceuticals. Ernst continued, "After they isolated the gene that causes the anomaly, they bought the rights to it from the family involved. Last month they successfully synthesized the gene. Currently, it must be administered by injection because the gene is destroyed by the digestive process. However, they're working toward a formula that would allow ingestion. Preliminary test results have shown a significant lessening of occlusion, ten times that of anything currently available. This therapy doesn't simply stop further plaque build-up, it reverses it. This super gene could be a cure, not just another treatment, a 'magic bullet,' so to speak."

Bitterman's face took on a look of deep concern as he pondered what he had just heard. "Do you have any documentation to substantiate your claim?" asked the skeptical executive. Ernst reached for his briefcase. He opened it and pulled out a manila envelope and handed it to Bitterman.

"It's all there: the history, the pharmacology, and the test results. You should know that I took great risks in obtaining these documents."

"Yes, I'm sure you did, and you've been compensated handsomely throughout our association," he said as he stowed the pilfered documents in his own briefcase. He thanked Ernst, but didn't offer him his hand as he left him sitting alone in the booth staring across the table at a cold untouched cup of black coffee.

As soon as Bitterman returned to his office, he summoned Andrew Dixon, Freiz's chief financial officer, to his office. After briefing him on what he learned from Ernst, he sat back in his chair and said, "Andy, I want you to evaluate Expharmica's financials. I intend to present a plan to purchase Expharmica at our next board meeting. After they hear what you've heard here today, I'm confident of their approval. We will then move quickly with an offer to purchase Expharmica. If they refuse to be acquired, I intend to go directly to the stockholders with an offer. One way or another, Freiz is going to own Expharmica. When can you get back to me with the numbers?"

"I'll have my people get right on it. I should be able to have it together by tomorrow afternoon."

A meeting was set up at Freiz corporate headquarters among Bitterman, Dixon, and the heads of other leading pharmaceutical companies including Theodore Allen, the CEO of Expharmica. The reason given for the meeting was to develop a strategy with which to approach the Food and Drug Administration with the intention of shortening the time between the discovery of a new drug and its final approval.

When Theodore Allen walked into Bitterman's office and saw only Andrew Dixon at the table, he knew there was more on the agenda than the FDA and their mutual concern of bringing new drugs to market sooner.

Bitterman opened the meeting by briefly discussing the issue with the FDA. Allen took a sip of coffee, then said, "Now Brett, let's get to the real reason for the meeting." Bitterman smiled as he looked at Dixon. "There's no fooling Ted Allen," he said patronizingly. Then, he turned serious.

"Look Ted, Andrew has evaluated your financials and it's obvious that Expharmica is in some trouble. After studying the situation, we are prepared to tender a mutually beneficial offer for the purchase of Expharmica."

"Brett, what makes you believe we are for sale? We've not put out any feelers of any kind to indicate that we are looking for a suitor, and why would you be interested in a company with such weak financials?" Allen knew the answer to his own question; someone on the inside had leaked the discovery of the Sicilia Gene. "I'm sorry, Brett, Expharmica is not for sale."

"Ted, let me be frank with you. Freiz is going to purchase Expharmica with or without your cooperation. We are prepared to go directly to the shareholders if necessary."

"I will fight you all the way," he said with determination.

"And you will lose," said Bitterman. "A public fight in which the outcome is assured would be foolhardy on your part and counterproductive for all of us. Ted, Expharmica is a small fish in a big pond. You're a smart man. You know you can't match our resources." Allen sat speechless. He had been blindsided. He knew everything Bitterman had said was true, and he also knew his options were few.

Bitterman continued, "Let Andrew show you our tentative proposal, which, I might add, contains a generous compensation package for you and your executive officers." Dixon handed Allen a folder containing the offer. "You may take the proposal with you to share with your fellow officers and board of directors. However, before you leave, I would like you to review the section on your compensation package." Allen still hadn't responded to Bitterman's comments, but did as he was asked. Bitterman and Dixon sat in silence while Allen read. At one point they observed him raising his eyebrows. They looked at each other and thinly smiled.

When he was finished, Allen closed the folder and stood. "I'll take this back for review and consideration."

While shaking hands, Bitterman said, "The compensation package is flexible; everything in it is negotiable. We would appreciate a response within two weeks."

"I'll get back to you," Allen said dryly.

After Allen left, Dixon turned to Bitterman. "What's your take?"

"He may come back for more money, but I think it's going to happen."

"Come back for more money?" said an astonished Dixon. "Twenty million dollars in cash and stock is a lot of dough. You think he'll have the balls to ask for more?"

"I would," replied Bitterman. "He's no fool. He knows what's at stake here. He'll be back."

As predicted, Allen did return a few days later for more money, and after tweaking his compensation package, he signed on the dotted line. A formal signing ceremony was arranged and a joint press release was issued, stating that this purchase will prove to be in the best interest of the public they serve.

It took the better part of six months before all of the regulatory agencies would sign off on the buyout.

Bitterman's first official act following the completion of the deal was to shelve the Sicilia Gene Project, thereby protecting Freiz's dominant market share of the statin drug Torvistat. His second act was to summon Max Trammel to his office. "Max, it appears that our association with Seymour Ernst has outlived its usefulness. I want you to take care of him. Do it today. He'll be at the College Diner at one o'clock to pick up the bonus I promised him. Loyalty from one's employees is essential, especially in an industry like ours. It's clear, based on his history, that he cannot be trusted. There is no room for a disloyal employee at Freiz."

Two days later Seymour Ernst's lifeless body was found on the side of the residential street on which he lived, an apparent victim of a hit-and-run accident.

CHAPTER TWO

WHEN the phone rang the first time, David Roy was dreaming about running. He was running—not from or toward anything—just running. He ran long, and slow, and easy, like he had as a boy during the summers on his grandfather's farm. Running, his awareness filled only by the steady push and pull of his own breathing. He was running like a young gazelle across the golden fields of sun-kissed wheat, with the summer wind warm and full against his face.

David was running like he had as a boy, but in the dream he was no longer a child. He knew this because when he looked down, the hands that pumped back and forth at his sides were broad and thick; the backs scarred and faintly lined by the years. He could feel his age in the sturdy weight of his body, and by the way his feet pressed firmly and deliberately into the ground with each stride. This was his adult body, and yet, surprisingly, he did not feel old. Gone was the clinging tightness in his chest. Gone was the heaviness of his limbs. Gone was the fatigue. The pain and weakness he had learned to expect seemed to have faded, miraculously replaced by the easy strength of his youth. In the dream, David leapt high into the air and began to laugh.

When the phone rang again, he was just reaching the northern edge of his grandfather's farm, which was thick with firs, pines, and oaks. As a child, he had spent hours and hours running along this forest's perimeter, though he had never dared to venture inside its shadows. Instead, the forest had been a source of endless mystery, filling his imagination with its grandeur and its secrets. Barely awake, he reached for the phone that had accidentally fallen from the night stand onto the floor just below his pillow.

"David? David Roy?" The voice on the other end of the phone sounded excited, and vaguely familiar.

In the darkness of his room, David pulled himself up onto one elbow and grimaced. The dream, and the feelings of health and exhilaration that had come with it, quickly slipped away. "Yeah," he said, forcing the word past the thickness in his throat. "Who is this?"

"I'll be damned!" the voice said, and then laughed. "It's really you."

"Apparently," David said, sleepily. He rubbed his eyes and squinted at the green digits on his nightstand clock; it read one-thirty. He sighed and said, "Who is this?"

"It's me, Mikey Fitz. Mikey Fitzgerald, from New London."

The haze of sleep was gradually lifting, and David's

mind abruptly seized on the image of an energetic, freckle-faced boy with a fiery red cowlick. It was an old memory. One buried deep in the recesses of his consciousness, layered over with years and years of living.

"Well, I'll be damned," David said, echoing the other man's surprise. "Mikey Fitzgerald ... Mikey Fitz." He drew the name out, announcing it as though it were a title of a song that he had suddenly remembered after years of trying. "Mikey Fitz," he said again, this time with a smile on his face.

The two of them had been best friends for thirteen years, back when they were both growing up in identical, white clapboard houses on Beech Rose Avenue. *Inseparable*, their mothers called them.

And for thirteen years, they were. For thirteen years they had played, and fought, and schemed together. They had learned to crawl together, and to walk, and later, to swim, fish and to sail. They had been the proud builders of the most enviable fort in the neighborhood—a two-story tree house that had taken one and a half summers to build. *Two peas in a pod*, their mothers called them.

And then one morning, Mikey's father walked out of the Fitzgerald's front door and never came back. Just got into his car and drove off. David still remembered that day, and the day two weeks later, when Mrs. Fitzgerald piled herself and her three young children into a taxi and went down to New York to live with her mother.

"It's been what, twenty-five years?" David said, finally.

"Twenty-eight," Mikey Fitzgerald said. "But who's counting."

David remembered that they had tried to keep in touch by mail and the occasional phone call. But the months and the years, along with the miles, had gotten between them. By the time high school started, David knew no more about Mike Fitzgerald than the occasional rumors around town.

"I heard you were wounded in Kuwait during the first Gulf War," David said now, because he had been thrust back into his memories from long ago, and because he was still groggy from sleep.

His old buddy laughed. "You heard right," he said. "Lost a leg six months into it, came home, met the woman of my dreams and had a kid. You know how it is."

"Yeah," David said, even though he didn't. He had been in his final year of grad school at Connecticut College when the war ended, and his subsequent marriage to his college sweetheart had ended without children. He passed a tired hand over his eyes. "Sorry about the leg," he said, feeling the inadequacy of his words.

"Nah," Mike answered. "That's neither here nor there. It got me out of the army early, anyway." That's one way to look at it, David thought dryly. He paused, trying to picture his lively childhood friend making do with only one leg, but he couldn't.

"So," he said, forcing himself to push the depressing image away, "how are you doing now?" Mike laughed, and it was the same laugh that David remembered from their childhood, only deeper.

"I'm doing okay, but I've gained a lot of weight, fat, but healthy as a horse."

"Fat," David repeated more as a question, unable to

picture his old friend being fat. When he had last seen him, Mikey was tall and skinny, his knees and elbows seemingly too large for their limbs. David sat up and turned on the light, wincing in the sudden brightness. His bedroom surrounded him in shades of white and beige—his ex-wife's choice. She had wanted calm sophistication, but he felt it was simply bland, if not downright boring. Now he wondered why he never changed it.

"The wife's Greek," Mike continued, like this explained everything.

"Ah," David replied.

"She makes the best damn Greek food this side of the Atlantic. And her *baklava*, man..." he trailed off, momentarily distracted. David offered a small grunt of appreciation, which seemed to pull Mike back into the conversation. "God, I'm sorry," he said, sounding a little embarrassed.

"Enough about me, right? You must be wondering why the hell I'm calling you in the middle of the night."

"No, no," David lied, as he again squinted at the clock...it read one forty-five. "I had just gone to bed. Besides, it's great hearing from you."

"Don't be ridiculous," Mike said cheerfully. "You always were a bad liar, you know." David smiled at the warmth that lay beneath the deep tenor of his childhood friend's voice. "Really, though, it's fine," he said. "I just can't get over the fact that I'm talking to you after all these years. So why *are* you calling me in the middle of the night?" They both laughed.

"Shocking, huh?" Mike said. "Well, wait until you hear

what I've got to tell you. It's big news, man, really big. That's why I couldn't wait until the morning to call."

"It *is* morning." David interjected. Mike's demeanor turned serious. He lowered his voice to almost a whisper. "If anyone asks, you didn't hear it from me, okay?"

Sitting now on the edge of his bed in the stark emptiness of his bedroom, the phone cradled against his shoulder, David was reminded of the time when they had strung a tin can telephone between their bedrooms so that they could talk after their bedtime. It hadn't worked, of course; the string got tangled in the massive pine tree that stood sentinel outside David's window. Instead of discreetly whispering their secrets, the two boys ended up fairly shouting at each other from their windows.

David switched the phone to his other ear, and settled back into the pillows. "Sure, Mikey," he said. "What's going on?"

"Well," he took a deep breath and exhaled into the phone. "To make a long story short, after my wife Arianna and I had our first daughter, I knew that there was no way I was going to be able to support my family by working the register at the local Wal-Mart. So I went to college, got my degree in medical technology. Luckily for me, Arianna's old man had some pull at a couple of places, and the next thing I know, I've landed a job at Freiz Corporation."

"Damn," said David. "Those are some connections." The Freiz Corporation was the largest research and development-based pharmaceutical company in the world. "That's great, Mikey." It felt strange, a little weird, calling his now adult friend, Mikey, instead of Mike or Michael.

Michael sounded too formal for old friends, so he decided on Mike.

"Tell me about it, I mean, it's nothing huge—I'm a lab technician. But the work's interesting and it puts food on the table. The only bad part was that we had to leave New York and come back to Connecticut. Guess where?"

"New London?"

"Close, Waterford."

"Same difference," David said, and they both laughed.

"Well, anyway," Mike replied. "As I said before, I'm a lab tech. I work at their research facility in Norwich."

"How did you find me?"

"I was looking over the list of potential candidates and I saw your name. I was hoping it was a different David Roy."

David forced himself to give a short laugh. "Sorry to disappoint."

"Man, I'm sorry you're having so much trouble with your heart."

David closed his eyes and thought about the heart attack, the numerous catheterizations, the four angioplasties, and the failed triple bi-pass he had undergone during recent years.

"Anyway, I saw your name and wanted to see if it was really you, so I did some detective work," he laughed. "The list had no other information except your doctor's name and a reference number. So, I went to classmates.com and *voila!* I knew it had to be you by the bio. They don't give phone numbers, so I called information hoping your number was listed and *voila* again. And, here I am, old buddy."

"That's amazing. I'd forgotten that I ever signed up for classmates.com. Anyway, what's this list for?" he asked with a larger measure of interest.

"Have you ever heard of the Sicilia Gene Trial?"

"Jesus," David said. "I've read about it, but that was over twenty years ago. What's going on now?" David sat up, swung his legs over to the floor and walked to the window. It was raining and rivulets ran down the windowpane, illuminated by the amber glow of the streetlight.

"All I know is that Freiz is going to be conducting a long-term trial on a drug called apoA-1 Sicilia. The word is it's some sort of miracle drug."

"Hey, I requested to be included on any list of participants in future cardiac related trials." David interjected.

"Well, old buddy, there are three thousand names on the list, including yours, but only five hundred will be chosen to participate. The good news is you should be getting a call from your cardiologist within the next few days. If there are no overriding reasons why you can't participate, you'll be added to the pool of prospective participants. That's where I come in. I work closely with the trial administrator and I'm certain I can get you in. Better yet, I can almost guarantee that you will not be in the control group. No placebo for you, old buddy."

"Jesus, God, Mikey, I don't know what to say, except, thank you."

"That's good enough for me. I'm just happy I can help you. I'll call you tomorrow—at a more respectful hour, to touch base with you. Hope you can sleep," he said with a jab. "Goodnight."

David let the phone drop to the floor. He pressed his forehead against the windowpane. The coolness helped relieve the flush that ran through him. He took a long deep breath and thought: *maybe there is hope*.

CHAPTER THREE

As hard as he tried and as fatigued as he was, the sleep David so desperately needed eluded him. The best he could achieve was a kind of twilight, where the possibilities of a better life flitted in and out of his semi-conscious mind. Thoughts of being able to exercise again without the gnawing pain of angina, of ascending a flight of stairs, or taking a brisk walk without having to stop to catch his breath, excited him. He would intermittently caution himself not to be too optimistic. After all, this was only a study, and any new drug, even if fast-tracked, probably wouldn't be available for two to three years. But, the possibilities ... *the possibilities*, he thought.

He had for so long harbored nothing but negative thoughts about his deteriorating physical condition. Thinking the end could come at any time, he was often depressed. On one occasion, he even contemplated suicide. That had scared him and he sought help. Although the Paxil helped with the depression and the nitroglycerin helped with the angina, he always felt listless and fatigued, and not very optimistic about his future.

Having given up any chance of getting any meaningful sleep, David rolled out of bed. The green LED on the clock radio read 4:23 a.m.. He slipped into his slippers and shuffled to the bathroom, then to the kitchen, where he put on a pot of coffee. While the coffee brewed, he fetched the newspaper from the front porch. It lay at the foot of the front door. *The paperboy was uncharacteristically accurate this morning*, he thought as he smiled thinly.

David sipped his coffee and scanned the headlines of *Newsday*. Nothing caught his interest. He was simply preoccupied. He recounted his conversation with Mikey ... Mike Fitzgerald from the night before. "Have you ever heard of the Sicilia Gene Trial?" he had asked. He vividly recollected reading about a possible breakthrough in the treatment and prevention of cardiovascular disease many years ago, but then nothing. There were no follow-up articles or news stories. It was as if the original article was just a figment of his imagination. He remembered thinking it was probably too good to be true anyway, and forgot about it ... until Mike had told him that a long-term trial on the drug was to be conducted. He wondered, why the lapse of more than twenty years? Why has it surfaced now? As he pondered these questions, he sipped his coffee.

His thoughts drifted to Sally. *She will be happy for me*, he thought. It wasn't his heart trouble or another man that caused her to leave him. It was because he was unable to give her what she wanted most in life, a child. He was infertile. A bout of mumps, exacerbated by orchitis, when he was thirteen had left him sterile. He would make light of his condition by telling her that many great men, George Washington among them, were incapable of making babies. She would smile and say, "It's okay, honey." But David knew it wasn't okay, and if there was one issue that could come between them, it was his sterility. David suggested adoption, but Sally wanted to bear a child. David understood. As time went by their relationship became strained. The issue was never far from the surface. Then, one frigid January day, five years ago, she asked for a divorce. David was devastated, but not surprised. He had been expecting the inevitable for some time.

It was an amicable break-up as break-ups go. David kept the house in Greenport and Sally moved to New York City to pursue a career in fashion design. David continued teaching high school mathematics until he suffered his heart attack two years after the split. He missed her dearly and thought of her often. For the first year, she touched base with him occasionally. Then, the calls stopped. He'd heard from a mutual friend that she'd met someone. Aside from his physical problems, the loss of Sally only deepened his depression.

David was brought back to the present by the alarm clock's buzzing. He had forgotten to shut it off when he got up. He shuffled into the bedroom, hit the button and quietly returned to the kitchen. He didn't know why he went through the pointless exercise of setting the alarm in the first place. He was always well awake before the set time.

He noted the time and decided to shower now, so as not to miss the call he hoped was coming.

As he entered the bathroom, he noticed the first light of day breaking to the east. It would be a beautiful spring day. *Spring*, he thought, *a time of renewal.*

CHAPTER FOUR

D AVID jumped at the sound of the first ring and snapped up the phone well before it had a chance to ring a second time. "Hello?" he said, with anticipation. He was disappointed with the response. "Davey, its Mike."

"Morning Mike. What's up?"

"You don't sound happy to hear from me, old buddy. Is something wrong?"

"No, not at all. I was just anticipating the call you said to expect from my cardiologist."

"Oh. Well, I've got some good news. If you get past the screening process, you're in, if you know what I mean."

"That's great, Mike. I'm eager to start the trial. I'm sick and tired of feeling sick and tired."

"I hear ya, man. Listen Davey, we just got out of a meeting with the administrator. The trial is scheduled to start in the middle of June."

"Damn, that's more than three weeks away. I was hoping it would be sooner, like tomorrow."

"I can understand that. By the way, where is Greenport?"

"It's about twenty miles southwest of New London, across the sound. It's a small town at the end of Long Island's north fork. It's where my ex is from."

"I didn't know you were divorced. Sorry to hear it. Man, we got a lot of catching up to do. Any kids?"

"No," David said without elaboration.

"Well, that's one saving grace." Mike chuckled.

"Yea, I guess so." Wanting to change the subject, David asked,

"Mike, what can you tell me about this trial? I mean, there were some articles on the Sicilia Gene back in the late seventies or early eighties, then nothing. What gives?"

"I wish I knew. They give us information on a need-to-know basis. We've been told very little, actually, mostly just some basics and our role in administering the trial. Even the trial administrator, who I've worked closely with in past trials, has been tight lipped. He's already done me some personal favors, so I don't want to push him."

"Sure, I understand." Just then, David heard the call waiting tone. "Look, Mike, I gotta run, I've got another call coming in. It could be my cardiologist."

"No problem, Davey. I'll talk to you soon."

"Thanks for the info. And Mike, I haven't been Davey in almost thirty years."

"Sorry, old buddy. What do you go by now, Dave or David?"

"David will be fine. And Mike ... thanks again. I owe you big time."

"Anytime, Davey, old buddy."

David hit the flash button on the phone. "Hello?" he said.

"Hello, Mr. Roy?" David recognized the voice of Doctor Howard, his cardiologist. He felt a surge of adrenalin shoot through his body.

"Yes doctor, how are you?" he said awkwardly.

"I'm fine, thank you. Now getting directly to the reason for my call: Mr. Roy, do you recall our discussion regarding an upcoming trial of a potential new therapy for cardiovascular disease to be conducted by the New England Clinic for Cardiac Care?"

"Yes, of course I do."

"Well, I just got off the phone with Doctor Charles Bauer. He's heading the trial. They are preparing to conduct a clinical trial on a new therapy. I, and all the other cardiologists from the tri-state region, were solicited by the clinic some time ago to submit potential candidates for an upcoming clinical trial."

"Yes, I remember you asking for permission to submit my name."

"Well, congratulations, you were chosen as a prospective participant."

"That's great news! Thanks, Doc, I really appreciate your doing this."

Howard continued, "The trial will last six weeks and requires all participants to sign releases giving NECCC control over their cardiac care for the length of the trial.

This control gives them exclusivity regarding any medical care you may need, excluding emergency care, of course. Dr. Bauer, the head of the trial for Freiz, has committed to keeping me informed if your cardiac condition changes in any way. Are you comfortable with their terms so far?" David responded immediately.

"Yes, of course, why wouldn't I be? I'm on borrowed time. I'll try anything that may help improve my health or delay the inevitable."

"I understand, but I must warn you, your participation in the trial is not without significant risk and the possibility exists that you may be given a placebo." *Not if Mike can do what he promised*, David thought. "Aside from possible negative side effects, you will be subjected to a battery of tests, some invasive, like an angiogram, for example."

"Doc, based on my current quality of life and my life expectancy, I have no choice but to give it a shot. I really don't have much to lose, if you think about it. When I go to bed each night, I wonder if I'm going to wake up the following morning, and when I do awake, I'm as tired as I was when I went to bed. Because of my condition, I have no personal life. I can't do the things I've always enjoyed, like working-out and running. I can't even have sex, for Christ's sake. I'm forty-one and I feel like my life is over. What the hell do I have to live for?" David caught himself. "I'm sorry, Doc. I'm just tired of living like this, and it gets to me sometimes."

"I understand, David," he said, dropping the formal address. "I'll send a copy of your medical records to Doctor

Bauer. I'll need you to come in to the office and sign the authorization form."

"I'll come over right away."

"That'll be fine. Let me give you the number to Doctor Bauer's office. He said you may call anytime during normal business hours."

David dialed the number and waited. His heart pounded to a rising pulse as he waited for someone to pick up on the other end. He took in a long, deep breath and exhaled slowly in an effort to calm himself.

"Hello, NECCC, how may I direct your call?" said a woman with a pleasant voice.

"Extension 219, please," David responded. Again, the phone rang in his ear. He felt another adrenalin rush, and again, he took a deep breath.

"Hello, Doctor Bauer's office, Kate speaking, how may I help you?"

"Uh, yes, my name is David Roy. I'm calling about the clinical trial. I was given this number to ca—" The female voice cut him off.

"Yes, Mr. Roy, we were waiting for your call. Well, yours and about five hundred others." She laughed. Her tone was decidedly less formal than the receptionist's. "As you already know, you've been chosen to participate in a clinical trial that will begin on June fifteenth. I need to ask you a few short questions: Are you willing to sign an agreement giving the New England Clinic for Cardiac Care exclusivity regarding your cardiac care for the term of the trial?"

"Yes, I'll agree to that."

"You will be required to make at least six visits to our

clinic, maybe more. Of course, they will be scheduled long enough in advance so as to accommodate any other obligations you may have. Is that also agreeable to you? And you will need to submit to an angiogram at the beginning and the end of the trial, as well as some non-invasive testing."

"Yes, of course."

"Very well then. An orientation meeting will be held one week prior to the start of the trial. It's scheduled for June 7th at ten o'clock in the morning, here at the clinic headquarters in Boston. I'll send you a package that will explain everything. In the meantime, if you have any questions or concerns, please feel free to call me."

"Thanks, Kate, I appreciate your help." David hung up. Too nervous to sit, he had paced from room to room throughout the conversation. Now, feeling drained but still excited, he plopped into his easy chair in the den, closed his eyes and thought, *the ball is rolling. This is really going to happen.* Then realizing he had one more chore to do, he jumped up and headed for Doctor Howard's office.

CHAPTER FIVE

BRETT Bitterman personally greeted each director as they entered the lavish boardroom for their
monthly meeting. He had been the Chairman of
the Board and CEO of Freiz for over twenty years. And in
that time, he had taken Freiz from a moderately successful
company to the largest and most profitable pharmaceutical company on the planet, earning him the respect and
admiration of his peers and Wall Street moguls. He had the
reputation for being not only smart, but also tough. He had
cleaned house when he arrived at Freiz, firing two-thirds
of the incumbent management team and replacing them
with the brightest business minds from this country and
abroad.

Bitterman demanded the most from everyone who
worked for him. Success was rewarded with promotions
and bonuses, but failure was not tolerated. By all accounts,
he was a fair, but difficult man to work for. He subscribed

to the Machiavellian Theory that it is better to be feared than loved.

The seven men and two women took their seats in the high-backed leather chairs that surrounded the custom-made oval, black walnut table. Each director was supplied with bottled water. Note pad and pen were placed neatly in front of each chair, and pitchers of orange juice and carafes of coffee, both high-test and unleaded, rested at each end of the table. Against a wall, a cloth-covered table adorned with a bright flower arrangement held fresh fruit and Danishes.

Bitterman opened the meeting: "Welcome, everyone. Today's agenda is short, but nonetheless, of vital importance, so let me get right to it. While Torvistat remains the best selling statin in the world at twelve billion in sales last year, and demand is at an all-time high, there is a real potential for trouble in the not-too-distant future. Haber Pharmaceutical's statin, Zimstan, the second best selling statin, is coming off patent at the end of the year. I have learned from a friend of ours in Washington that when that happens, Medicare will no longer cover Torvistat for Medicare participants, but instead, will switch to the generic form of Zimstan. Even without taking into consideration the loss of revenue from the general population, losing the Medicare market will result in nearly three billion six hundred million in lost revenue." Eyebrows furrowed as they realized the negative ramification of what they were just told.

"Is there anything we can do to convince Medicare to do otherwise?" asked a director.

"Probably not, but before everyone gets too concerned, let me explain our strategy for protecting our market share. We are currently working on two new drugs that increase the levels of High Density Lipoproteins—the good cholesterol. Our plans are to bind one of them to Torvistat and apply for a new patent for Bi-Torracept-T. Torvistat with the addition of the new drug, Bi-Torracept, will be far superior to anything out there now. It will be the first drug capable of doubling one's HDL level. Our R&D Department also believes that neither drug under development will easily lend itself to duplication, as is the case with the current statin drugs, without infringing on our pending patents. Therefore, our competitors will not be able to produce a similar drug by slightly altering our chemical composition."

The board listened intently, but the mood around the table brightened considerably as Bitterman continued. "As I said before, we have two new drugs in the pipeline. The first one is in the final stages of development, and the second will be evaluated in a clinical trial, which will begin in two weeks.

"In order to protect our market share until the first of our new drugs is available to the public, which should be in approximately eighteen months, we need only to convince the folks at Medicare to delay the removal of Torvistat from their list of approved medications."

"And just how do we accomplish that little feat?" asked one skeptical director.

"Our lobbyists are putting a full-court press on our friends in Washington—both houses, I might add. In addition, I plan to make a visit to see my old friend, Bruce Richards. I'm confident I can convince him to help us."

"Brett, friend or not, that is not going to be an easy task. He would be taking an enormous political risk in helping us," said a doubtful director.

"I agree," said another.

"It's no secret that Richards would like to run for president. I don't think he'll risk losing any political capital, even for an old friend," said another.

"I don't see how you can be so confident that he'll cooperate with you, considering his aspirations," added a third.

For the first time since the meeting started, Bitterman managed a thin smile. "I guess I'll have to make him an offer he can't refuse."

CHAPTER SIX

DURING the next two weeks, David thought of the upcoming trial and little else. As each day passed, his anticipation grew. Although his thoughts were mostly positive, occasionally some negative ones crept into his head. When they did, he tried to dismiss them, but he was not always successful. *What if, after my pre-trial physical, I'm rejected for some reason? What if Mike can't pull it off and I end up in the control group? What if...* As the trial date got closer, David became more and more apprehensive. After all he'd been through, he couldn't bare the thought of something going wrong. This was more than likely his last and best chance of reversing, or at the very least, slowing the progression of his atherosclerosis.

The sun's rays warmed David's face as he drove east from Greenport to Orient Point where he would catch the ferry to New London, Connecticut. From there, he would drive to Boston, home of the New England Clinic for

Cardiac Care where he was to report tomorrow morning at eight. There, he would join an elite group of people, all of whom, he surmised, were hoping to get the real thing and not a placebo. He felt a pang of guilt for having the luxury of knowing he would not be in the control group, but it left him quickly. He'd received few good breaks in his life; he felt he deserved this one.

When he arrived at the ferry terminal at Orient Point, he was instructed to park in one of the many lanes designated for ferry loading. After doing so, he went inside the ferry office to collect the ticket he had purchased by telephone the previous day. By the time he got back to his car, the attendants were starting to load the boat. David started his car and inched along until he reached the loading ramp of the huge vessel. The ferry company took great pride informing its patrons that they would be crossing Long Island Sound on a World War II vintage LST landing craft. The boat actually participated in the D-Day invasion of Normandy. Of course, it had been retrofitted and renovated and could accommodate up to ninety cars and nine hundred passengers. The only problem for David was that the cars were parked on the lowest level and the passenger area was on the top level. A long staircase connected the two. He would have preferred to stay in his car for the hour and forty-minute ride, but the ferry company did not allow it.

He made his way up the metal staircase, stopping at times to rest and allow more able bodies to pass. By the time he reached the cabin, his breathing was labored and he started to experience angina. He quickly fished a small, glass nitroglycerin sprayer from his pocket and sprayed a dose under his tongue. Soon the pain subsided and his breathing eased.

The beautiful, late spring day was too nice to waste sitting inside the cabin, so David decided to grab one of the seats outside. The calm air promised a smooth ride across the placid sound. The smell of the salted air reminded him again why he could never live far from a body of salt water. The ferry turned north toward Plum Gut, where the waters from the bay and the sound met, or more accurately, collided. Normally, this stretch of water between the point and Plum Island was one of the angriest found anywhere. *The Gut*, as the locals called it, was respected and even feared. But today, a combination of calm winds and a slack tide made for easy passage for the ferry and the numerous small fishing and pleasure boats that glided through the mirrored waters.

As the ferry made its way through the Gut, it passed the Orient Point Lighthouse on the left and the infamous Plum Island Animal Disease Laboratory on the right. The place was shrouded in secrecy. It was a highly secure island off limits to non-employees. The local population believed there was more happening on the island than they were led to believe. Its mystique grew even larger when it was mentioned in the movie "The Silence of the Lambs" as a place where the fearsome cannibal, Hannibal Lector, could be securely held.

As they moved out into open water, the boat picked up speed. Its forward motion created a cool, gentle breeze that reminded David of his dreams of running—running without pain or shortness of breath. He closed his eyes, inhaled deeply and thought, just maybe, his dream would be realized.

David looked around at the other passengers. More of them had decided to enjoy the ride on the outer deck. He wondered where they all were going. He noticed families with small children in tow, elderly couples, and a few young lovers. The ones who chose to stay in the cabin and play cards were obviously going to one of the casinos: Foxwoods or Mohegan Sun. David noticed an elderly man sitting alone reading a newspaper. What caught his attention was the oxygen bottle sitting next to him with its clear plastic tubes that snaked their way to his nostrils. *My God, that could be me.* The thought depressed him. He pushed it aside, instead concentrating on the possibilities that lay before him. Until a few weeks ago, there was little prospect of any new medical breakthrough. Oh sure, articles were written in various magazines and trade publications on the prospects, but their promise of fruition always lay somewhere over the rainbow. It was always, "In the not too distant future … blah, blah, blah." But, now … this! He almost had to pinch himself. He was so excited after getting the news that he wanted to call Sally. He knew she would be happy for him, but he thought better of it. Besides, he didn't even have her number, and it would mean going to a mutual friend to get it. *No*, he thought, *let it be. Better to wait and see if the trial is successful.* He didn't want to put the cart before the horse. But, if it worked, he would definitely call her.

The ferry slowed as it entered the mouth of the Thames

River. The city of New London was approaching on his left and Groton to his right. Groton is the home of submarine builder Electric Boat, and a Navy submarine base, and New London boasts the United States Coast Guard Academy, and Connecticut College. It also hosts the oldest collegiate competition in the country: the annual four-mile boat race between archrivals, Harvard and Yale, which dates back to 1852. More recently, New London had gained nationwide notoriety when the United States Supreme Court upheld the city's right to invoke eminent domain on private property; not for the traditional purpose of condemning private property for public use to build roads and bridges, but instead to give private entrepreneurs the opportunity to redevelop the site in order to increase the tax base. Many believed this to be one of the worst decisions ever handed down by the court.

As the converted LST maneuvered to dock, David thought fondly about his childhood in New London and the enumerable, subsequent trips he and Sally had made across the sound, most of them in winter, on their way to one of the many sky resorts in Vermont. He had always enjoyed the boat ride, even in rough seas, but none were as enjoyable as the one he took today. The sound of the water-drenched tow lines tautly rubbing against the craft's metal siding created an eerie screeching sound as they tightened their grip and slowed the ferry's momentum. The bang of the loading ramp as it dropped onto the pier below was a familiar sound that signaled their arrival.

CHAPTER SEVEN

D AVID was a full twenty minutes early for his eight o'clock appointment. So full of angst, he slept little the night before. He approached the reception desk and gave his name and the reason he was there. A slight, distinguished, older lady with silver-gray hair, he guessed her to be in her mid-to-late sixties, took his name and said with a pleasant voice, "Please take a seat, Mr. Roy." She pointed to a small waiting area that was furnished with industrial looking metal and plastic chairs. "Someone will be with you shortly."

"Thank you." David scanned the magazines in the wall rack. Most were dog-eared and none he saw were anywhere close to being current. *Typical*, he thought.

He was thumbing through an old issue of *Newsweek* when he heard the revolving entry door turn. He looked up to see a woman emerge. He was immediately taken by her countenance. He scrutinized her every movement as she strode across the marble floored lobby with long, purposeful strides. Her shiny dark hair was pinned up in a loose bun, which contrasted well against her white lab coat. She had a china-doll like complexion that was devoid of any detectable make-up. As she approached, he could see her facial features clearly: her brown eyes were big and bright and her cheekbones high. Beneath her perfectly shaped nose were the most beautiful lips he had ever seen: full and deep with color—even without lipstick. They reminded him of Angelina Jolie's. As if sensing his stare, she turned her head toward him as she passed, giving him a thin smile without breaking her stride. David smiled back and felt a rush of blood fill his face as she turned and disappeared down the hall. He didn't mean to ogle, but she was striking. She looked to be in her mid-to-late twenties. *Too young for me*, he thought. And although he couldn't tell if she was wearing a ring, she was probably married. Women with her kind of looks were almost never unattached at her age. He closed his eyes in contemplation. *It would be nice to meet someone like that.* He missed not being in a relationship, not having someone special. After Sally left him, he was a basket case, and then he got sick. *Maybe one day I'll be well enough to handle a relationship.* He started to fantasize about his youth when he was brought back to reality by a loud male voice.

"Davey?" David's eyes snapped open to see before him the adult Mikey Fitz. He stood up and instinctively both men gave each other a bear hug. "Mike, man, it's great to see you after all these years. Hey, you're not that fat." David said, mockingly.

"Gee, thanks for the compliment, but I am. And you don't look that sick."

"Thanks, but I am," he countered. "Otherwise I wouldn't be here."

"Yea, yea, I hear ya, man. Hopefully, that will all change for the better in the next few months."

"I'm counting on it, Mike." David turned serious. "It's been a rough few years, with no end in sight. At least now, I have some hope for a better life."

"Listen, Davey … Dave, sorry, old habits are hard to break. I've got to check in. Someone will be with you in a few minutes. I'll see you inside. See ya later, old buddy and remember we've got to be careful not to let anyone know we're old friends."

"Sure thing, Mike." David watched Mike disappear down the same hallway as the woman had a few minutes earlier.

It was now eight forty-five and the lobby was filling up quickly. Most of the people, David observed, were much older than he. At forty-one, he figured he was a good fifteen to twenty years younger than most of the others. It was now getting crowded and the room was abuzz with chatter. Anxious people made small talk as they waited for the orientation to begin.

A woman's voice called for attention. The loud chatter quickly abated to a murmur and then to silence. "Good morning everyone. Please follow me to the lecture hall for final processing and orientation." She turned and motioned for all to follow.

The tiered lecture hall was a large room stacked with

several semi-circular levels designed to give participants an unobstructed view of the lectern located at the bottom center. The eager candidates were led in and directed to their seats. After all were seated, they appeared to fill only about half of the room's seating capacity. David found himself in the third row from the bottom near the end, closest to the door. Seated in a row behind the lectern were employees of Freiz and the New England Clinic for Cardiac Care. The NECCC had been selected to administer the trial. He spotted Mike among them. To his surprise, next to Mike sat the woman he saw in the lobby earlier. She looked up and caught his gaze. He quickly looked away. *Damn*, he thought, *that's the second time she caught me staring*. He wanted to look at her again, but resisted the urge. Through his peripheral vision, he saw Mike discreetly trying to get his attention. He casually looked in Mike's direction and gave him a guarded smile in return. The woman glanced in his direction, and David thought, *oh no, she thinks I'm smiling at her*. He felt his face redden again. He was rescued … somewhat, when he saw Mike lean close to her and whisper something. She again looked briefly in David's direction before redirecting her attention to the podium.

A smartly dressed middle-aged woman approached the lectern. She tapped the microphone to make sure it was on before she spoke. "Good morning, ladies and gentlemen. My name is Doctor Monique Rentz. I am the head of Research and Development at Freiz Pharmaceuticals. As you already know, we have developed a new therapy, which has shown great promise. We anticipate the clinical trial, which you have agreed to participate in, will provide proof of its efficacy. The trial administrator will be Doctor Charles Bauer. He has been affiliated with the New England Clinic for Cardiac Care for over thirty years and is their chairman of cardiology and chief trial administrator. Before I turn the microphone over to him, let me wish you all the very best. Thank you and good luck." With that, she handed the microphone over to Doctor Bauer.

As Doctor Bauer was preparing to address the assemblage, David took a chance and again glanced at the dark-haired woman who had left such a strong first impression. He hoped he wouldn't get caught looking a fourth time. Her gaze was fixed on the back of Doctor Bauer. David stared for as long as he dared, and then, he, too, turned his attention toward the doctor.

Doctor Bauer laid out the day's agenda. First, there would be more paperwork to fill out. This solicited a collective sigh from the group. There would be more releases to sign and forms to fill out, both there and at home. After a short break, they would be instructed as to how and when they would receive the therapy and explained the measures to be taken to evaluate its effectiveness. A one-hour lunch break would follow, after which they would be assigned a trial and group number. Lastly, they would be sent to examining rooms for an EKG and a final cursory physical examination before being scheduled for an angiogram and first injection.

David looked around at the other participants. They were all hopeful, but only half would receive the actual drug, the other half, a placebo. *How unfair life can be*, he thought as he was again struck with another pang of guilt.

CHAPTER EIGHT

A T the break, Doctor Bauer announced that there were refreshments in the adjoining room. David wanted to make a bee-line to Mike, but instead wandered inconspicuously in his direction. "Mike, can I talk to you for a second?"

"Sure," he said, as he filled his cup with coffee. "Let's grab a table." Mike walked to an empty table as David followed close behind.

"Mike, who was that woman sitting next to you?"

"C'mon, Dave, I haven't seen you in years and all you want to know about is Gina. Man, we have a lot to catch up on."

"Mike, we'll have plenty of time for that. It's just that my time here is short."

"I know, I know, everybody wants to know about Gina. Look, man, you're wasting your time. She doesn't date."

"So, she's not married."

"Yes, but she is committed."

"Oh, I see, she doesn't like men, is that it?"

"No, that's not it at all. As far as I can tell, she's heterosexual."

"Then what's the story? She's certainly attractive enough to draw men to her... like flies to honey."

"No doubt about it, she's a looker," Mike replied. "Can you imagine what she would look like if she was gussied up?" The thought had already crossed David's mind. "But beyond that," Mike continued, "she's a good person. I've worked with Gina for quite a while, and I can tell you, they don't come any better. Her mother died when she was a kid. When she was a senior in high school, her father had a serious heart attack that left him in a very weakened state. She has dedicated herself to his care, which, I might add, is quite admirable, but very demanding. She claims she doesn't have time for a relationship."

"I can understand that, but she's also entitled to a life of her own."

"She doesn't think so," responded Mike.

"What?" David gave Mile a puzzled look. "Why not?"

"Because she thinks she caused her father's heart attack, and as a result, partly out of love and perhaps out of guilt, she feels obligated to tend to his care."

"That's crazy. How could she have caused his heart attack?"

"Well, as she tells it, after her mother died, her father never remarried. He never even dated, as far as she knew. He instead took on the responsibility of raising her on his own. The problem was he was ill equipped to be both mother and father. Before her mother died, he doted over Gina. He was very loving and affectionate, always hugging her and giving her butterfly kisses, and rarely scolding her. And she loved it when he gave her butterfly kisses. According to Gina, her mother was the one who always meted out the discipline. After she died, her father inherited this responsibility, and to her dismay, his demeanor hardened and he became a strict disciplinarian. He never laid a hand on her, but he was overly restrictive. Consequently, like most teenagers she began to rebel. She said a weekend didn't go by when they didn't argue. Mostly, the arguments centered on curfew times or whom she was dating.

"One night in her senior year, she and her father had a huge blowout. She stormed out of the house and didn't come home until three in the morning, two hours past her curfew. As she and her boyfriend drove down the street toward her house, she saw lights flashing. They looked to be in front of her house. As they got closer, she could make out an ambulance and a police car. She told me she almost died right there on the spot. When they reached her house, EMTs were wheeling her father out on a gurney. His eyes were closed and his ashen face was covered with an oxygen mask. She ran for the gurney, but was intercepted by a police officer who explained that her father had suffered a heart attack.

"Her father survived, but his heart was severely damaged and he became a cardiac invalid. Gina told me that she grew up that night. She accepted responsibility for her actions and vowed to take care of her father...and that's what she's done."

"That's some story, but I—"Mike cut him off.

"Hey Dave, here she comes. I'll introduce you." Gina, along with the rest of the group, was beginning to return to the lecture hall. As she was about to pass them, Mike waved her over to the table. They both stood as she approached. "Gina, I want you to meet David Roy." Mike leaned in close to her ear and whispered, "Please keep this between us; he's an old friend of mine." Then he straightened and continued the introduction. "David, this is my favorite coworker, Gina Coletti." Gina graciously extended her hand and David eagerly accepted it. Her tender but firm grasp emitted a warmth that seemed to flow throughout his entire body. He wondered if what he felt was real or imagined.

"Pleased to meet you, David," she said, smiling.

"Same here," he replied, awkwardly.

"Break's over," injected Mike. "We'd better get back. We can talk later."

As they walked back to the lecture hall, David and Gina made small talk, mostly about his high hopes for the trial.

CHAPTER NINE

A FTER the participants filled out the last of the forms, Doctor Bauer explained the tests that would be conducted to measure their progress. They would each receive an electrocardiogram and an angiogram at the start and conclusion of the trial, along with two intravascular ultrasound tests in between. As he spoke, his staff handed out detailed instructions and a schedule to each participant.

As Doctor Bauer spoke, David's thoughts and gaze drifted back to Gina. The guilt trip her father's heart attack had caused was certainly unjustified. The underlying cause was already there, and the attack would probably have happened anyway, maybe not just then and there. Although the sacrifice Gina was making was both admirable and laudable, it was also somewhat pitiful because she was entitled to a life of her own. Was she so guilt ridden that she felt compelled to immerse herself so totally in her father's care that she excluded the possibility of entering into a personal relationship with anyone else? These thoughts, rather than the ones about his own illness, raced through David's mind as Doctor Bauer spoke.

His attention was redirected when he accepted an envelope from a staffer that contained the forms and schedule Doctor Bauer had referred to earlier. A paste-on label was affixed to each envelope that gave the participant the time and room number for their pre-trial physical and EKG. David's read: Kennedy Building, room 103, 3:15 p.m. It was now 11:55 a.m. Doctor Bauer informed the group that lunch would be served, buffet style, in the same room where they had taken their break. "Enjoy your lunch, and if anyone has any questions, please feel free to ask me or any of my staff whom I have asked to join you for lunch. Thank you and good luck to all."

After choosing from the clinic's heart healthy selections, David and Michael made their way to an empty table in a far corner of the room, passing Gina in the process. Michael asked her to join them and then gave her a wink. She responded to the wink with a quick look of puzzlement. At the table, Michael spoke nonstop while shoveling in food at the same time. "Gina, please keep this to yourself. Dave and I were like brothers when we were kids. We lived next door to each other in New London. One day while ice-skating together on Perry's pond, I fell through the ice and couldn't pull myself out of the water. David crawled across the ice, and as it cracked around him, he pulled me to safety. From that day forward we were inseparable until I moved to New York."

David offered, "That's right. Unfortunately, sometime after Mike moved we lost contact. Coincidently, this trial has brought us back together."

"That's right. And man, do we have a lot of catching up to do."

"I'll bet you do," she said with a soft smile. "You'd better be careful though, you might just get him kicked out of the trial."

David's eyes were drawn to Gina and he had to make a conscious effort to keep from staring at her while conversing with Mike. Mike continued. "David, I want you to meet my family. You'll like them. My wife, Arianna, is a great cook. Did I mention she's Greek? Ah man, she makes the best Greek food. If you like eggplant, her *moussaka* is to die for and her *Baklava,* well, it's by far the best this side of Greece."

"Sounds like you did all right for yourself."

"He certainly did. I've met Arianna. She's a great person," said Gina.

"I can't wait until you meet her." Mike replied. "We've got to get together sometime real soon. You too, Gina," he said enthusiastically. David instinctively looked for her reaction. "I'd love to, Michael, but you know how busy I am with work and things at home. We'll see," she hedged. *Things at home,* David thought, nothing specific, just *Things at home.*

"C'mon, Gina, you're entitled to give yourself a break once in a while," said Mike as his cell phone started to ring.

"Michael," said Gina, "You know you're supposed to turn your phone off when you're in here."

"I know, I forgot, sorry," he said loud enough for others to hear. He looked at the display and said, "Ah, speak of the devil, it's the wife. Excuse me for a minute," he said and headed for the hallway.

After he watched Mike exit the room, David turned to Gina with a smile and tugged on his earlobe. "See this?" he said holding his earlobe so Gina could see the scar that ran down the middle. "I can thank Mike for that. One frigid winter day we got the bright idea to go fishing for flounder down by the oil docks on the Thames. We weren't there five minutes when the hook of a lure from an overhead cast by Mike caught me right here." He again tugged on the ear for emphasis. "I was so startled that I stumbled forward, falling off the dock into the icy river."

"Ouch, that must have hurt," Gina said with a grimace.

"As a matter of fact, it didn't. I was so shocked by the cold water that the only thing I could think of was getting out. I know the Bible tells us that only one man ever walked on water, but that day I came close to being the second." Gina put her hand to her mouth trying to stifle a laugh.

"Oh, that's horrible," she said.

"That's not the worst of it. After a three-mile walk to the emergency room at Lawrence Memorial Hospital for the removal of the hook and a couple of stitches, my parents read me the riot act for being down at the river. We were eleven at the time, and the river was off-limits. After the dressing down, my mother came over and hugged me until I couldn't breath." Gina, thinking of her own mother, gave David a contemplative smile, but said nothing.

David and Gina sat amid an uneasy silence when David said, "He's right you know. You are entitled to a little down time, some R&R so to speak. Why don't you take Mike up on his offer? It sounds like it would be fun. And, who knows, you might like the company," David said with a mischievous grin.

Gina's demeanor turned serious, "David, I just met you. You seem like a nice guy. God knows, Michael thinks the world of you, but you don't know me. You don't know my circumstances."

"I'm sorry if I offended you in any way. I certainly didn't mean to. It's just that I believe that everybody, regardless of their circumstances, is entitled to some personal downtime."

"With all due respect, I don't think you are in any position to give me advice." David, seeing that she was getting annoyed, backed off.

"You're right, I'm sorry if I've upset you."

She studied him briefly before she spoke. "Just how much *do* you know about me," she said suspiciously.

"Listen, you're right, it's none of my business. I shouldn't have said anything. Let's just change the subject."

"No, let's not, I want to know. You obviously know something or you wouldn't have tried to give me your sage advice," she said sarcastically.

"All I know is that you take care of your father—"

Gina interjected, "That damn Michael, I love him to

death, but sometimes he just doesn't know when to keep his mouth shut. What did he tell you?"

"Not much, just that your father had a severe heart attack that left him in need of constant care, and you're the one who provides that care."

"I don't mind doing it. He is my father after all. What else did he tell you?"

"Not much," David said, feeling he'd said too much already.

Michael was still on the phone when he opened the door and peeked in. He pointed to the phone to let them know he was still engaged in his conversation with Arianna. David gave him a quick wave of understanding; Gina gave him a look that could kill. Michael quickly disappeared back into the hallway.

"Go ahead, I'm waiting."

Oh, what the hell, David thought. Although he didn't want to upset her further, it was too late to be diplomatic. "Mike said that you are too hard on yourself. He said you don't spend any time on yourself."

"What does that mean, exactly?" David sensed things were going in the wrong direction. "Look, I'm going to be straight with you. Gina, I find you extremely attractive. After all, you are a beautiful woman." Embarrassed by the comment, she turned her head to the side.

"Is there anything else?" she said.

"Mike told me about the circumstances that you believe led to your father's heart attack." Gina closed her eyes, but remained silent. "It wasn't your fault, plain and simple. It would have happened anyway, maybe just another time or place. You're a medical professional, you know I'm right."

"Is there anything else?" she snapped. Gina quickly gathered her things. "Thanks for the compliment—and the unsolicited advice. I've got some things to do before the afternoon session."

David sat back in his chair and exhaled loudly in frustration as he watched Gina snake her way between the tables toward the door. Seconds later Mike came in with a confused look on his face. "What happened, Dave? Gina is really ticked off at me. What the hell went on after I went out to talk to Arianna?"

"I butted in where I shouldn't have. I didn't mean to upset her. I'm sorry, but she's really mad at you. It's my fault. I guess you're not the only one who doesn't know when to keep his mouth shut."

"Huh?"

"Oh, never mind. Mike, do you know her home or cell phone number?"

"Hey man, she's already pissed at me. If you want her number, you're going to have to get it from her."

"I understand," David said as he scribbled his phone number on a scrap of paper. "Listen, Mike, do me a favor, give this to Gina, It's my cell phone number. Ask her to call me. Tell her I'm really sorry that—"

"You can tell her yourself. She will be giving you your EKG later this afternoon."

CHAPTER TEN

AVID sat in the reception area along with several others who were also waiting for their EKGs. Thoughts of his exchange with Gina brought on a flurry of emotions, not the least of which was regret. He should have known better—he did know better—so what happened? Although he was sincere in what he had said, it wasn't his place to say it. The longer he thought about it, the angrier he became with himself. His one and only chance to make a good first impression squandered, he sank into a funk.

"Mr. Roy?" David looked up to see Gina standing in the doorway scanning the room. He quickly raised his hand to catch her attention.

"Mr. Roy, please come in," she said in a professional and detached manner. Conflicting thoughts flashed thought his mind as he walked passed her while she held the door. Should he apologize yet again or just keep his mouth shut?

"Please unbutton your shirt and lie on the table." David did as ordered. Gina pushed up his pants cuffs and pulled down his socks. She squirted a gel-like substance on various parts of his chest and legs. The gel was cold and the first squirt got David's attention. "Hey, that's cold," he protested.

"Sorry, I should have warned you," she said with a sly smile.

"You look like you enjoyed it."

"No, don't be silly, of course I didn't," she said as her smile broadened. "Well, maybe just a little."

David felt her professional façade was beginning to melt away. He was eager to say something, to apologize, but he didn't want to interrupt her while she was administering the EKG.

The test took only a few minutes. Gina removed the results from the printer and briefly glanced at them before placing the printout in a manila envelope. She handed it to David with instructions to return to the waiting room. "You will be called in for your physical shortly. Please give that to the doctor," she said, pointing to the envelope.

It's now or never, David thought. "Gina, listen, I really am sorry for getting you so upset. It was none of my business, and I should have kept my mouth shut. It was thoughtless and stupid. Please forgive me," he said earnestly.

"It wasn't thoughtless or stupid, it was sincere. I know you meant well, so let's just forget it ever happened." David stuck out his hand and said, "Friends?"

"Friends," she said shaking his hand. He wanted to say more but decided not to push his luck.

At the conclusion of his physical, David was given an appointment for an angiogram scheduled for the following morning, a test he was thoroughly familiar with, and one he did not look forward to having. Undergoing the test was not without risk, but it was necessary to determine the level of occlusion in his arteries in order to establish a baseline to measure future tests against.

David arrived back at the Holiday Inn in Boston, where the clinic had made arrangements to house the trial participants, and headed straight for the bar. He ordered a Bud Light from the tap, one of the two drinks he allowed himself daily. He was nursing his brew and thinking about the day's events when he felt a tap on his shoulder. He turned to see Mike who was sporting his omnipresent smile. "Hey old buddy, mind if I join you?"

"No, not at all, but won't you get in trouble for fraternizing with the troops?"

"Hey, I'm on my own time. What I do with it is my business. Besides, I'm only having a friendly drink at the bar. No big deal," he said as he signaled the bartender and ordered a Guinness from the tap. After a long pull, Mike wiped the creamy foam from his upper lip and said, "Ah, the nectar of the gods. So, how'd the rest of your day go?"

"Well, I passed my physical and I'm scheduled for an angiogram in the morning."

"I *know that*. I pulled your chart before I left."

"Then why did you ask?"

"C'mon Davey, you know what I mean—Gina, how'd it go with her?"

"I apologized again and she accepted."

"And?"

"And what? That's it—period,"

Mike changed the subject. "Arianna and I would like to have you over on Saturday. She can't wait to meet you."

"Mike, I'm going home to Long Island tomorrow evening right after I get my first injection."

"So? You're only a ferry ride away. You don't even have to bring your car over; I can pick you up at the dock."

David hesitated briefly, then said, "Oh, what the hell, why not, I would like to meet your family, too. But you don't have to pick me up; I'll take my own vehicle."

"Great. I'm also inviting Gina," he said, raising his eyebrows.

"Fine, Mike, but don't push her. She's felt put upon enough already."

"I hear ya, man."

"By the way, Mike, how did you get to know her?"

"As I told you, we worked together in Norwich at Freiz. When her father's heart condition worsened, she moved back to Boston to care for him. I really missed her. She was a great coworker and a really good friend. Arianna and the kids loved her too. It's great to see her again. "Davey," Mike said looking at his watch, "I gotta run. I'll call you to firm up plans for Saturday."

The long day had left David exhausted. He wasn't very hungry so he ordered a turkey sandwich on whole wheat, which he ate at the bar. He washed it down with another beer. He had declined an offer from Mike to have dinner with him and a few of his friends, which didn't include Gina. Although she lived locally, Gina was undoubtedly home tending to her father's needs. He wondered if he would have accepted the offer if Gina was going to attend. As tired as he was, he knew he would have.

David recounted how Mike again reminded him that the two of them would have to be discreet because the staff was instructed not to fraternize with the participants even though they were encouraged to mingle at breaks and meals to answer their questions and address their concerns. David thought about his upcoming visit to Mike's home. The thought of seeing Gina made his stomach twinge. Though he was doubtful she would actually show, it gave him something to look forward to.

Back in his room, David stretched out on the bed and started to skim through the voluminous material he was given. He was amazed at the amount of paperwork he'd have to complete during the trial: there were questionnaires, evaluations, and surveys to be submitted periodically; some weekly, others monthly. Some were the annoying kind with multiple choices such as: often, somewhat, very little, or never. There were questions like: Have you experienced angina in the last week? If yes, how severe? How long did it last? At the end, there was space to add any personal observations. This was a small price to pay if, as a result of the trial, his health improved.

David rested the paperwork on his chest, closed his eyes, and drifted off to sleep.

David found himself swimming. This had always been his favorite form of exercise and relaxation. Taking long powerful strokes, he glided effortlessly, as he had in his youth, through the clear, azure water. Gradually the water became more viscous, its consistency changed to that of oil, and then to that of quicksand. He tried to stay afloat, but the task was overwhelming. His efforts exceeded his body's ability to provide enough oxygen to satisfy his starving muscles. His breathing became labored as his lungs struggled to take in that one last breath of fresh air. He felt a stabbing pain radiating from deep within the center of his chest. He began to lose consciousness as his face dipped below the surface and he slowly disappeared into the darkness beneath.

He bolted up in bed and gasped for air. After catching his breath, David made his way to the bathroom. He splashed cold water on his face, and then looked at himself in the mirror. *How many more episodes like this one can I endure before my heart can take no more?*

What would it be like, he thought—to die? He often contemplated his death. His medical condition forced him to confront his mortality. Would he experience a long agonizing death or painlessly sink into the big sleep, never to return to the conscious world—or would he cross over into an afterlife, a heaven of some sort? He didn't believe in Purgatory or Hell; living on earth provided enough of both. No, it was either heaven or nothing. He hoped it was heaven.

He had always struggled with the conflict between faith and science. To him the notions of The Big Bang Theory and Creationism were, by themselves, equally implausible. The concept of all matter in the universe being compressed into a speck slightly larger than a grain of sand, then exploding to create the ever-expanding cosmos was, in his mind, ludicrous. Just as absurd was the contention that the world was created in six days when scientific evidence indicated the earth to be over four and a half billion years old. Given the fact that science cannot explain where the matter for the 'Big Bang' came from, and considering the possibility The Bible was not meant to be taken literally, perhaps the real answer lies somewhere in between. Maybe God created the 'Big Bang' on the first day. And who's to say a day referred to in The Bible wasn't a twenty-four hour period, but instead, a time span of billions of years. After all, the last book of the New Testament, Revelations, is written in riddles and certainly is not to be interpreted literally. If this is the case, why must the first book of the Old Testament, Genesis, be interpreted in such a manner? David pondered these questions periodically, knowing that no living person knows the answers.

He splashed his face one last time, toweled, and returned to bed. He always had trouble falling back to sleep after one of these episodes. After tossing and turning for some time, he turned on the light. The clock read one-thirty. He sighed in resignation as he reached for the book he had taken along just for such an occasion. He read for almost an hour before falling asleep.

CHAPTER ELEVEN

D AVID awoke at five-twenty after another fitful
night of sleep. He shut off the alarm, which was
set to go off at six thirty. He wondered again why
he engaged in this exercise in futility. He couldn't remember the last time he was awakened by an alarm clock.

He opened the drapes, revealing a strong, late spring
storm. The wind-driven rain pelted the window before
gathering in rivulets that further obscured his view of the
outside world. He never liked this kind of weather. The
gray pall dulled the vibrant colors of the season. Normally,
the sight would be depressing, but today the dank weather
couldn't dampen his mood. After all, this was the day he
had long awaited.

After David showered and dressed, he went down to
the lobby, which he found deserted except for a lone clerk
who stood behind the counter at a computer. He was likely

playing a video game to pass time, David surmised. The clerk noticed him. "Good morning, sir."

"Good morning," David replied with a smile.

"It doesn't look like it's a very nice day out there."

"No, but it's still a good morning."

"Sir?" said the confused clerk.

"I'm anticipating a good day, that's all."

"Oh, I see. Is there something I can do for you?"

"No thanks, I couldn't sleep. I'm just killing time until I leave for an appointment."

"Well, if you're interested in breakfast, the café opens at six." He said looking at his watch. "It should be opening right about now. We also offer complimentary coffee and newspapers, if you like. They're over there," he said, pointing to a service table.

"Thanks, I think I'll take you up on that." The clerk went back to his computer. David passed on the coffee, but walked over and picked up a copy of *The Boston Globe*. Except for a sip of water to wash down his daily medication, he was restricted from food and drink until after the completion of his angiogram.

David sat on one of the overstuffed chairs that, along with a few sofas, were arranged in clusters throughout the lobby. He tried to read the paper. He turned from section to section, from the lead stories to business to sports, but found concentration impossible. His thoughts vacillated between his pending test and Gina. Just a few short weeks ago he was in despair. With little to look forward to, he was in a perpetual state of depression that was only partially relieved with medication. Then suddenly, everything changed. The excitement and promise of the trial, and chance encounter with Gina had lifted his spirits. He felt alive again. Sure, there were no guarantees on either front, but he chose to be optimistic. His sense of hope had been restored, and he relished the feeling.

David checked his watch. It was almost seven o'clock. He decided to leave for the clinic. He would be early for his eight o'clock appointment, but he could just as easily wait there as he could in the hotel lobby, and who knows, maybe he'd run into Gina. Remembering the poor choice of recycled and tattered magazines provided at the clinic, he took the paper with him.

The clinic waiting room was empty when David arrived. He signed in and chose a seat that gave him the best view of the entry door.

He tried to keep his mind occupied with the paper's crossword puzzle, quickly filling in the easy clues; the ones that required little thought. He was penning in the answers when Mike entered through the front entrance. He immediately noticed David was sitting alone and detoured in his direction. "Well, old buddy, this is the big day, cath and injection number one. I'll bet you're excited, huh?"

"I'm a little apprehensive about the angiogram, but yes, to answer your question, I can't wait." Mike patted the side of David's arm and said, "Good luck, David." He gave a thumbs-up as he disappeared down the hallway.

He was about to go back to his puzzle when Gina came flying through the door. She, too, noticed David and waved and said, "Good morning." Disappointed she didn't stop to talk, David blurted out, "Will I see you at Mike's on Saturday?"

"I'm going to try," she said unconvincingly, before proceeding into the hallway.

I'm going to try. Her words rang with uncertainty. David wondered if she would really make the attempt or was it just a convenient answer meant to discourage any further attempts at obtaining a commitment. He was mulling these thoughts over when a nurse appeared. "Mr. Roy?" she inquired.

"Yes?"

"Please follow me. We're ready for you."

David was placed on a gurney, and wheeled into the catheterization lab by Patty, one of the two nurses who would be assisting the attending physician, and the one who would prep him for the procedure. He was amazed by the way medical professionals could remain so detached while poking around in the most intimate areas of a patient's body. Here she was, shaving around his genitals while making small talk with the other nurse as if she were doing nothing more than peeling a banana or pouring a cup of coffee. David always disliked this part, and despite the fact that he'd been through it many times, he always felt embarrassed by it.

For some inexplicable reason, he was far more nervous than he had been in the past when he had undergone the same procedure on a half dozen other occasions. Perhaps he believed he could not continue to defy the odds and emerge from the test unscathed and without complication. Maybe it was his dreadful phobia of hospitals and doctors that developed during his father's ten-year struggle with emphysema, and his mother's lengthy battle with lymphoma. Or maybe it was the simple reality that, this time around, he had more to lose, because he wasn't trying to avoid death. This time he was hoping to reclaim his life.

David felt a chill pass through his entire body, and he began to tremble uncontrollably as his gurney was swiftly placed in the center of the room. Was it incessant fear, or just his inability to quickly acclimate to the lab's cool temperature and sterile environment, he wondered? To his right was a round table covered with instruments and syringes, and to his left, a rather large, intimidating monitor. Before he could collect his thoughts, he was approached by a man and a woman, who appeared to be in their early forties, and each, like Patty, were dressed in light green scrubs. "I'm Doctor Payne." *Oh God, you've got to be kidding me.* "Do you have any questions before we proceed?" he inquired before being politely interrupted by Patty who suggested that an additional sedative be administered because the patient seemed more nervous than most. "Yes, that will be fine, but I want him fully alert to comprehend any directions that I need to give during the procedure." Patty proceeded to fold back several layers of warm compresses, exposing his genital area to all. David couldn't help but think of all the nurses that had viewed his private parts throughout the years. Although no one had seemed terribly overwhelmed by what they had seen, he was grateful that none had seemed unimpressed.

"Do you prefer that I enter through your right or left side?"

"The left will be much more comfortable for me," David replied. He felt the numbing sensation of the local anesthetic being applied to his groin area just seconds before hearing and feeling the puncture of the catheter as it entered his body. It was such a weird sensation to feel a foreign object being firmly threaded through the entire length of his artery to the very core of his being. Even more incredible was his ability to view the entire procedure on the adjacent monitor. *God, one slip of the hand!* He didn't want to think about the repercussions. He knew a tear in the vessel would most likely result in emergency by-pass surgery or death. The first few minutes were difficult, but the pain subsided once the catheter had passed through the abdominal area. As in the past, he then felt a burning, tingling sensation that at times reached his throat and lower jaw. Within minutes it was over. Thank God retrieving the catheter was much less annoying, and far more expedient. He now looked forward to his first injection and his dinner with Mike and, hopefully, Gina.

The angiogram went well and David was relieved that he had made it over the final hurdle. The test results revealed severe occlusion in each of his three major coronary arteries. He didn't need a risky invasive test to tell him that. After all, any moderate exertion reminded him that he was, indeed, on borrowed time. The Sicilia Gene therapy was his one and only hope.

David was one of the first to arrive for lunch the following day. He made his choices and found an empty table. Shortly after, Mike came in with a few coworkers. He saw

David, and after filling his tray, he made his way to David's table. "How'd you make out with your angiogram?" Mike said with concern.

"I do have severe blockages in all three of my main arteries."

"Of course you do, otherwise you wouldn't have been selected for the study."

"Listen, Mike, I know I'm in bad shape. I live with it twenty-four-seven. We both know I didn't need an angiogram to tell me that. But I'm happy that all of the interviews, paperwork, and pretests are behind me. At one o'clock I get my first injection, and *that* is something to be happy about."

"How long ago did you have your bypass?"

"Three years ago. I had just turned thirty eight."

"Wow, and your arteries are that clogged already?"

"Yeah, they used the artery from my left forearm, which they thought was going to be more durable than the ones from the leg, and both mammary arteries. They've since discovered that the arteries from the arm remain open for only one to five years. Mike, I am the antithesis of the people with the Sicilia Gene. They were gifted with a super HDL that keeps their arteries clean. I, on the other hand, am predisposed to very high levels of LDL and inefficiently low levels of HDL. The Torvistat helps somewhat, but not enough. I guess you could say that my body chemistry is programmed to self-destruct." He looked at Mike and shrugged.

"Man, you were dealt a tough hand. I sure hope the

gene therapy works for you. You're way too young to be this sick, old buddy."

"Mike, I'm well aware that this is my only shot. Until I got your phone call, I was resigned to living a life of despair with little hope for any measure of longevity. Now, even before I get my first injection, I feel more alive. I have something to cling to—hope. Anyway," he said, changing the subject, "I'm looking forward to meeting your wife and family on Saturday. What time do you want me to be there?"

"Anytime after noon is good. What time does the ferry get in?"

"Well, if I take the ten o'clock boat, I'll get to New London around eleven forty. By the time I get to your place, it should be almost noon."

"Sounds good to me. Let me give you directions to the Fitzgerald homestead." Mike proceeded to write out directions on a paper napkin, after which he looked at his watch and said, "Time to get back to work. If I don't see you this afternoon, I'll see you on Saturday. Good luck with your injection."

"Thanks, Mike. Oh, wait a second, what can I bring to your house?"

"Just yourself, old buddy. Arianna's got everything covered."

"Well, I'm not coming empty handed. I'll think of something."

"Don't worry about it. Just don't miss the boat," he said with a chuckle.

David checked the number on the door before entering. He was greeted by a nurse who had her hands full. She was carrying a box of syringes and a metal holder that held several vials of what David assumed was the medication. "Hello, I'm David Roy. I have a one o'clock appointment."

"Welcome, Mr. Roy," said the plump, middle-aged woman. "We're ready for you. Please follow me." She headed for a door and awkwardly tried to push it open. David quickly moved in to open it. "Thank you, Mr. Roy."

"I wouldn't want you to drop that," he said pointing to the vials. She looked at him and smiled. After placing the box and vials on a table, she turned to David.

"Okay, Mr. Roy please pull up your sleeve." He pulled up his short-sleeved shirt to reveal his upper arm. The nurse wiped his arm with an alcohol swab, and then without fanfare she filled the syringe from one of the vials and injected him with the clear liquid that contained the synthesized version of the apoA-1 Sicilia Gene. "That's it, Mr. Roy, we'll see you in one week for your second injection. Do you have any questions?"

"Uh, no, I'm okay. Thank you."

"See you next Friday," she said with cold efficiency.

"Thank you," he said as he headed for the door. Once back in the lobby he paused to digest what had just happened. He had been looking forward to this for several weeks and in seconds it was over. It all seemed so anticlimactic. The few other people in the lobby looked strangely at him when he laughed out loud, but he didn't care. The only thing that mattered was knowing that the cleansing Sicilia Gene was now flowing throughout his body.

David Roy returned to the hotel, packed his bags, checked out, and headed for home.

CHAPTER TWELVE

D AVID drove off the ferry in New London at eleven forty-five on Saturday morning. Before leaving Greenport, he had stopped at a local florist to pick up a potted plant for Mike's wife, Arianna. He didn't know the name of the plant, but it was colorful with big red blossoms. He was sure she would like it.

He followed the directions Mike had given him and arrived at the quaint Cape-Cod style house a few minutes before noon. The home's white exterior, accented by its slate colored roof, pale blue shutters, and white picket fence that ran parallel to the road, provided a picture-perfect image of a traditional New England setting. He checked the cars parked in the driveway and on the street, looking for a Massachusetts license plate. He heart sank when he saw none.

Mike met him at the door and greeted him with a big

smile. "Hey, right on time. Come in. Come in," he said as he motioned with his free hand.

David noticed Mike was wearing shorts. He had seen prosthetic legs before, but not this closely and not on someone he knew. His eyes were drawn to it. "If it makes you uncomfortable, I can put on long pants."

"No, no, I'm sorry, I didn't mean to stare. It's just that I've never seen one up close," David said awkwardly as his thoughts vacillated between the Mike he saw and the one he remembered from his youth.

"No problem. It's pretty high tech, state of the art. I'll show you how it works later." David was less than thrilled at the prospect. "Arianna!" Mike shouted, "David's here." She seemed somewhat embarrassed as she appeared from the kitchen. Her slightly overweight torso was wrapped in a white bathrobe and she was drying her shoulder-length jet-black hair with a towel.

"Sorry, as you can see we're running a little late."

After introductions, David presented Arianna with the potted plant.

"Oh, thank you so much. What a beautiful Amaryllis. Look at the size of the blooms, and what a vibrant red color," she said, holding it up for all to see. "That was so thoughtful of you. Mike told me you are really a nice guy. I can't wait to talk with you."

"C'mon, Davey, I'll show you around." Mike gave David a tour of the impeccably kept house and manicured yard. It was obvious to him that Mike was proud of his family and home.

As they walked around the back yard David said, "Do you take care of the yard yourself?"

"Yup, and the garden too," he said pointing to a small plot in the rear of the yard where David saw rows of staked tomato, cucumber, and bean plants.

"I'm impressed."

"I love working in the yard and garden. It's a great diversion and it keeps me out of Arianna's hair—and vice versa—if you know what I mean."

"You have a wonderful wife and home, Mike. You're a lucky man," he said, wistfully.

Mike was describing the many varieties of hydrangeas in his perennial garden when he heard his wife's voice emanating from the house. "Oh my God, it's so good to see you!" Mike turned to David. "Gina's here." Before he could respond, Arianna called from the house, "Michael, come on in, Gina's here."

"I'm surprised she came. I really thought she wouldn't," said David.

"Actually, I'm a little surprised myself. Since her father got sick, she has focused on nothing but his care. Anyway, I'm glad she came and I know you are too," he said with a wink.

When they reached the house, Arianna and Gina were standing in the kitchen talking. When David saw Gina, he felt a flutter in his stomach. She was beautiful. She had on white Capri pants and a sleeveless black top. She was wearing little makeup, which further accented her natural beauty. Her hair was pulled back into a ponytail, which complimented her casual attire.

When their eyes met, Gina smiled softly and said, "It's good to see you again, David."

He smiled. "I'm happy you could make it."

Arianna glanced at both of them and said, "Why don't the two of you go into the living room. Michael and I have some things to do in the kitchen. We'll be in shortly." Michael looked quizzically at his wife. She nodded toward the kitchen and he got the hint.

Gina sat on the edge of a Queen Ann chair while David sat opposite her on the sofa. He looked around the room and said, "Mike's done all right for himself, great family and a nice home. What more could any man want? I don't know how he pulled it off." They both laughed and then David said, "I'm really glad that you're here. I hoped you'd come, but I had my doubts. To be honest, you didn't sound too convincing when you said, 'you would try.'"

"I truly wanted to come. I mentioned it to my father and he told me that if I didn't go he would cut me out of his will. We had a nice long talk and he mentioned some of the same things to me that you had said. At the end, he promised to stay alive while I was away. My father has a sick sense of humor. So, here I am. I really wanted to see Arianna and the kids again—and you, too," she said as she leaned forward, reached over and affectionately patted the top of his hand.

They talked for some time before Mike and Arianna reappeared. It wasn't long before all were enjoying a glass of Merlot from a bottle Gina had given Arianna. Mike and David reminisced to the delight of the two women.

After hearing several stories from Mike and David's

childhood and sharing many laughs, Arianna excused herself to finish preparing dinner. Gina offered to help, and they both left the room.

"Well, are you having fun yet?" asked Mike.

"You can't imagine how much I'm enjoying myself."

"Wait till you see what the wife has made for dinner. She's an amazing cook." Mike wasn't exaggerating. Arianna put out a sumptuous display of delectable Greek dishes, including: Spanakopita, Greek salad, moussaka, and roast leg of lamb.

Arianna culinary skills proved exceptional as everyone enjoyed the dinner and the jovial conversation that filled the room with laughter. Just when everyone thought they couldn't eat another thing, Arianna made coffee and served a platter of baklava along with a bottle of ouzo and Metaxa.

After the gluttonous repast, Arianna and Mike began to clear the table.

"Why don't you two take a little walk while we clean up?"

David looked at Gina and said, "Sounds good to me. What do you say?"

"I definitely could use a walk. I haven't eaten this much in—I don't when. Arianna, everything was delicious."

"I'll second that," said David.

Gina and David strolled beneath the large oak trees whose enveloping canapé silhouetted against the moonlit sky. They seemed to command a presence of their own as they outlined both the street and the manicured lawns and quaint houses. A few minutes into their walk, David burst out laughing.

"What's so funny?"

"Arianna."

"What?"

"Not only is she a great cook, she's also the social direc-tor." Now, it was Gina's turn to laugh.

"I noticed that too, but she means well."

"I know she does. It just struck me funny, that's all."

They walked for a while longer before David broke the silence. "You know, Gina, I had a great time today. I really enjoy your company and I would like to see you again. Maybe we could have dinner sometime, or see a show, or do something of your choosing."

"David, I'm not too sure about this."

"C'mon, you know you'll have a good time. Besides, you know I'm harmless and you'll be perfectly safe with me."

David felt a sharp pain in the pit of his stomach because he realized, although he meant well, this was not something a man would or should tell a woman he wished to court.

Gina unsuccessfully tried to stifle a laugh and said, "I'm sorry, I didn't mean to make light of your condition, but I don't think of you as being harmless."

"I guess it is a rather poor choice of words, but you know what I mean."

"Yes, I do, but it was never a concern."

"By the way, David, aren't you forgetting one little detail?"

"And what might that be?"

"That I live in Boston and you live on Long Island.

That's a long way to go to pick up a date. Besides, you know we're not allowed to fraternize with our patients. I could lose my job and you could be sent home."

"My time is my own. I could drive up on the weekend and get a room—for one, of course."

She gave him a look that acknowledged his lame attempt at humor, and then said, "We'll see." David was disappointed with her tentative answer, but at least she left the door open.

They circled the block and soon found themselves back at the house. Mike's son and daughter had returned from a neighbor's birthday party, and Mike and his son were playing catch with a football in the backyard while his daughter was attempting to jump rope. When Mike spotted David and Gina, he called out to David, "Go deep!" David put up his hands and said,

"Are you trying to kill me? No, you throw me the ball and you go deep." Mike tossed him the ball and started gimping across the yard. David pumped his arm and let fly a perfect spiral that hit its target. "Nice pass," remarked Mike.

"Wow, I'm impressed," said Gina.

"I was a pretty good athlete before I got sick." David said proudly.

"By the looks of it, you haven't lost it all."

After hesitating, he said, "No, not totally."

Gina looked at her watch. "It's getting late. I should be going. I'd like to get home before dark. I never liked driving at night."

David concurred. "I need to head back to the ferry

myself. Mike and Arianna had asked me to stay over. I told them I had plans, but would take them up on their offer another time."

After they said there goodbyes to the Fitzgeralds, David walked Gina to her car. "May I call you?" he asked.

"Okay," she said looking up at him and smiling, "but not this weekend."

It was time to bid farewell and David, feeling awkward in the moment, stuck out his hand. Gina glanced at it, then leaned forward and kissed David on the cheek. "I had a wonderful time today."

"So did I."

Gina got into her car. After starting it, she put it in gear and gave David one last smile before pulling away. David suddenly realized he didn't have her phone number. He ran after the car and shouted for Gina to stop. At first he thought she didn't see him, but then he saw her brake lights. Out of breath, he walked toward the car as Gina backed up.

"What's wrong?" she asked.

"I just realized that I don't have your phone number." She waved him off saying, "Don't worry, I have yours, I'll call you."

"Sure you will," David replied.

"No, really, I'll call you. I promise," she said and drove away.

CHAPTER THIRTEEN

D AVID spent much of Sunday thinking about the day before at Mike's. It was great meeting Mike's family, but the highlight of the day was the time he spent alone with Gina. For some inexplicable reason, he was unusually comfortable around her. With other women, he believed his health was an issue, but not with her. Perhaps it was due to her chosen field of work or because she lived with someone whose life had been traumatically altered by the same dreadful disease, or maybe it was simply because he sensed she was special. Whatever the reason, he was grateful he didn't have to deal with the issue—at least for the time being. Eventually, he knew he would, especially if she fell for him and the therapy didn't work. He couldn't expect anyone to commit to a long-term relationship with someone with such a dubious prognosis. For now, he would take it one step at a time.

It was eight o'clock on Monday night and David was

lamenting the prospect that Gina had changed her mind and decided not to call him. Maybe after thinking about it, she came to the conclusion that committing to a relationship with someone in his physical condition wasn't the most prudent course of action and chose to opt out. She did kiss him though, albeit on the cheek. Nevertheless, it was still a kiss, and somewhere from deep within he knew it was more than just a kind gesture. *Besides, it has been only two days, and between her job at the clinic and attending to her father's needs, there are great demands on her time.*

He was contemplating these conflicting rationales when the phone rang. He glanced at the caller ID display. He didn't recognize the number, but he did the area code— 857—Boston. He snapped up the phone.

"Hello," he said with anticipation, using all his resources to hide his excitement.

"Hi, David, it's Gina."

"Gina, hi, how are you?"

"You sound surprised to hear from me."

"I am a little, but pleasantly so."

"I was going to call you yesterday until I realized that I left your phone number on my desk at work. I wanted to thank you again for Saturday. When I got home, I was thoroughly debriefed by my father."

"Oh, really, and?"

"David, you have to understand, my father lives in fear that his daughter, his only child, will end up an old spinster. He has been encouraging me for the longest time to get out more. So, he was thrilled when I said I was going. He wanted to know all about you."

"And what did you tell him?"

"By the way," she said quickly changing the subject, "are you into baseball?" David sensed she didn't want to talk about it, so he didn't press the issue. He wondered if she had told her dad that he had suffered from the same debilitating disease. *Probably not*, he thought.

"Oh, yeah, I follow baseball. I'm a huge Yankee fan."

"Oh God, I should have known. My team is the Red Sox and we love to hate the Yankees."

"What a surprise. Does that mean we are doomed?"

"Well, I guess if Mary Matalin and James Carville can get along, I guess we can too.

"The reason I asked is because my father has season tickets. When I was young, he and I would attend almost all the home games. He's had them ever since I can remember, and even though he doesn't use them anymore, he refuses to give them up. Now, he usually gives them to my nephew.

"Anyway, as I'm sure you are aware, Boston is playing New York this coming weekend, and I was wondering if you'd like to go to the game? That is, if you think your heart is strong enough to handle seeing the Bronx Bummers—I mean Bombers lose to the better team."

"Fat chance, and yes, I'd love to go, if only to see you eat your words."

"We'll see," she said with confidence. "What time is your appointment on Friday?"

"Three thirty. Why do you ask?"

"Well, if you don't mind waiting around until five, I could show you where I live. I wouldn't want you to get lost on Saturday. In case you haven't heard, Boston is not the easiest city to drive around in. Also, there is a Holiday Inn less than five minutes from my house. It's a lot closer than the hotel near the clinic."

"Sounds good to me."

"I can look up the number if you'd like."

"That'd be great, thanks."

After Gina gave David the number, they continued talking for well over an hour, each asking questions of the other; quickly removing the self-imposed barriers that restricted them from getting to know one another. Each began to slowly realize that they shared a common bond.

Their hardships had merely stifled, not deadened, their desire for companionship. He told her about his failed marriage, but left out the infertility part. He knew if their relationship continued that he would eventually have to tell her. Fortunately this was not the time, he concluded.

When David arrived at the large two-story Victorian style house in Boston's Italian north end at eleven thirty, he found Gina sitting in a rocker on the wrap-around porch. She was wearing jeans, sneakers, and a T-shirt emblazoned with *Red Sox* across the front, and her ponytail stuck out of the back of the team cap. A mitt lay in her lap. The scene reminded him of his youth and his trips to Yankee Stadium. Gina began to laugh because David was also wearing a baseball cap and carrying a glove in hopes of snagging a foul ball.

They exchanged smiles as David made his way up the walk. "I can see that you're ready to go."

"I am, but before we go, I want you to meet my father.

He doesn't like me to date anyone he hasn't met. Come on," she said as she took his hand and led him into the house. David observed how cute she looked. *Beautiful and cute—what a great combination.*

The furnishings, although in good condition, appeared old. David surmised that little had changed since her mother had died. Gina led him into a room that appeared to be a combination den and library. Its walls were paneled in rich cherry. A built-in bookcase covered one wall from ceiling to floor with a break in the middle to accommodate a large window. Its top shelves were stocked mostly with what looked like law books. Gina told David that before her father had gotten sick, he was one of the most prominent attorneys in Boston. The remainder of the shelf space was filled with expensive-looking leather-bound classics and other volumes of various sizes. Another wall, perpendicular to the bookcase, was covered with framed photographs.

Alphonso Coletti was sitting at his desk. His back was to the bookcase, and light from the mid-day sun filled the room from the window behind him. *The Globe's* sports pages were spread out before him.

David was taken aback at the sight of the frail man whose clothes hung from his shoulders like those on a coat hanger. An oxygen tube snaked its way down from his nostrils and disappeared beneath the desk. "Daddy, this is David...David, my father." David moved quickly, approaching the desk and offering his hand in hopes that Mr. Coletti wouldn't try to stand. He sensed David's motive and stood erect as they shook hands. "I'm not totally incapacitated. Nice to meet you, son." David's face reddened at the realization that her father recognized his transparent, although sincere, gesture.

"Nice to meet you too, sir."

"Name's Alphonso, but everyone calls me Al. According to the paper, it looks like we could see a pitching duel today."

"Yes sir, it sure looks possible, although I'd much rather watch a slugfest. But it really doesn't matter as long as the Yanks win."

"Well, whatever happens, I hope that traitor, Johnny Damon, goes O for four. You'd never have seen Ted Williams or Yaz jump ship like that Benedict Arnold."

"I agree, sir. There is no team loyalty today. As in most everything else, money rules." As he spoke, David scanned the wall of photos. He saw many of Gina, her father, and a woman he assumed was her late mother. He noticed one where Gina and her father were posing with Boston great Carl Yastrzemski. Written across the front was: "To Al and Gina, two of my most loyal fans. Best Wishes, Carl Yastrzemski." Another photo showed a proud Alphonso Coletti standing with his arm on the shoulder of another famous Red Sox slugger. The caption simply read: "Best wishes, Ted Williams."

Al noticed David's gaze and chimed in, "Ya know son, it was said that Ted Williams could read a license plate when most other people couldn't see its color and Yaz... nobody could play a carom off the green monster like he could."

"I must admit, they were pretty good," David conceded.

"It's getting late. We'd better get going or we're going to miss the first pitch," Gina said, as she looked at her watch.

"Nice meeting you, Mr. Coletti."

"Al, son, call me Al. I'll be watching the game on TV. Maybe I'll see you two," he said with a laugh. Gina gave her father a hug and said, "I left your lunch on the counter."

"Thank you, honey. You two have fun."

As David drove to Fenway Park, they made small talk in between Gina's directions. "Your father seems pretty perky for someone in his condition."

"Sometimes I think he puts on a show so I won't worry, but I've seen him gasping for air after very little exertion. I go along with his little charade just to appease him, but he doesn't fool me one bit."

"Have you ever tried getting him into this or any other trial that might help his condition?"

"Unfortunately, he's not a viable candidate. His heart muscle is too badly damaged."

"Well, it's clear he adores you."

"I know he does. Sometimes I wonder if I'm worthy," she said, more to herself than David. He let the comment pass.

The stadium parking lot was filling fast as they arrived. After parking, they made their way to the box seats, which were located directly behind Boston's dugout, but not before stopping to buy a program and scorecard.

"You do take your baseball seriously, don't you?"

"Is there any other way?" she said pertly.

David expected the roar of the crowd when the Sox were introduced, but he had to laugh when thunderous booing erupted when his Yankees took the field. Gina turned and gave him a big smile.

It was much as Mr. Coletti had predicted, a pitchers duel. The final score was two to one, Boston.

As they exited the parking lot, David asked Gina to recommend a good restaurant. "David, you didn't mention anything about dinner. Besides, I wouldn't want to go out looking like this. Before you came this morning, I made a tray of Chicken Marsala. I'd like it if you'd stay for dinner, and based on the results of the game, I know my father would enjoy your company." This was not how David had envisioned their first dinner date, but she was right, they hadn't firmed up any plans for after the game.

"I'd love to. I'm looking forward to you and your father razzing me a little."

"A little? You Yankee fans are insufferable. When we get the chance to get you back, we have to take advantage of the opportunity."

"That's fine with me, I can take it. It doesn't happen very often."

"Touché."

The conversation at dinner was predictable, and the Marsala was exceptional. David mentally added one more item to her list of assets, Chef de Cuisine.

After dinner, David and Gina sat on the two-person swing on the front porch. "The Chicken Marsala was great. Did your mother teach you how to cook?

"No, I was too young when she died. I taught myself. If you can read, you can cook. I always liked to cook and I have a fairly sizable collection of cookbooks."

"Well, I'm impressed. It was delicious."

For the next several minutes they sat swinging in silence; a scene reminiscent of a more innocent and far less complicated period in time.

"I know it has only been a little over a week since I received my first injection, but I swear I'm feeling better already."

"It does seem a little early to see any results, but who knows, Dr. Rentz seemed very optimistic at our last staff meeting."

"Maybe it's just the result of getting out and enjoying myself. I haven't done anything or gone anywhere in so long I'd forgotten what it feels like to have some fun."

"Maybe it's the company you're keeping," she said coyly.

"I'm absolutely sure that has something to do with it."

"It could be the medicine … or maybe it's just the placebo effect. In every double blind study there are positive reports from both groups. It's psychosomatic. You know … the power of positive thinking." Gina suddenly realized what she was saying and added, "I'm sure that's not the case with you. I mean … I don't know, but I'm sure it's the drug that's making you feel better."

It was at this moment that David realized that Michael had not told Gina that he had gotten him into the non-placebo group. Why hadn't he told her? Did he not totally trust her? For now he decided to cast his reservations aside because he recognized Gina's comments had placed her in an awkward position. He gently took her hand in his and peered directly into her dark eyes. Her gentle smile affirmed what he already knew. Gina fully understood he was referring to more than his health.

CHAPTER FOURTEEN

GOOD things were happening to David. Certainly, his admittance into the Sicilia trial and his bourgeoning relationship with Gina were the two that most affected his well-being. As a result, he felt more alive than he had for nearly a decade. But he knew his body, and something more than his newfound happiness was making him feel physically better. He refused to believe that it was psychosomatic, as Gina had suggested. The truth was, he was sleeping better and he felt less fatigued. He needed to prove to himself that these improvements were real. Somehow, he had to quantify them. He decided to take a walk. He took walks most days, but he kept them short. He knew his limits, and would stop before he felt any tightness in his chest. Today, he would test those limits. He threw on shorts and a T-shirt, and after lacing up his sneakers, headed out the door. He walked his usual route, but at a slightly faster pace. No pain or tightness—*so far, so good.* He stepped up the pace another notch and repeated the route. This time he was slightly winded, but still experienced no angina. He was pleased with his performance. It was enough for one day; he didn't want to push his luck. Two weeks ago he would have been winded after the first few minutes. He had proven to himself that it was not in his mind; he was not only feeling better—he was getting better. Whatever the Sicilia Gene serum was supposed to do, it was obviously doing. He never expected to see results this quickly. After years of despair, his optimism was growing and with it, his confidence in the future.

The following week, David and Gina spoke every day. They talked about many things, but not of his improving condition. David kept the results of his self-tests to himself. He knew she harbored doubts about his claim and wanted to wait until they were together to show her firsthand.

On Friday, as in the previous week, after his appointment, he again met Gina. This week, to avoid any suspicion, he drove directly to her house. And this time he had confirmed dinner plans at a restaurant of her choice.

While Gina readied herself, David visited with her father. He liked Al and he had the impression the feeling was mutual. Al loved talking baseball. And David added the element of doing it with an adversary, something Al, as an attorney, enjoyed. The series between the Yankees and Red Sox had ended with Boston winning three of the four game series, and Al couldn't pass up the opportunity to do a little piling on. David let him have his fun, knowing his turn would come.

Al Coletti turned serious. "David, if you don't mind,

I'm going to be a bit forward. Gina thinks the world of you. As you might expect, we are very close, and she has always confided in me. We've spoken about you on many occasions. At the risk of violating her confidence, I must tell you, she's hoping the relationship will grow into a long-term one." David felt a sudden wave of elation as Al continued.

"Now, as you can imagine, I adore my daughter. She has devoted her entire adult life to my care ... something I am not entirely pleased about. She deserves a life of her own ... to be happy, and that is something I would like to see before I go. I have encouraged her to date, but she would have none of it. That is until she met you, and even then I had to threaten to disinherit her if she didn't go," he said with a weak laugh. "I wouldn't want to see her hurt, so I ask that if the feeling isn't mutual, please don't lead her on. And I do have one other concern ... your health. All Gina will tell me is that you are a participant in one of her company's trials. Professional ethics prevents her from telling me more. Pardon me if I'm being too personal, but would you mind giving me some insight as to the state of your health? I'm sure you understand my concern."

"Mr. Coletti, I appreciate your concern for Gina, but I can assure you the feeling is mutual. Until now I had the same concerns myself. It's good to hear that she feels the same way. As far as my health is concerned, I am on medication for high cholesterol, and the medication I'm receiving at the trial promises to reduce it to more normal levels." He hoped that cursory explanation would satisfy Al Coletti.

"That's good. I needed to hear those things from you— and David, let's keep this part of our conversation between us." David nodded his understanding as Gina entered the room.

"What are you two talking about? You both look like the cat that swallowed the canary."

"I was trashing those bums from the Bronx."

"Careful, Daddy, you know what they say about paybacks."

"Yes, yes, I know, but one must take his shots when they come along," he said as he winked at David. "You two have fun. Oh, and Gina, one more thing. I think you should follow my suggestion." David wondered what he was referring to, but decided it best not to ask.

After they got into David's Jeep Grand Cherokee, Gina asked him if he had checked into the hotel. "No, I came directly to your house. I thought I could swing by and do it on our way to dinner."

"Well, Daddy and I think it could get expensive staying in a hotel, especially if you plan on coming up on a regular basis. He suggested you stay with us. Our home is certainly big enough."

"Your father suggested that? So that's what he was referring to when we left? I thought he was talking about a certain restaurant or a specific dish to order. He's okay with me staying in your house?" David said, sounding a little surprised.

"Relax, David. The offer was to stay at our house, not in my room. And besides, you told me your intentions are honorable, aren't they?" she said coyly.

"Well, maybe not a hundred percent," he retorted with a sly grin.

Gina playfully punched him in the arm and said, "I'm not worried, Daddy has a gun and he taught me how to use it."

"Oh, now that's a comforting thought."

"But don't worry, neither one of us has shot anyone lately."

"Another comforting thought. You sure know how to make a guy feel right at home. I just hope I don't run into your father on the way to the bathroom, especially if he's packing."

"You don't have to worry about that. He sleeps on the ground floor in the parlor that we converted into a bedroom because he's too weak to climb stairs."

"Ah, the infamous stairs. Thank you for bringing that up."

"Should I make up a cot in my father's room for you?"

"Very funny. Not to worry, I think I can handle a few stairs."

Gina had selected a cozy trattoria not far from her house. It was housed in an old brownstone in Boston's north end. If it didn't have a sign above the front door, it would look like most of the other houses on the block. The small family-owned restaurant, which seated no more than thirty people, had skillfully positioned its tables and booths to provide an intimate dining experience.

The matronly hostess greeted Gina at the door with a big hug.

"Gina, it's so good to see you. You look wonderful. How is Alphonso?"

"It's good to see you too, Anna. Daddy is holding his own. As you know, he doesn't get out much anymore because if he did, you would see him at his favorite restaurant."

"Oh, you're such a sweetheart," she said and gave Gina another hug.

"Give him our best." Anna turned her attention to David.

"Anna, this is my friend, David Roy. He's visiting from Long Island. He tells me the best Italian restaurants in the country are there. I had to bring him here to prove him wrong."

"We'll do our best. Come, let's start off with the best table in the house."

They followed Anna to a table nestled in the niche of a large bay window. David pulled out the chair for Gina, and then seated himself at the white linen-covered table illuminated by a single candle placed at its center.

"Well, Mr. Roy, do you have your heart set on a particular dish or are you interested in a dining adventure?"

"Pardon me?"

"David, when Daddy and I come here we don't order off the menu. We let Anna bring us what she wishes, and I have to tell you, we are never disappointed."

"Sure, it sounds like fun. But I must tell you, I don't eat red meat."

Anna clapped her hands. "Very good," she said. Before she left for the kitchen David ordered a bottle of Amarone Della Valpolicella Classico, 1995. "Wow," said Gina, "I'm impressed."

"It's a great wine. It can stand up to the best the French have to offer."

"Yes, and very expensive. Is the gentleman vying for favors?" she said in a mock English accent.

"I would be no gentleman if it were true," he retorted. "But they would not be rejected if bestowed upon me."

"All comes to he who waits," she said laughing. "By the way, your English accent needs some work."

"I would have practiced if I knew I'd need it tonight." They were both laughing when Anna appeared with a huge platter of hot and cold antipasto.

David and Gina enjoyed a delicious meal of Italian dishes prepared by Anna's husband, Carlo. To their delight, Anna brought out small samples of many entrees. David loved eggplant, but never had Eggplant Parmesan that wasn't breaded. "This is great."

"I knew you'd like it. Try some of the chicken francese. It is the best you'll ever have." They ate until they could not eat another bite. They declined dessert and opted for only cappuccino.

"I hope you saved a little room for one more course."

"Are you kidding? I'm stuffed."

"Oh, c'mon, there's always room for a little crow."

"Not so fast. The meal was excellent, but don't make a judgment until I take you to one of my favorite restaurants on the island."

"Fair enough, but you must admit this will be hard to beat."

They were sipping their cappuccino when David said, "Gina, I know you think it's all in my head, but I can tell you for certain that it's not. I am getting better. I'm sure some of the improvement, at least the mental part, has to do with you." Gina smiled softly as David continued. "But physically I can do things I couldn't just two weeks ago. This stuff is doing its job, it's really working. I can't remember when I've felt this good."

"I think you may be right. A week ago I had my doubts, but during this past week I heard the same type of comments from several other participants. There are too many of them to chalk it up to coincidence. It is becoming increasingly clear who is getting the Sicilia serum and who is in the control group. I've even discussed it with Doctor Bauer. The results seem to be so dramatic that he wants to do an intermediary study on the participants. He's planning to conduct an additional angiogram on a few randomly selected participants to see if there is any lessening of occlusion. He's so optimistic; he's notified Doctor Rentz from Freiz."

"When are they planning to perform the tests?"

"I'm not sure, but Doctor Bauer seemed pretty excited. I wouldn't be surprised if he discussed this with you during your next visit."

"Wow, that is exciting. So many positive things are happening to me lately that I think I'd better pinch myself."

"I'll save you the trouble," she said as she leaned across the table and gently pinched his cheek. "It's real David ... all of it."

When they arrived back at the house Gina excused herself and checked in on her father. He was asleep with only the flickering light from the television illuminating the room. She walked to his bedside and kissed him on the forehead before turning off the television and quietly closing the door.

"My father is sleeping. He has a habit of falling asleep with the TV on. Come on, I'll show you your room." David followed Gina up the wide oak staircase and down a hallway. "This is your room, sire," she said as she bowed and waved her arm across her midsection. David laughed.

"I'm not going there again," he said waving her off.

"The bathroom is over there," she said pointing to a door across the hall. "Come down after you get settled."

David surveyed the large room. All of the furniture seemed oversized and antique. In the middle of the room against the far wall stood a huge four-poster bed with a canopy. A wooden step stool provided access to the high mattress. He quickly unpacked the few clothes he'd brought, and after putting his toilet bag on the vanity in the bathroom, he went down and rejoined Gina, whom he found in the kitchen. "Would you like a little more wine," she said holding up the unfinished bottle of Amarone that Anna had allowed them to take home. "Only if you join me." Gina grabbed two wine glasses from the cupboard. "It's such a nice evening, why don't we have this on the porch?"

They sipped their wine and talked while gently swinging. Gina prodded David a little on his failed marriage. He wasn't ready to get into it, so he skirted the issue and she didn't push it. For a period they swung in silence. David put his arm around Gina and she leaned in close and laid her head on his shoulder. The wine and the rocking motion of the swing soon lulled Gina to sleep. David was perfectly content to sit there and listen to the rhythmic cadence of her breathing. After some time passed, David didn't know how long—nor did he care, Gina suddenly woke with a jerk. "Oh, I'm sorry I fell asleep. How rude of me."

"Don't be silly. It's been a long week. I'm a little tired myself."

"Maybe we should call it a night."

"I guess we should," David replied as he gently placed his arms around her, offering an affectionate hug before retiring for the evening.

They climbed the stairs together; David going to the left and Gina to the right.

David lay in bed unable to fall asleep. His hyperactive mind wouldn't allow it. His thoughts were vacillating between his evening with Gina and the apparent success of the Sicilia Gene therapy when he heard a soft knock on the door. "Yes?"

"It's me," Gina said as she entered his room. David hunched up on his elbows. The ambient light from the full moon enabled him to see her slender form. She was wearing a full-length nightgown. David reached for the light. "No, don't turn the light on. I just wanted to thank you again for a lovely evening. I thoroughly enjoyed myself." She bent down to kiss him. As their lips met, he instinctively pulled her toward him. The innocent kiss turned passionate and she hesitated for a brief moment before pulling away. "Maybe this wasn't such a good idea."

"Please stay," David whispered.

"I want to, but I'm not sure. If I stay, will you promise to behave?"

"Of course. Believe me; I would never do anything to make you feel uncomfortable."

"I do believe you, David. Do you think it will be okay if I just lay next to you?"

"Yes," he said while pulling her close.

They cuddled for a time before Gina drifted off to sleep. David was tired, but didn't want to sleep. It had been a long time since he felt a woman next to him. It was comforting to feel her body heat radiate through him, to hear the rhythm of her heartbeat, and to smell the sweetness of her hair. He fought it for as long as he could, and then, he too, drifted off to a peaceful sleep.

CHAPTER FIFTEEN

ON Sunday afternoon, David headed back to Greenport. Leaving Gina was difficult, and the thought of not seeing her for another five days was disheartening. If this relationship was to continue to grow, as he hoped it would, other arrangements needed to be made. But he was getting ahead of himself. In the short term, seeing Gina on weekends would have to suffice.

On Monday, as usual, he awoke before dawn. He wasted no time, as he was anxious to take his walk—to further test himself. Instead of taking his usual route, he decided to walk the half-mile to the tiny village.

Greenport had once been a thriving, whaling port rivaled only by its neighbor, Sag Harbor, located across the bay on Long Island's south fork. After the whaling industry died, the locals turned to fishing and harvesting oysters and bay and sea scallops for their living. Today, all that remain are a few commercial fishermen and bay-men. Gone are the oysters and their processing plants with their huge mounds of shells that most villagers used to cover their dirt driveways. Gone, too, are the huge wooden bunker boats with their tall center mast on top of which sat a crow's nest where spotters sat for hours looking for schools of bunker that were netted for their oil.

Now, the vast majority of fishing is recreational and the commercial boat docks have been replaced by waterfront restaurants and marinas complete with all the amenities of a first class resort. Not only has the village been transformed by necessity and time, but the entire north fork has been forced to adapt to the modern world. The once dominant potato farm has given way to vineyards and wineries that dot the expanse from Aquebogue to Orient Point. The few remaining farmers have had to accept new ideas and terms that at first seemed strange, like *agratainment*. Instead of just planting a field of corn for harvesting, now farmers plant fields with the sole purpose of creating a corn maze. Day trippers by the thousands clog the inadequate roads that lead east, making stops at the many farm stands and wineries as well as the pumpkin and Christmas tree farms that line Routes 25 and 27, the only two roads on and off the north fork.

David took in a heaping breath of the cool, damp morning air. He loved this time of year, a pleasing respite between the cold raw winters and sticky hot summers.

As he walked down Front Street, he glanced to his right. He could see the few remaining commercial fishing boats that made their home at the railroad dock, which marked the end of the line on the north fork for the Long Island

Railroad. In years past, the train would actually venture out over water; today the bulkhead was safely on terra firma.

He reached the corner of Front and Main where he stopped for a cup of tea at the Coronet restaurant. He kibitzed with the locals and the natives while sipping his tea. The native-born Greenporters had made it clear when David married Sally and moved to Greenport that he could eventually be accepted as a local, but never a native; something in which the natives took great pride. Although it was all said in jest, he had the impression that the natives took it more seriously than the locals.

After his tea break, David headed down Main Street toward the bay. On the way he passed Goldsmith's toy store, an old fashioned proprietorship whose wooden floors, narrow aisles, and vast inventory would immediately transport any baby boomer back to his childhood. Toys of every kind could be found in small bins, stacked on shelves, and even hanging from the ceiling. It was truly a child's wonderland. The street ended at the Claudio complex on the bay front. Claudio's restaurant, billed as the oldest family-owned restaurant in the United States, faced the water. The old wooden two-story structure had a dinning room on each level, and an ornate antique bar of dark mahogany accented by a brass foot rail as its centerpiece. It was well documented that during prohibition it was used by rum-runners as a transportation hub and by bootleggers as a distribution point. Since the restaurant was built partially over water, the rumrunners would maneuver their boats under the restaurant and unload the contraband through a trap door into a windowless room. From there the whiskey was delivered to speakeasies across Long Island and New York City. David was fascinated by the village's colorful past, and he wondered what it would have been like to live during that historical period in time.

David stood on the pier at Claudio's and looked across the bay to Shelter Island, an enclave for the rich that was nestled between the north and south forks of the island; hence its name. From his vantage point, he could see the many sailboats moored at The Shelter Island Yacht Club in Dering Harbor. He watched as two ferries passed each other on their way from one island to the other. It was an especially beautiful morning. David was mesmerized by the sun's rays shimmering off the bay. Gina would like Greenport, he thought. He decided that instead of spending the next weekend in Boston, he would invite her to visit his adopted hometown. He wondered if she would come, recalling the difficulty he'd had in getting her to leave her father's side for a two-hour date. *All I can do is ask.* He took in a few deep breaths of cool salt air before starting for home.

Encouraged by his successful trek into town, David jumped into his Jeep and drove to Sixty-Seven Steps on Long Island Sound. The beach was so named because there were sixty-seven steps on a wooden staircase that led from the top of the sound bank to the beach below.

As he stood on the top landing overlooking the sound, he was overtaken by a wave of nostalgia. He and Sally had come here to swim in the summer and walk the boulder-laden beach the rest of the year. He shook it off and contemplated his next move. There was a landing half way down. *Surely I can make it there and back*. He started down. When he reached the landing, he stopped and considered his options: start back up or continue to the bottom. Although he had a fleeting thought that he might be biting off more than he could chew, he hesitated for only a few seconds before descending. When he reached the beach he walked to the water's edge and stopped. Again, thoughts of Sally came to him. They had come here many times. However, he hadn't been back since the divorce. *If Gina does come, I'll take her here. I'll start new memories.* He turned and looked back at the staircase—Sixty-Seven Steps—and it looked much higher than he remembered. He wondered if he had made the right choice by coming all the way down. He started up slowly, not wanting to overexert himself this far down. He climbed steadily, five steps, then ten, fifteen steps, then twenty-five. At thirty-four he reached the landing and still wasn't experiencing any signs of fatigue or angina. Excited by his renewed sense of confidence, he hesitated only briefly before starting his final ascent. When he reached the top, he was winded, but still felt no pain or discomfort. Before going home, he took one last look over the water to Connecticut. On clear days it was visible to the naked eye. He wondered what was in store for him on his next visit to the clinic.

He was eager to talk with Gina about his accomplishments of the day, but also somewhat anxious about asking her to come to Greenport. He called her at the usual time, 8 p.m. They talked for a while about some mundane things until

David couldn't hold back any longer. "Gina, you'll never guess what I did today."

"So, tell me."

"This morning I walked the half mile to town and back—"

"That's great, David."

"No. No. That's not it. I felt pretty good when I got home so I decided to try something else. I drove to the sound, to a place called Sixty-Seven-Steps. That's how many steps there are down to the beach. I went to the bottom and walked halfway up before taking a short breather. Then, I walked up to the top. I was winded, but I had no adverse reactions, no angina...no anything. Sixty-seven steps equates to more than five flights of stairs. I used to have trouble with one."

"David, that is wonderful!" There was a short pause before she spoke again. "Hmm, I guess we know what that means don't we?" she said in a suggestive manner. David felt his face redden and he became flustered.

"I didn't mean for you to think that I was trying to insinuate that I am now able to—"

"Relax, Sweetie, I know what you meant and I'm happy for you, but I also know what it means as far as you and I are concerned...and I'm happy for us as well. Let's just leave it at that for now."

"Fair enough. Gina, there is one more thing. I was thinking it would be nice if you could come to Greenport this weekend. I think you'd like it. It's a great little town, especially this time of year." He anticipated an excuse but none was forthcoming.

"I'd love to come to Greenport, it sounds lovely. I was wondering when you were going to invite me."

"You were? I didn't ask sooner because I didn't think you'd accept with your father's condition and all. As a matter of fact, I expected you to beg off this time."

"You know that Daddy and I are close. We talk about everything. The subject has come up in our conversations. He's convinced me to take you up on the offer if and when you made it, although I must say it didn't take much convincing. Daddy's also assured me that he can survive without me … at least for a while."

"A wise man that Al Coletti," David said with a chuckle. The remainder of the conversation centered on Gina's pending visit and David's next appointment at the clinic.

That night David had trouble falling asleep. The conflicting emotions of anticipation and apprehension kept him awake well into the night. On one hand, he looked forward to his next visit to the clinic and Gina coming to Greenport. On the other hand, there were issues the two of them had to deal with. He finally rationalized that whatever happened, for the most part, was out of his control. *If I can't control it, there's no sense worrying about it.* He did his best to only think of the positive things in his life, and eventually he drifted off to sleep.

On Wednesday morning, David received a call from Dr. Bauer asking if he would agree to submit to a second angiogram, which he did without hesitation. Because he was vague as to its purpose, except to say it was needed for an intermediate study, Doctor Bauer appeared somewhat surprised that David seemed eager to undergo another angiogram so soon. He then gave David the same pretest instruction he'd heard so many times before. He could recite them in his sleep, but he listened patiently. David had some questions, but thought better of it and held his tongue. The doctor thanked him for his cooperation and hung up.

In his wildest dreams, David never thought he would be looking forward to having another angiogram.

CHAPTER SIXTEEN

D AVID arrived at the clinic on Friday with great expectations. He waited anxiously to be called for his angiogram. The seven a.m. appointment necessitated his coming over the night before and getting a hotel room.

He was flipping through an old issue of *Time* magazine when Mike came through the front door in a rush. He waved to David as he raced through the lobby, uttering with a wide grin, "Late, as usual." David returned the smile and shook his finger at him in mock disdain before going back to his magazine. He looked at his watch; it read ten past seven. He waited impatiently until seven twenty-five when Mike appeared and called him into the office. Dr. Bauer didn't seem to be as personable as he had been during prior visitations. He appeared preoccupied, distant, as if something was bothering him. David looked at Mike quizzically and nodded toward Bauer. Mike answered by shrugging his shoulders. Dr. Bauer turned to David,

"Mr. Roy, I hope we haven't inconvenienced you too much, but I'm told another angiogram is no longer required." David was taken aback.

"Really? What's changed, Doctor?"

"Well, I was late calling you in this morning because I was on the phone with Doctor Price, NECCC's head administrator. As you may know, we have been performing angiograms all week. Doctor Price believes we have ascertained enough information for the time being. Again, I'm sorry if we've caused you any inconvenience."

"What does this new information show, Doctor?"

"I'm sorry, Mr. Roy, I'm not at liberty to say. Any information regarding the study will come from Doctor Price's office. Michael, could I ask you to go to the lab and pick up the serum for Mr. Roy's injection?"

"Oh, it's here in the fridge. I picked it up yesterday afternoon."

"Evidently, there's been some sort of mix-up. I'm told we have the wrong serum," Doctor Bauer replied.

"I picked it up myself, Doctor. It's the right stuff."

"Mr. Fitzgerald, please, just do as I requested."

"Sure, Doc," he said, and left the room.

Dr. Bauer busied himself with paperwork while waiting for Mike to return. David sat in the uneasy silence wondering what was going on. He had an unsettling feeling about what had just transpired. Something didn't seem right from the moment he entered the room. Dr. Bauer's uncharacteristically dour mood concerned him. *Something is going on here, and it can't be good.*

After having some blood drawn and receiving his injection, David made his way to the cafeteria. He sat there nursing a cup of green tea, waiting for Mike to take his coffee break. He was pleasantly surprised when he saw Gina enter the room. He waved her over. He instinctively rose as she approached the table. He was ready to embrace her when he realized where they were. He begrudgingly settled for a simple, less-than-satisfying hello. She smiled and took a chair across from him. Then she leaned in and whispered, "I can't wait to come to Greenport." David raised his eyebrows, but before he could say anything Mike clumsily grabbed a chair and joined them.

He looked at David and said, "What's going on, man?"

"You're asking me? If you don't know, how the hell would I?" David turned to Gina. "They cancelled my angiogram and then there was a problem with the serum. On top of all of that, Doctor Bauer was not the same. He seemed to be in a bad mood. Something is going on around here, and Doctor Bauer isn't talking." There was a pregnant pause before Mike broke the silence. He glanced around before he spoke.

"Listen, man, all I can tell you is that this morning we were all instructed by Doctor Bauer to keep all trial test results confidential. I'm not talking about violating a patient's confidentiality, we know better than that. I'm talking about the compilation of statistics from the recent angiograms and blood tests as they compare to the base line numbers established at the beginning of the trial. As of today, we are no longer going to compile the test data. All test results are to go directly to Doctor Bauer. And, we were further instructed not to discuss the test results, even among ourselves."

"But why?" David asked

"That's the sixty-four thousand dollar question. Out of the blue, we were called in this morning and reminded of our confidentially agreement. Then they told us about the restriction on information sharing. That was it. The whole meeting took less than five minutes. I'm going to snoop around and see what I can find out."

"Michael!" Gina said sternly, "You could lose your job. Don't do anything stupid. You've probably said too much already."

"What's that supposed to mean?" David interjected.

"There is a time and place for everything, and this is neither." Then turning to David, she said, "On a more positive note, I've arranged to get off early, so you won't have to wait around all afternoon. I'll meet you at the hotel in about an hour. That way I can follow you to the ferry. I also took half a day on Monday, so I don't have to leave Greenport on Sunday. I can take the early ferry on Monday."

"That's great!" David said, immediately forgetting about the day's events.

"What's this, a weekend get-away to Long Island?"

"Oh, Michael, be quiet. Do you want to get us all in trouble?"

"Okay. Okay," he said as he got up to leave. "Have a fun

weekend. I'll see what I can dig up around here," he said in a hushed voice.

"Michael, I'm serious, don't do anything that could jeopardize your job. Remember, you've got a wife and family to think about. You know how strict they are about this kind of thing."

"Don't worry. I'll be careful."

"Oh, you're impossible," Gina said as Michael was leaving.

Just before the lunch break, Doctor Bauer informed Michael he would be leaving for the day due to an unscheduled meeting with Doctor Price and Doctor Rentz.

"We are meeting at the Colonial Arms. I left the number on my desk in the unlikely event you need to contact me."

"Sure thing, Doc, enjoy your lunch." Doctor Bauer gave him a halfhearted smile and left.

This is my opportunity. I didn't expect one so soon. Doctor Bauer and Doctor Rentz will be out of the building. That means I can take a look around both offices and the lab. I'd better get moving.

Michael quickly scoured Dr. Bauer's office looking for anything that might explain the sudden shift in tactics. He searched his desk. The drawers were unlocked, but he found nothing. Next, he tried to access e-mails from Bauer's laptop, but it was password protected. "Damn," he said to himself, and headed directly for Doctor Rentz's office. He knocked on her office door and waited—no answer. He looked both ways before turning the knob. He feared the door was locked. To his surprise, it wasn't. He looked around one more time before entering. He closed the door behind him and flipped on the light. His heart was pounding. He could explain being in Doctor Bauer's office and the lab, but Doctor Rentz's office was another matter. He wasted no time. He thumbed through the few pieces of paper on her tidy desk. They revealed nothing. Next, he tried the drawers. *Damn! They're locked.* He grabbed the computer mouse and the screen saver disappeared revealing an opened e-mail. Mike read its contents. *Monique, after evaluating the data contained in your preliminary report sent via e-mail, I agree, the results are incredibly impressive. I have decided to immediately implement the first course of action of the contingency plan we discussed with Price. So, go with the placebo for all immediately. If this fails to produce the desired effects, we will meet to discuss a more aggressive course of action to bring the trial to an end. Also, submit your formal report as soon as practicable. Brett.* Mike turned on the printer next to her desk and printed the message. Then he went back to the computer and scanned her sent messages. He opened the one addressed to Brett Bitterman. *Brett, as you can see from the figures provided by Doctor Bauer, the results of the preliminary tests are nothing short of astounding. The average lessening of occlusion in the group receiving the Sicilia gene serum is 10%. While that may not seem significant to the average person, it should be noted that what took years to form on the artery walls was removed in a few short weeks. Unfortunately, I believe we may have discovered the magic bullet. I trust you will use this information to best serve the interest of our Freiz shareholders. Monique.* Mike was stunned at what he'd just read. He sent this message to the printer too, and then reset the computer to the way he found it. His heart was pounding like it wanted to escape his chest. He quickly stuffed the printouts into his pocket, turned out the light, and slowly opened the door. Once out of the office, he felt slightly less nervous.

Michael then made his way to the lab. His job required that he have access, so he could explain his presence if required. He swiped his security key card and entered the lab. First, he checked the lab to make sure no one else was there. Satisfied that he was alone, he headed straight for the refrigerator where the serum was stored. He heard the security door close. Someone was coming. He made himself look busy as the door opened and a coworker entered.

"Hi, Mike. You're working through lunch too, huh?"

"Yeah, I want to leave a little early this afternoon."

The coworker took some supplies from a storage shelf and said, "Have a good weekend."

"Yeah, you too." As soon as he heard the security door close again, he opened the refrigerator and removed a vial of serum from the same lot that Doctor Bauer had him return the previous day. He slipped it in his sock and hurried back to the examining room, hoping to catch Gina before she left, but there was no sign of her. He wanted to share with her what he'd found. And even though he still wasn't sure of its significance, he sensed it was big.

CHAPTER SEVENTEEN

David stood with his arm around Gina on the top deck of the ferry as the Connecticut shoreline faded into the distance. They watched as pleasure crafts passed and small fishing boats angled for blue fish, fluke, and striped bass. David pulled her closer, turned, and kissed her forehead. Gina smiled and laid her head on his shoulder as her hair flew freely in the stiff breeze. For some reason, he was more at ease with Gina than ever, and even as other passengers milled about, he felt an intimacy that was new to him. Maybe it had something to do with the absence of Gina's father. Al never bothered them, but he was always within earshot. And even though he believed Al would never do such a thing, it was always in the back of his mind that Al might show up during a particularly tender moment. He wondered if Gina had similar feelings.

As the ferry made its way past Plum Island and the Orient Point Lighthouse and started its turn toward the ferry slip, they scurried along with the other passengers headed down to their cars.

After disembarking, David took the only road that led west to Greenport, proudly pointing out historical landmarks as they drove through the quaint, tiny village of Orient.

As they approached the causeway connecting Orient and East Marion, Gina commented on the beautiful vistas on both sides of the road. On the left there were sprawling fields of tomatoes and beans that stretched nearly a quarter mile to Orient Harbor, whose waters glistened in the late afternoon sun. To the right was picturesque Dam Pond, where a lone, derelict rowboat was moored to a crooked locust pole. Beyond the pond lay a stretch of beach that separated the pond from Long Island Sound. "Oh, David, this is gorgeous. There is a picture perfect postcard in every direction." David smiled and nodded his head as if to say, *I told you so.*

They turned left onto Main Street. A right turn would have taken them to Sixty-Seven Steps. As they headed south, they passed a number of large Victorian style houses and the historic Townsend Manor Inn which sat on Sterling Harbor. As they approached the village, they passed the several art galleries that dotted the narrow street. At Front Street, David made a right and again headed west. Main Street and Front Street were the only two commercial streets in the tiny village. Gina looked from side to side as they passed cafes, pubs, and boutiques. At Mitchell Park located on the bay side of Front Street, brightly painted horses on the carousel bounded up and down with the organ music to the delight of the children who straddled their wooden backs.

At Fourth Street, David made a left turn, and within seconds pulled up to a modest two-story wood-framed cape. "Here we are."

"Oh, David, it's charming. You didn't tell me your house was on the water."

"You never asked. C'mon, I'll show you around," he said as he grabbed her suitcase.

When they reached the front door, David leaned down and picked up a long, slender box that was leaning against the door and handed it to Gina. "I believe this is for you," he said while unlocking the door. They stepped into the foyer. Gina held the box close to her as she looked around the room in awe. The foyer was opened to a great room, which overlooked the bay. "Wow, what a gorgeous view," Gina said, while still holding the box close to her.

"Aren't you going to open it?"

"Oh, yes, of course." Gina removed the red ribbon that adorned the box and opened it. Inside were a dozen red roses and a card. She opened the card. It read simply: *Dear Gina, Welcome to my home. Love, David.* "Oh, thank you, they're beautiful!" She reached up and gave him a peck on the cheek.

"C'mon, I'll show you your room," David said as he led the way down the hallway with her bag in tow. He entered a bedroom and laid her suitcase on a chair. Gina looked around the room and then at David. With a smirk she asked, "And where is your room?" David pointed across the hall. Gina craned her neck to catch a glimpse. "Oh, your room has a nicer view," she said coyly.

"Oh, you want my room instead," David replied in a boyish and naïve manner. Gina, taken aback by his sincerity and generous offer, began to laugh.

"Okay, okay, I didn't want to be presumptuous or take anything for granted. I have to admit, this is a little awkward. I wasn't quite sure how to handle this part. I didn't want to offend you."

"You did the right thing. I would have been a little disappointed if you'd done anything else, but if you don't mind, I'd like to stay in your room."

"I hope you mean in my room ... with me."

"Oh, no, you get the guest room," she said mockingly. "Of course, with you, silly." David shrugged his shoulders and without another word, transferred her bag to his room. "Listen," he said, "it's been a long day, so I figured we'd eat in tonight and go out tomorrow night ... if that's okay with you."

"That's fine with me. It'll be nice just to relax tonight."

"That's exactly what I was thinking. I'll let you get situated. When you're ready, you can find me in the kitchen."

"Okay. I just want to freshen up a little and get out of these work clothes."

The aroma of sautéing garlic wafted through the kitchen and into the hallway toward Gina. "Something smells good," she said as she entered the kitchen. "What are we having?"

"Shrimp Scampi," said David as he stirred the chopped garlic in the bubbling butter and olive oil mixture.

"Oh, we're having Shrimp Shrimp. Very nice."

"What? Whatta'ya mean…Shrimp Shrimp?" David said with a confused look.

"Well, Scampi means shrimp in Italian. You said we are having Shrimp Scampi…shrimp shrimp," she said smiling and tilting her head for emphasis.

"Okay, wise-ass, very funny. Thanks for giving this Anglo a lessen in the Italian language."

"Happy to oblige. Is there anything I can do to help?"

"Uh, yeah, you can peal, de-vein and butterfly the shrimp for the shrimp shrimp," he said with a wide grin.

"Ugh, sorry I asked," she said with a contorted look. "Where are they?" she said carefully scanning the counter and sink area.

"They're in the fridge." Gina removed a large glass bowl from the refrigerator and set it on the counter. After removing the plastic wrap, she looked at David. "Hey, these are already cleaned."

"Gotcha!"

"Touché."

"What you can do is grab the bottle of wine from the fridge and pour us a glass. The cork is loose. I opened it earlier." Gina did as requested. After accepting his glass from Gina, he raised it and offered a toast: "To a wonderful weekend." They tapped glasses and sampled the wine.

"This is very good, David," she said as she examined the bottle. "*Santa Margherita* Pinot Grigio…very nice."

"A special wine for a very special person." Again he lifted his glass before drinking.

"Flattery will get you nowhere, Mr. Roy."

"No, but hopefully the wine might…keep drinking." Gina playfully punched him in the arm. "Really, is there anything I can do to help?"

"Yes, actually, you can take that package of pasta and put it in the pot when it starts to boil."

Gina slipped the pasta into the rolling water as David emptied the bowl of shrimp into the piquant sauce. He moved the shrimp around constantly with a wooden spoon, making sure they all got coated with the scampi sauce and cooked evenly. He threw in a large pinch of freshly chopped parsley and continued to stir. He removed the pan from the heat just before the shrimp were cooked and lightly sprinkled Italian bread crumbs over the top of the dish before placing it under the broiler for just a few minutes to slightly brown the crumbs. He moved quickly now, removing a prepared bowl of salad from the fridge and quickly dressing it with olive oil and vinegar, then to the oven to check on the scampi. It was done to perfection. Gina handed the drained pasta to David. He emptied it into the sauce and gave it a good stir. He handed Gina a butane stick lighter and asked her to light the two long white candles that stood in cut crystal holders on a table set with a crisp, white linen tablecloth and napkins. David was moving with purpose now. He placed the salad plates on the table and then with tongs, he plated the entrée. He returned the pan to the kitchen, turned off the lights, and then re-entered the dining room with a bottle of wine. After filling their goblets and dimming the chandelier, David took a seat across from Gina. Pleased that everything had come together, he let out a sigh of relief, and hoped she appreciated his efforts. He didn't have to wait long to find out. Gina reached across the table placing her hand upon his. "Oh, David, everything is just perfect. Thank you."

"And you're perfectly welcome. Dig in before the Scampi gets cold."

The conversation during dinner centered on David. Gina wanted to know about his family, but David never mentioned his divorce. Gina avoided the subject as well, not wanting to possibly ruin the weekend. He knew they needed to discuss his failed marriage and the reason for it, but now was certainly not the time.

After dinner, Gina helped David clean up. When they were finished, David opened another bottle of wine, grabbed two clean glasses and said, "C'mon, let's go sit on the porch."

"More wine? Are you trying to relieve me of my inhibitions, Mr. Roy?"

"Can wine do that?" he said while feigning a stunned expression.

They sat in the screened-in porch on a white, wicker love seat and sipped their wine. The full moon's silvery light glimmered on the bay, causing eerie shadows. Gina got up and walked to the screen. "Is that yours?" she said pointing to a boat that was barely visible in the ambient light. David joined her. "Yes, the boat and the dock are mine. We...," he caught himself, "At one time I used it to putter around the bay, do a little fishing, or take it over to Claudio's on the weekend when they had live music, that sort of thing."

Gina intuitively said, "It's okay, David, when you're ready. There's no rush, I'm not going anywhere." Her reassuring words put him at ease.

"Anyway," he continued, "I haven't used it since my heart attack. I have it put in the water every spring," he laughed, "but it just sits there all summer. I can take you out in it tomorrow or Sunday, if you'd like."

Gina took his hand. "I'd like that."

Gina snuggled up to David as the night air took on a chill. "Maybe we'd better go in, it's getting a little too cool out here." Once inside, David put a CD, of Johnny Mathis ballads, into the player, and then sat on the sofa. He patted the cushion nest to him, inviting Gina to join him.

"No, no," she said as she grabbed his hand and pulled him up. "Let's dance." They danced slowly, in a close, gentle embrace to the velvety voice singing *The Twelfth of Never.* Gina said, "I love his music; his voice is unique."

"You know his music? I'm surprised. His heyday was even before my time."

"His stuff is timeless. Daddy told me my mother loved his music and bought all his albums. He still has them. He said they used to dance to his songs all the time … just like we're doing now."

They continued to dance through *Chances Are* and *It's Not For Me To Say.* In the middle of *Wonderful, Wonderful,* David gave Gina a long passionate kiss. She responded by pressing herself into him. Feeling the softness of her warm body against his, David felt the stirrings of desire well up within him, but at the same time he felt unsure of himself. He hadn't been with a woman since Sally. Their kissing became more passionate, and soon his self doubts melted away with the heat of the moment. Suddenly, Gina pulled back. She took his hand and in silence, led him to the bedroom where again they kissed. David ran his hands up and down her curvaceous body. He slid his hand down to her hips and around to her buttocks and then up her sides to her smooth, firm breasts. Their breathing was heavy now. Again, Gina slowly pulled away, this time to disrobe. David eagerly followed her lead, and after casting aside the sheet, he welcomed her into his bed. At first their lovemaking was slow and gentle, but soon became intensely passionate. Again, they slowed the pace for they both wanted the moment to last as long as possible. David felt a blissful communion with Gina that went far beyond the physical act.

Afterward, they lay on their backs with David's arm around Gina, holding her close, her head against his chest. She said sounding concerned, "David, we didn't use any protection. I'm a little worried because I'm in the middle of my cycle."

David inhaled deeply and exhaled in a rush. "You don't have to worry."

"I don't, why not?"

"It's been weighing on my mind for some time. I was waiting for the right time to tell you this, but I guess there is no right time. I've put off telling you for too long already. I should have told you sooner, I'm sorry."

"Tell me what?" she said, impatiently.

"About my marriage...or I should say my divorce.

When I was a kid, I had the mumps. There were some complications from the disease that left me sterile. I didn't find out about my condition until I was married and we were trying to have a child. Sally wanted to have children in the worst way, and when we found out I couldn't—"

"She left you … she left you because of that?" She said incredulously. "I'm sorry, David, but didn't she take an oath, part of which said, for better or worse?" Gina sounded annoyed. He was worried about how she would take the revelation. Oddly, her reaction gave him a small measure of solace, but what he still needed to know was how this new information would affect her attitude toward their relationship. "I mean, you don't leave someone you're married to, and supposedly love, because you can't have children. I think that's terrible."

"What if you're not married?" David asked.

"Well, that's a little different. Without the bonds of marriage to consider, it could be a tough call. I guess it depends on how strongly one feels about it." Her answer was too ambiguous; it didn't tell him what he needed to know.

"Gina, I don't care what someone else might decide to do; I need to know how you feel about it."

Gina sat up in the bed, hugged her bent legs and said, "I really haven't given it much thought. It never entered my mind that you would be sterile. And yes, growing up I always looked forward to being a mother one day. But after taking care of my father for so many years, I no longer have an overriding desire to have children. Besides, my prime childbearing days will soon be behind me. So, to answer your question, it's not a problem with me. Now don't concern yourself about it anymore." She then turned and started tickling him. He retaliated. They rolled around for a few seconds, which immediately reignited their passion.

They made love again before falling into a contented sleep.

CHAPTER EIGHTEEN

On Saturday morning, after a leisurely breakfast, David gave Gina an extensive tour of Greenport that included Sixty-Seven Steps, where they took a long walk along the boulder-strewn beach.

Once back in David's Jeep, Gina commented on his improved endurance.

"Are you referring to today's activities or last night's?" he quipped.

"Actually, I'm impressed with both."

"You know what amazes me, the rate at which my health is improving. To think that just a few weeks ago I wouldn't have dared to navigate a staircase that long. Heck, I wouldn't have tried one half that size. It's really remarkable."

"It is remarkable. At the rate you're going, you'll be running in next year's Boston Marathon."

"Yeah, right," he said and then changed the subject.

"What do you think happened at the clinic yesterday? With all the procedure and rule changes, it all seemed so dark and secretive."

"Oh, don't concern yourself with any of that. It's not that unusual. They often make midstream adjustments during these trials."

"Maybe so, but Mike seemed baffled and more than a little concerned."

"You know Michael, he overreacts to everything."

"Well, maybe you're right," he said and let it go. "Why don't we walk around the village, visit a few galleries, and then have lunch at Claudio's?"

"Sounds good to me."

They were sitting at an outside table watching the water traffic go by and sharing a dozen littlenecks on the half-shell when Gina's cell phone rang. She quickly fumbled around in her pocketbook and fished out the phone. Out of embarrassment, she turned it off without answering it. "I'm sorry," she apologized as she looked around. "It is so annoying when people use their cell phones in restaurants. I forgot to turn it off when we sat down." David scanned the other patrons and none seemed to notice Gina's faux pas.

"No problem, but aren't you going to check to see who called?"

Gina pushed a button on her phone. "I don't recognize the number. Maybe it's a wrong number." She checked her voice mail. "Whoever it was, they didn't bother to leave a message. I guess it can't be that important," she said making sure to turn off the phone before placing it back in her bag.

After lunch they sat for a while soaking up the sun and enjoying the reggae band, *Jamaican Jam*, before heading home.

That night they supped at the chic *Frisky Oyster*, a trendy gourmet restaurant on Main Street. Gina especially enjoyed the local lobster prepared Thermador style. David chose the Chilean Sea Bass. They finished the meal with a shared dessert, a chocolate soufflé with a molten center topped with homemade vanilla ice cream.

After the sumptuous repast and especially decadent dessert, they were stuffed, so they decided to walk some of it off. They were strolling through the tourist-filled streets of the village, arm in arm, when it started to sprinkle. The sprinkle quickly turned to rain. They made a mad dash for the Jeep, but just before they reached it, the sky opened up. Once inside the Jeep they paused to look at one another. Their clothes were soaked through, and their hair matted and dripping. All they could do was laugh at the sight of one another.

Gina was toweling her hair when David knocked on the bathroom door. Gina opened it and David offered her his white terry-cloth robe, which she accepted with a smile and a thank-you. "When you're ready, I'll be out on the porch," David said as thunder rumbled above them and the lights flickered.

When Gina appeared on the porch, she was a sight to behold. She was wrapped in his robe, which was big enough for two of her, and her hair was wrapped in a towel-shaped turban.

"Pretty sexy, huh?" she asked

"Works for me." he said.

"Yeah, right. Your nose is growing."

"Here," he said, extending her a glass of wine. "This will warm you up."

Gina took the glass and sat down next to David. Suddenly, there was a flash of lightning and a simultaneous loud, snapping clap of thunder. The lights flickered and then they lost power. They both flinched. Gina let out a yell of surprise and grabbed David's arm. He put his arm around her and pulled her to his side. "Wow," he said, "That was close. The storm is right over us." They sat and watched as nature provided a spectacular pyrotechnic display for the next several minutes.

After the storm moved out, they sat by the light of a lone candle and talked, losing all sense of time. When they realized it was after midnight, they decided to call it a night.

When Gina woke on Sunday morning, she found herself alone in David's bed. She slipped on his robe and followed the aroma of freshly brewed coffee to the kitchen where David was preparing waffles.

"Homemade waffles? Do you cook like this all the time?"

"Usually not, but I do like to make a nice breakfast on Sundays." After a short pause, he added, "I haven't done it in a while. Actually, I haven't done a lot of things in a while. It feels good to start living again. Thanks to you."

"And the trial," she added.

"Yes, and the trial. But you, Miss Coletti, are single-handedly responsible for the profound improvement in my emotional well-being."

"I'm sure the trial's effects have had something to do with that as well, but it's still nice to hear you say that."

While they were cleaning up after breakfast, David looked outside.

"It's a beautiful day for a boat ride. There's no wind and the bay is like a mirror. Whatta ya say?"

"Sounds like fun."

After they finished in the kitchen, they headed for the dock. David helped Gina into the boat before he untied the lines. He choked the engine and to his surprise, it started right up. He adjusted the choke and pushed away from the dock. Within a few seconds they were skimming across the placid blue waters of the bay.

David stood at the wheel and motioned for Gina to take it. She gave him a "who me" look, but then moved over to take it. She stood at the center console with her hands firmly attached at ten and two o'clock. David moved behind her and placed his hands on top of her white knuckles. "Relax. Steer it like you would a car, nice and easy, no sudden hard turns." He removed her right hand from the wheel and placed it on the throttle. "Forward for more speed and back for less ... simple." David then pushed the throttle all the way forward before moving to the side and letting Gina take full control. The ninety-horsepower Yamaha engine roared with power and leapt ahead at a speed that was much too fast for Gina's inexperienced piloting. She let out a scream and quickly pulled back to a more manageable speed. "David, are you trying to get us killed?" David waved her off. He was laughing too hard to answer.

When they neared other boat traffic, David retook the wheel. He showed Gina how to navigate around other craft and how to cross a wake properly.

Once back in open water, he handed the piloting duties back to Gina, who, this time, took the wheel with slightly more confidence.

"Let's ride around Shelter Island," David said, pointing in the direction he wanted Gina to take.

While circumnavigating the island, Gina felt her cell phone start to vibrate. She wanted to ignore it, but thought it might be her father, so she retrieved it from her pocket and glanced at the caller's number. It was the same number that had called the previous day. She turned off the phone and placed it back into her pocket. She looked at David and shrugged it off. David was curious, but didn't question her, thinking it would be an invasion of her privacy to do so.

When they returned to the dock, David hosed down the boat. Gina excused herself saying she wanted to call her father. Once in the bedroom, she dialed the number of her two-time caller. The phone was answered after two rings. "Hello, Gina? Why haven't you taken my calls or called me back?"

"Michael, why are you calling me at David's? What's so important that it couldn't wait until I saw you at work?"

"Listen, Gina, I'm sorry I bothered you at David's, but we need to talk and it can't be at work. You won't believe what I found out on Friday after you left for the weekend.

I haven't told a soul, but I need to talk to you. And please don't mention anything to David until after we talk."

"Michael, don't tell me you were snooping around the clinic after I told you not to. Did you?"

"Gina, I found something very interesting and I need to share it with you. We need to figure out what to do with the information."

"What's this 'we' stuff? Michael, I want no part of whatever you're doing or what you've done. It can't bring anything but trouble."

"Gina, just give me a chance to explain what it is. I think you might change your mind once I do. Please, Gina, you are the only one at work I can trust."

"Oh, Michael, you're impossible. I'm not coming back to work until Monday afternoon. It'll have to wait until after work."

"Thanks, Gina. Can you meet me at my hotel room right after work?"

"It's against my better judgment, but okay, but only for a few minutes. I'll need to get home."

"Great. My room number is 231. See you Monday."

After Gina hung up she heard David enter the house. She hit the speed dial on her phone and waited. "Hi daddy, it's me. I just wanted to make sure everything's okay with you." She walked into the kitchen while talking. "Yes, yes, I know. Yes, I'm having a wonderful time," she said, and threw David a smile. "Yes I will. See you tomorrow night. Love you too," she said before hanging up. "Daddy says hello. He's happy that I'm enjoying myself."

"He's not the only one," David responded.

Later at dinner, David observed a change in Gina's mood. She seemed preoccupied and distant. "Is everything all right?"

"I'm a little worried about Daddy. He was upbeat and said he was fine, but he sounded so tired. I'm sorry, David. I didn't realize it showed." She didn't want to share her real concerns with him. *The less he knows the better.* "I guess I just worry too much. It's one of my faults."

"I'd call it caring, and it's anything but a fault."

"Well, regardless, let's not let it spoil an otherwise perfect weekend."

"I'll toast to that," he said raising his glass.

The weekend was as close to perfect as anyone could expect. Until now Gina hadn't realized just how much she was missing in her life...and David was everything any woman could want. As for David, he felt life was worth living again for the first time in years. It all seemed too good to last...he hoped it wasn't.

CHAPTER NINETEEN

W HEN Charles Bauer arrived at the Colonial Arms, Thomas Price and Monique Rentz were already seated in the dining room. Price rose to greet him. "Please Charles, have a seat. The waiter should be right over."

"Actually, I'm not that hungry. I'm here at your request," he said tersely.

"Look, Charles, I understand why you're upset, that's why I asked you here—to explain our position."

"At a neutral site, to avoid any appearance of impropriety?"

"That's correct," Rentz interjected, "We are affording you the courtesy of an explanation of our recent decisions. Let me be frank with you, Doctor Bauer. Freiz and the NECCC, I might add, are in business to make money, and we make our business decisions accordingly. Besides the Sicilia Gene therapy, Freiz has another drug in the pipeline to treat coronary artery disease. Due to recent developments, we have decided to place our bets on Bi-Torracept-T. It is a wonderful new drug that not only lowers LDL, but it also raises HDL. It promises to be a blockbuster."

"But as preliminary tests show, the Sicilia Gene therapy appears to be a cure rather than a treatment. Wouldn't that trump anything else available?"

"Forgive me, Doctor Bauer, but please...don't be so naïve," Rentz retorted. "If we cured every disease that we treat, we wouldn't be in business very long, and I might add, if we cured coronary artery disease, the NECCC wouldn't be around long either."

"She's right, Charles," Price added. "Besides, it's not our call. Let me be perfectly honest with you, the clinic does a lot of business with Freiz, and I'm not prepared to put that relationship in jeopardy. Charles, I need your understanding and cooperation on this. Do I have it?" Bauer paused for a moment before answering.

"I'll do what's expected of me," he said reluctantly.

"Look, Doctor Bauer," Rentz piped in, "Freiz is looking for a quick way out of the trial. Going with placebo for the entire group, we feel, is the quickest and cleanest way."

"And how is that going to be a quick fix?"

"That's really not your concern. And one more thing, of course, you will have to adjust the current data to reflect a far less positive outcome."

"You mean fudge the numbers. Just call it what it is."

"Fudge is such an unappealing word. I like adjust much better," she shot back.

"As I've said, I'll do what's expected of me. Now if you'll excuse me, I have work to do."

"What do you think?" Rentz asked Price after Doctor Bauer left.

"He's obviously miffed, but don't worry. Charles is a good soldier. He'll come around."

"Good. I'll be meeting with Bitterman tomorrow morning, but before I do, you and I have something further to discuss."

Doctor Monique Rentz arrived at Brent Bitterman's office at seven in the morning, well before his staff started the workday. She found him in his office poring over the Sicilia Gene trial report she had sent him earlier.

"Quite impressive, I must say. An average of ten percent decrease in occlusion in just a few short weeks. It's rather amazing, really. I don't think any of us thought the results would be this remarkable. If this gets out, we would be hard pressed to explain why we're not pursuing this course of action instead of rolling out Bi-Torracept-T. Also, from your report it's evident that the majority of participants receiving the Sicilia Gene therapy have reported substantial positive results. Administering a placebo will not be enough to create the effect needed to justify abruptly terminating the trial. We need to mitigate the results using more aggressive means. Do you understand what I am saying, Monique?"

"I do."

"Good. Then I will leave the rest to you. And Monique, rework the numbers in the report and resubmit it to me.

I will destroy this copy and you do the same with whatever you have in your database or in hardcopy. I don't want this information floating around. Also, have the current database changed to reflect what we want...little or no improvement with moderate side affects."

"I've already taken care of it. Bauer will handle it."

"Can this Doctor Bauer be trusted?"

"Price and I met with him yesterday. Price tells me he'll comply."

"Listen, Monique, on another subject, I'm leaving for Washington tomorrow. I have a very important meeting with the vice president regarding Medicare's potentially devastating decision on Torvistat. I'll be doing some major lobbying and I want to have an ace in the hole. Bring me enough Sicilia serum for a full series of doses along with the syringes and alcohol wipes."

"I'll have it sent right up from the lab."

"No. I want you to hand deliver it to me. I don't have to tell you that we must be discrete in all matters pertaining to the serum and the trial."

After Doctor Rentz delivered the unmarked package to Bitterman, she went to her own corporate office and dialed the New England Clinic for Cardiac Care and asked to speak to the clinic administrator, Thomas Price. She informed him of a need to meet again, preferably first thing in the morning, before the staff reported to work, and this time it would be just the two of them.

Doctor Rentz again visited the lab. She searched the index and found where the clotting Factor V111 and vitamin K were stored. She then prepared the vials that would replace the ones containing the Sicilia gene serum. The combination would surely produce problematic blood clots in at least a few participants. That's all that would be needed to justify ending the trial.

After assigning some of her duties at Freiz headquarters to her subordinates, she prepared to leave for the clinic in Boston.

Rentz and Price met in his office at seven. Rentz placed an unlabeled box on Price's desk. "Thomas, I have here a new set of replacement vials containing placebo. They are coded as Sicilia, so they are indistinguishable from the real thing. The participants will have no idea they are receiving something other than the Sicilia gene serum. If you could make the switch this morning before your employees report, I'd certainly appreciate it."

"I'll take care of it."

"Thank you, Doctor Price."

As Rentz was leaving the building, she ran into Doctor Bauer. She greeted him tentatively, "Good morning, Doctor Bauer."

"Doctor Rentz," he replied with a nod.

"How has everything gone since our meeting?"

"I have complied with your request," he said curtly.

"Very good. Thank you, Doctor."

"There is one small problem. A vial of the Sicilia gene serum appears to be missing."

"What do you mean appears to be missing? It's either missing or it's not," she said sternly.

"Okay, a vial is missing. I have had no reports of breakage, so as of now it's missing. I will question the staff. I'm sure there is an explanation. I wouldn't be overly concerned at this point. More than likely, someone broke one and simply hasn't reported it yet."

"Is there anyone you suspect would have a motive for taking the serum?" she said pointedly. Bauer hesitated briefly before answering.

He looked her in the eye and said, "No ma'am, I surely don't." She accepted his answer, at least for the time being. She would have to address the missing vial, but not right away. She had enough on her plate already. *Besides the number of people who have access to the lab are few.* One thing was clear; she needed to speak with Doctor Price about increasing the level of security.

For now she was satisfied. The serum had been switched and the trial records fudged. *It was a productive day.*

CHAPTER TWENTY

WHEN Gina returned to work on Monday afternoon, she found the same dour pall hanging over the clinic. Dr. Bauer was pleasant, but his mood was sullen. Michael seemed on edge. Gina felt bad karma all around.

Unfortunately, no one on the staff, including Doctor Bauer, had any idea the serum they would inject into the participants this week was laced with a substance that would soon bring the trial to an abrupt end.

Gina wasn't there more than half an hour when Doctor Bauer called an impromptu meeting of the staff. Gina had to agree with Michael, strange things were happening at the clinic and no one was offering any explanations.

Doctor Bauer attempted to change that perception. He explained that while the treatments would continue, there was some cause for concern because a few abnormalities were discovered upon further testing of participant's blood samples. Michael threw Gina a knowing look. Then Doctor Bauer reiterated what he had expressed on Friday: all test results were to go directly to him. Finally, to stem a purported rumor that someone was leaking test results, everyone was again reminded of their confidentiality agreement. They were further instructed not to discuss the trial with anyone, including coworkers unless it was directly related to their job performance.

"Before I conclude, I need to ask if anyone has broken a vial within the last few days?" Michael felt a wave of anxiety at the question and a cold sweat erupted from nowhere. Some responded with a "no," while others nodded in the negative. Michael nervously did both.

"Well, that's very odd indeed. While checking the inventory against the amount of Sicilia serum used, I discovered there was one vial short. If anyone knows anything about this, please approach me in private. Any information offered will be treated with the utmost discretion."

It was customary to solicit questions at the end of staff meetings. This time, however, Bauer simply thanked everyone for their cooperation and left the room.

To Michael, the afternoon seemed to drag on forever. He was anxious to tell Gina what he'd discovered, and he had second thoughts about what he had done. *I should have listened to Gina.*

When the workday finally ended, he went directly to his room and waited for Gina. When she arrived, she barely got in the door before Michael started. "Gina, they're going to sabotage the trial."

"What? How can you make such an assertion? Why

would they want to sabotage their own trial? That's ridiculous, Michael."

"I know how it sounds, but just hear me out, okay? On Friday I went to the lab and snooped around a little."

"Oh, Michael, your incorrigible! What's wrong with you? I can't believe you would jeopardize your job like this. Do I have to remind you that you have a wife and family to think about?"

"Don't worry, I was careful."

"Michael, that's not the point! You have no business snooping around at work. You know how strict they are about their proprietary information."

"Calm down, you're the only person I'm telling... for now."

Clearly frustrated, Gina simply said, "Tell me what you found."

"Well, after our meeting with Doctor Bauer on Friday, I knew something was up. I could just feel it. So when everyone went to lunch, I made a little visit to his office and looked around. I didn't really find anything, so I checked Doctor Rentz's office. The door was unlocked—"

"I can't believe you did this."

"Anyway, as I said, the door wasn't locked so I took a quick look around. I found an open e-mail on her computer. It was from Brett Bitterman. He said—"

"Oh, Michael, this is getting worse by the minute."

"Gina, just let me finish, will ya? He said, among other things, to start giving everyone in the trial the placebo."

"Why in the world would they do that?"

"Because they want to end the trial."

"It doesn't make any sense."

Michael continued: "He also said he was impressed with the interim results of the trial. In an e-mail sent to him from Rentz, she said the participants receiving the Sicilia Gene serum had a ten percent lessening of occlusion. She said, and I'm quoting, 'unfortunately, I believe we may have discovered the magic bullet. I trust you will use this information to best serve the interests of our Freiz shareholders.' " With wide eyes, Michael leaned forward in his chair and said, "What do you think now?"

"I'm not sure what to think. It's all a little confusing to me. If they thought they discovered, as you said, the magic bullet, why would they want to sabotage the trial? You'd think they would want to follow it through to the end to see what the optimum result would be."

"I agree. I've been thinking about it all weekend. The only thing I can come up with is, the results are too good."

"What? That's crazy. Now you aren't making sense."

"I know it sounds crazy, but here's my theory: As we all know, Torvistat is the number one selling cholesterol drug in the world. It and Zimstan, its closest competitor, will be coming off patent soon. Currently, Torvistat accounts for over thirteen billion dollars in sales, fully a third of Freiz's total yearly revenue. When the patents expire, much cheaper generics will be cropping up to take a huge chunk out of the market share now held by Freiz and others, and while the Sicilia gene shows great promise, Bi-Torracept is close to FDA approval. It's simply a matter of economics; of protecting market share."

"But, Michael, everyone seems to think the Sicilia

Gene therapy is actually a cure as opposed to a treatment. Wouldn't that be the way to go in the long run?"

"You and I might think that way, but not if you understand the corporate mentality where increasing profit is their only objective. When you come down to it, that's Bitterman's only job. Listen, Gina, I know it sounds cynical, but huge corporations like Freiz don't give a damn about their customers except to get them to buy more of their product. It makes no difference if it's a drug or a cigarette, if it will lengthen your life or shorten it. It just doesn't matter to them as long as it produces profits. It's all about sales, sales, sales, and the profit those sales produce for the corporation and ultimately, the stockholders. It's capitalism at its best and worst. And worst of all, it's nearly impossible to hold them accountable. Just look at what the tobacco companies have gotten away with. The CEOs stood before congress and lied through their teeth. Everyone knew it, but none of them were held to account."

"In this case," Michael continued, "Freiz purchased the Sicilia Gene way back in the 90s. They sat on it all these years and now they want to shelve it again because they see a better profit opportunity with Bi-Torracept. Not a better product, mind you, just a more profitable one."

"If what you say is true, millions of people could have been saved over the years. If even half of the million or so who die every year from the disease were spared by the Sicilia Gene therapy, we're talking five hundred thousand people a year, every year, and that's a conservative estimate."

Thoughts of Gina's father popped into her head. *Could he have been cured when first diagnosed with atherosclerosis, before it caused his heart attack?* The possibility angered her. "It's hard to believe that any corporation could get way with something like this. It's criminal. Wouldn't you think that the press would be all over it?" she said with frustration.

"Sorry to say, it's not against the law; maybe it should be, but it's not and even if it was, who's going to stop them? Who stopped the tobacco companies? And, believe it or not, it was in the press back in the 70s. There were articles about Expharmica's discovery of the Sicilia Gene and later about its purchase by Freiz. Then, they abruptly stopped. We heard no more on the subject. People have short memories about such things and if they are not reminded every once in a while, things drop off their radar."

"Why do you think the media let it go?"

"I really can't say, but I wouldn't be surprised if Freiz's powerful influence had a hand in it. After all, they advertise in every major newspaper and magazine in this country and around the world."

"Oh, c'mon Michael, do you really think they would conspire to that extent?"

"There's no doubt in my mind. Based on what I've seen, it wouldn't surprise me in the least."

"If all what you say and think is true, which I must admit, seems far fetched, it is unconscionable. How can they ever justify their actions?"

"Gina, haven't you been listening? People who run corporations don't care about such things."

"So, now what are you planning to do with this information?"

"I'm not sure yet. I don't know where to start or whom

to trust. Plus, I'd like to gather as much evidence as possible before trying to expose them."

"Michael, you'd better be very careful with this. This is not some mom and pop organization you're taking on; you're messing with the big boys. Do you really think that is something you should get involved in? Don't bite off more than you can chew. Think about your future, your family."

"Gina, I am thinking about my family. What if my wife or I, or God forbid, one of my children could benefit from the Sicilia Gene someday and they couldn't because I didn't do what I could to make it possible. Think of all the people who already could have been helped or lives saved that weren't because of corporate greed." Gina again thought of her father … and David.

"No, Gina, I can't just turn a blind eye to this. I have to prove to someone who can and will do something about it that this is all real. I don't know just who yet, but I'll figure it out. If I can, Freiz will no longer be able to keep it from being developed and made available to anyone who needs it."

"Now who's being naïve? Michael, what makes you think you can take on the largest, most powerful pharmaceutical company in the world and win? You're dealing with extremely powerful people. I don't know, Michael, you'd better think about what you're doing. You could be getting in way over your head. They will not stand idly by while you attempt to show the world they are a bunch of corporate ogres."

"I know. I know," he said showing concern.

"Now, tell me about the missing vial," Gina said knowingly.

"Honest, Gina, I didn't—"

"Damn it Michael, be straight with me. I could tell by the look on your face when Doctor Bauer mentioned it was missing that you were the guilty party."

"Honest, Gina I didn't plan on taking it. After I read the e-mails I just acted impulsively. After I took it, I realized it was a stupid thing to do. What can I say … and what can I do about it now?"

"How about putting it back. Maybe then they won't pursue it any further. If you don't, you know they will, and if they find out it was you who took it, you will, at the very least, lose your job and possibly worse. Put it back, Michael. It's not your job to save the world."

"Let me think about it over the weekend."

"I wouldn't wait too long," she warned.

"I know. I know," he said nervously.

"You didn't take anything else, did you?"

"No—no, nothing else." Michael chose not to mention he made copies of the e-mails. He knew it would only upset her further. Then he added, "I know what I've said is hard to believe, but please, do me a favor and keep your eyes open at work. We wouldn't want to see anything happen to David."

"And Michael, speaking of David, don't say a word about this to him. He's been through so much already. Telling him would serve no useful purpose at this point. All it would do is cause needless worry and anxiety."

"Yes, yes, I know exactly what you mean."

CHAPTER TWENTY-ONE

The White House

MR. Vice President, Mr. Bitterman from Freiz is here. He is your ten o'clock. Shall I show him in, sir?" asked the receptionist.

"Please do." Bruce Richards had known Brett Bitterman since he was a congressman, and Bitterman a lobbyist for the pharmaceutical industry, some twenty years ago. They had a good quid pro quo relationship and even socialized on several occasions, but they hadn't seen each other since they changed jobs. They were too busy, Bitterman heading the world's largest pharmaceutical company and Richards running the world's most powerful government . . . behind an inept, lame duck president.

The door opened and the secretary announced, "Mr. Vice President, Mr. Brett Bitterman is here to see you." Richards dismissed her as he rose and walked from behind his desk and extended his hand. "Brett, how the hell are you? How long has it been?"

"Far too long, my friend. It's got to be over twenty years, and things couldn't be better with me, but to be candid, I am a little worried about you. All of this talk in the media regarding your heart condition has me a bit concerned and I thought that I may be able to offer you some help." Richards, intrigued by his statement, motioned for Bitterman to take the seat.

"So that's why the urgent request to see me?" Richards laughed. "Brett, I have the best doctors in the world attending to me. What help could you possibly offer that is currently unavailable to me? And what is it that I would be expected to do for you in return?" Now it was Bitterman's turn to laugh.

"You know me too well." His demeanor turned serious and after a short pause, he continued. "You are probably aware that our closest competitor's statin drug, Zimstan, which enjoys a twenty-five percent market share, is coming off patent protection at the end of next year."

"Yes, I'm well aware of that. But Freiz's Torvistat has something like sixty percent market share. Why are you so concerned?" Richards knew the answer to his own question, but sat back in his chair and remained silent, waiting for Bitterman to elaborate.

"My sources tell me that when Zimstan's patent expires, Medicare will no longer cover Torvistat and instead, under Part D of their prescription drug plan, will provide only the generic form of Zimstan to Medicare recipients, regardless of which Medicare prescription plan they have chosen. Twenty-eight percent of our market share is Medicare participants. Torvistat is our largest selling medication. It currently provides thirteen billion dollars annually in profit. We will lose market share from the general population, but an additional loss of nearly four billion from Medicare would be devastating. I don't have to tell you how that will impact the bottom line at Freiz and its consequences on the value of our stock."

"I understand your problem, but I'm not sure what I can do to help, and frankly, I don't see how you can help me."

Bitterman leaned forward to close the gap between the two men.

"I need your intervention, Bruce." Bitterman said sternly.

"How could I possibly help? I can't do anything to stop the expiration of the patent on Zimstan, and I can't prevent Medicare from switching to the lower cost generic. Brett, you know I would help if I could. I just don't see how I can," Richards said, raising his hands in emphasis.

"Bruce, please don't state the obvious. And, don't patronize me. We've known each other too long. You've been in this town over thirty years, and you know how the system works. I need your help and I need it now." Bitterman became more assertive. "I need you to delay the move by Medicare for a minimum of eighteen months. I know you can do it, Bruce."

"Brett, you're putting me in a tough spot. You know the pressure we are under to cut costs. Even if I could do it, how would I justify it?"

"Listen, Bruce, you're the vice president of the United States, for God's sake. You can get it done. It's only for eighteen months."

"Brett, it's no secret that I have my sights on the Oval Office. If I were to help you and it got out, my political career would be over. As you mentioned earlier, I have some health issues to deal with that will undoubtedly work against me. That issue alone may do me in. My opponents, both in the primary and general election, if I get that far, are sure to keep it in front of the voters. I don't need to give my opponents any more ammunition than they already have." There was a deafening silence. "I'm sorry, I can't do it."

Bitterman stood and walked to the window, his back toward Richards.

"Bruce, trust me. The benefit to you far outweighs the short-term political fall-out. The next presidential cycle is more than three years away and a lot can happen between now and then."

"Benefits to me, what benefits to me?" he snapped. "And just why is this eighteen months so damned important anyway?" Richards was becoming agitated.

"Let me answer the second question first: We have developed a new and exciting drug that dramatically increases the good cholesterol, the high density lipoproteins. The statin drugs now in use do a great job at lowering the bad cholesterol, or LDL, but they do little to raise the HDL. Although this drug, Bi-Torracept, is quite remarkable by itself, we plan to bind it to Torvistat, thereby enabling Freiz to apply for a new patent which is, in reality, a new and improved form of Torvistat. Our researchers believe that the formula of the new drug, Bi-Torracept-T, will not be able to be duplicated in a different form like they are able to do with other statins. We will become the only company to have a drug that will lower LDL and substantially raise HDL levels in one medication. We will corner the market. It promises to be a blockbuster.

"We're confident that we can fast track the drug. To date, Bi-Torracept-T has no known side effects, something that is unheard of in this business. If we can make our case before the FDA—and I think we can—eighteen months should be adequate." Bruce Richards sat speechless, wondering just how this new drug could do any more for him other than forestall the inevitable.

Bitterman continued, "Now, for the best part, as far as you are concerned. Bruce, everyone knows you aspire to be president. Everyone also knows that you've had two heart attacks."

Richards quickly interjected. "Yes, that's true, but the last one was three years ago and it was fairly minor. I'm taking Torvistat, eating better and even exercising, which I must say, I disdain. The doctor says I'm in fine shape for the shape I'm in." He laughed, trying to inject a little levity.

"Bruce, what if I could give you a drug that would not only stop the progression of atherosclerosis but reverse it? What would you say?"

"I see," snickered Richards, "I agree to do as you ask with the promise of getting a wonder drug in eighteen months. Is that it, Brett?"

"No, Bruce, it's not Bi-Torracept-T. It is something quite different. I can give it to you now, by injection. By the time eighteen months rolls around, you'll have the arteries of a twenty-year-old vegetarian. Richards sat forward and put his hands on the edge of his desk and stood, pushing back his chair with the back of his legs.

"Are you serious?" Still skeptical, he asked, "How do I know it will work on me?"

"Bruce, you will see results in a matter of weeks. You will receive an initial injection and booster shots, one weekly for the next six weeks."

"This sounds too good to be true, Brett. And, you know what they say: if it sounds too good to be true, it probably is."

"Listen, Bruce, you are the only person outside of a very select group of people that knows about this, and I promise you: this is real. It's a magic bullet—sort of a rotor-rooter for the arteries. You'll be amazed with the results."

"Brett, if it's that good, why not simply market it on its own instead of putting all your effort in Bi-Torracept-T?" Bitterman hesitated, reluctant to answer the question.

Finally, realizing he had no other choice but the truth, he said, "Because, what you're getting doesn't simply treat atherosclerosis—it cures it."

The vice president rounded his desk and walked toward Bitterman shaking his head. "Brett, just what in hell is this all about? You've got me totally confused. Now, please, explain yourself."

Richards motioned for Bitterman to take one of the two seats in front of his desk; Richards took the other. Bitterman inhaled deeply and emptied his lungs in a rush. "Bruce, everything I've told you so far is true. What I am about to tell you, you must never repeat—to anyone. Do I have your word on it?"

"Oh, stop the cloak and dagger crap and get on with it." He snapped.

"No, Bruce, this is serious business. I need your word on this."

"Okay, okay, you've got it, now go on."

"Some years ago a small pharmaceutical company, Expharmica, made a startling discovery on the island of Sicily. While studying why some people get clogged arteries and some don't, they came across one family in particular that had no history of arterial disease as far back as the late seventeen hundreds. That in itself is not so peculiar. What perplexed the researchers was the fact that of the fifty living family members tested, all had high cholesterol. Stranger yet, they had high LDL levels and low HDL levels. Just the opposite of what one would expect to find." Richards listened intently as Bitterman continued. "After much research, they discovered that while their HDL levels were low, the HDL molecules that they did have, worked very efficiently and kept their arteries clean. Maybe there is something in the soil or the water there. At any rate, Expharmica eventually isolated the gene and synthesized it."

Richards piped in, "How come I've never heard of any of this. It seems to me it would have been big news."

"Indeed, it would have, except, Freiz found out about the discovery—

"A little case of industrial espionage?" Bitterman ignored the comment.

"At any rate, Freiz purchased the company."

"And when exactly did this discovery occur?"

"Some years ago."

"How many?"

Bitterman paused, "Twenty some odd."

"What! You've known about this for over twenty years and did nothing to bring it to market. You bastards! Do you have any idea how many lives you could have saved in that time? This is insane." Richards was now pacing the length of his office.

"Calm down, Bruce. Let me explain. I'm sure you'll agree with our reasoning. Although self-serving, we needed to protect our position as it related to Torvistat and its modified version already in clinical trial. Besides, our industry makes money by treating diseases, not curing them."

"Now let me explain why it is in your best interest that we not make this available to the general population. Even with the proven efficacy of the statins, almost a million people in the United States alone, still die every year from some form of vascular disease. Now, let me ask you: what would happen if at least five hundred thousand more people each year were added to the rolls of Social Security and Medicare?" Bitterman looked at Richards with wide eyes and waited.

"My God, Brett, the ramifications would be devastating. The financial burden would make the federal budget bleed enough red ink to fill oceans."

"Exactly, Bruce, and that's not even taking into account the impact on the private sector. Cardiac care, especially bipass surgery, is a lucrative source of income for the medical establishment. There are clinics and hospitals all over this country that operate near bankruptcy. This would push many over the brink. Is that the kind of situation you want going into a presidential campaign?"

"I see your point."

"I thought you would. It makes good business sense all around. So what do you say?"

Richards hesitated briefly before answering. "When do I get my first injection?"

"I'm prepared to give it to you now. Now, if you'd just roll up your sleeve," he said while opening his briefcase. Richards seemed a little surprised, but did as requested.

"Excuse me for asking, Brett, but when was the last time you gave anyone an injection?" he said with some concern.

"Not since I joined the management ranks at Freiz, but don't worry, Bruce, it's not something one forgets how to do." Bitterman removed several vials and syringes and placed them on the vice president's desk. He inserted a needle through the top of one of the vials and drew the clear liquid into the syringe. After wiping Richard's arm with an alcohol swab he injected the life saving serum into him.

"That's it?" asked the vice president as he rolled down his sleeve.

"That's all there is to it, Bruce. The next injection should be one week from today and weekly until all the vials I've given you are used. I can show you how to store it properly and give the injections to yourself, if you'd like."

"That won't be necessary; I'll have my personal physician attend to it."

"Won't he demand to know what he's giving you?"

"Don't worry. I can assure you, it won't be a problem."

"Bruce, I want to thank you for your time and cooperation. I hope to see you soon and find you feeling chipper when I do," he said as they walked toward the door.

"Brett, wait a second, I have a question. Who else gets this wonder drug?"

Bitterman smiled and said, "Only the chosen few, my friend. Only the chosen few."

CHAPTER TWENTY-TWO

NECCC head administrator Doctor Thomas Price was on the phone with Doctor Monique Rentz when his secretary announced the arrival of Doctor Bauer.

Price advised Rentz that he was placing her on the speaker. He advised her to be silent so, unbeknownst to Bauer, she could hear their conversation. Then he carefully placed the receiver on the cradle and called in Doctor Bauer.

Price greeted Bauer with a handshake and offered him coffee, which he respectfully declined. "Please, Charles, have a seat." Bauer took one of the two chairs directly in front of Price's desk as Price took his own seat behind the large mahogany desk. "Charles, as you can imagine, Freiz is extremely concerned on many levels about the missing vial of the Sicilia serum. Have you made any progress in determining its whereabouts?"

"I don't know. It could be anywhere. It may have simply been dropped and broken. Although, if that were the case, it baffles me why the person who broke it wouldn't just come forward. These things happen, but to answer your question, no, I don't know what happened to it. I did mention it at a staff meeting, but no one offered any information."

Price pushed a button on a remote control device and a white projection screen descended from the ceiling at the wall opposite Price's desk. Bauer repositioned his chair to face the screen. "Charles, I think you'll find this interesting," Price hit another button on the device and automatically the drapes were drawn and the lights dimmed. Another button was pushed and the digital video recording began. It showed the entire lab. The recording was taken from somewhere above the center of the lab. The figures walking in and out of the lab were recognizable although slightly distorted by the wide-angle lens. Bauer sat in silence as Price hit the fast forward button. The figures scurried around as if they were in an old-time movie. After several seconds, he hit play again, and the speed returned to normal. "Now pay close attention, Charles." Bauer remained silent. Then he saw Michael Fitzgerald enter the lab. After a brief exchange with a coworker, he walked over to where the Sicilia gene serum was stored. He opened the refrigerator, quickly looked toward the door, then took a vial and placed it in his sock.

There was a quick gasp from Bauer. "My God, Thomas, I never would have believed it. Why in heaven's name would he do such a thing?"

"That's what I'd like you to find out, but most importantly, Charles, we need to recover the serum. At this point I can't imagine what his motive is, but he obviously had a reason to take the vial."

"What exactly do you suggest I do? I'm a researcher, Thomas, not a cop or psychologist. Why not have security handle it?"

"Because you are respected and well-liked. He'll trust you. Let's try the good cop, bad cop method first. Pull him into your office and explain that we know he took the vial. Tell him we are livid, that we are going to fire him, and press criminal charges against him. That should get his attention. Then, go on to tell him how you went to bat for him, that you went way out on a limb for him. Tell him that you've convinced us to forget the whole thing if he returns the vial intact. Give him twenty-four hours—no more."

"And what if he denies taking it, then what do I do?"

"Call me immediately."

Before Bauer left his office, Price thanked him for his cooperation. As soon as the door closed, Price picked up the phone. "Monique?"

"Yes, Thomas, I heard everything."

"And what do you think?"

"Do you think we can trust Bauer to get it done?"

"That's another issue we'll have to address."

"I wish I knew what Fitzgerald's motive was. It worries me that we don't have a clue as to why he would take it."

"I agree. He's a good worker, does a good job, is liked by everybody, and he seems happy. I don't get it either. There is one other thing I could do. He's always been very friendly with another employee, Gina Coletti. I could have Bauer interview her. On second thought, I'll talk to her myself. Maybe she can shed some light on this."

"Are they an item, Thomas?"

"No, I don't think so, nothing like that. They've known each other for many years. They're just close friends, but continue checking the security's surveillance tapes to see if anything shows up. Ms. Coletti is single, but from what I've heard she is dedicated to taking care of her ailing father. I'm told he has acute heart disease. Rumor has it that for some reason she feels responsible and is therefore devoted to his care."

"Ah, I see," said Rentz. "Perhaps we can offer her something in exchange for her cooperation—like an offer to help her father, perhaps. That would be a powerful incentive. Don't you agree, Doctor Price?"

"It very well may be, but let me see how the interview goes first. I'll have a better feel for it then. However, I do agree, the offer of the Sicilia therapy could be a very persuasive incentive. Why don't you access his medical records?

"Let me go so I can get on this. I'll keep you abreast of any developments."

Price wasted no time. He immediately called Bauer. "Charles, have you summoned Fitzgerald yet?"

"Well, no, not yet, I just got back in the office. I'll do it right aw—"

"Its okay, Charles, I'm not rushing you. As a matter of fact, the reason for my call is to tell you to hold off until I can speak with Ms. Coletti. I understand they are friends. Maybe she can persuade him to cooperate. It's worth a try. Please have her report to my office."

Gina was taken aback when told by Doctor Bauer that Doctor Price wanted to see her in his office. *Why would the head administrator of the clinic want to see me?* Her intuition told her it must have something to do with the missing vial. *What other possible explanation could there be?* She nervously pressed the up button on the elevator and waited. It arrived almost immediately. She stepped in, took a deep breath, and punched the button for the top floor. *Damn that Michael! Always shooting from the hip. Always careless. He drives me crazy sometimes. I wouldn't be surprised if his cavalier attitude cost him his leg in Kuwait. I hate to think that way, but damn it! He doesn't listen to good advice. I told him not to snoop around. Now look what's happened—Doctor Price wants to see me.*

The elevator door opened to a plush hallway, far different than the nine floors below it. Instead of hospital green tiled floors and commercial florescent lighting, Gina walked out onto a shiny, intricately designed, Italian marble floor. The walls were papered down to a chair rail. The design of thick alternating vertical stripes of burgundy and cream along with the crystal chandeliers that hung from the textured ceiling gave it the look of an upscale hotel corridor rather than a medical facility.

Gina walked the length of the hall before reaching a large glass door trimmed with polished brass. Behind the door sat a receptionist. Gina entered with trepidation. The matronly receptionist looked up to greet her.

"May I help you," she said with a smile.

"Yes, I'm here at Doctor Price's request."

"Oh, yes, Ms. Coletti, he's expecting you." She dialed

the intercom and announced Gina's arrival before escorting her to his office. She opened the door and again smiled at Gina before abandoning her.

To Gina, Price looked bigger than life sitting behind his desk in a high-backed leather chair. "Welcome, Ms. Coletti. Please, have a seat." Gina took one of the two chairs directly in front of Price's desk. "Would you like some coffee or tea, or perhaps a soft drink?"

"No, thank you, Doctor. I'm fine."

"Very well," he said as he stood up and walked to the window. He looked out the window briefly before turning to Gina. "Ms. Coletti, I understand that you are good friends with Michael Fitzgerald?"

"Well, sort of," she said tentatively. "We've worked together over the years and I've socialized with him on a few occasions ... along with his wife, of course."

"Of course," he said with a quick smile. One that indicated to Gina that maybe he didn't believe their relationship was strictly platonic.

"Ms. Coletti, let me get right to the point. As you know, a vial of the Sicilia Gene serum is missing, and we want it returned." Gina, stunned at his sharp, terse statement, stood.

"Excuse me, Doctor Price, but what does that have to do with me? Surely, you don't think I had anything to do with its disappearance. I haven't got the slightest idea what happened to it."

"Please sit, Ms. Coletti. No one is accusing you of anything. As a matter of fact, we know who took the vial ... your friend Michael Fitzgerald."

"Michael? Are you sure? Why would he take it?"

"Yes, we are sure. I can't tell you how we know, but believe me; we know for certain he took it. As for why he did, we were hoping you could shed some light on that."

"I have no idea why he would do such a thing…if he did do it."

"Are you aware of any recent changes in his behavior? Some have noticed a change in his demeanor, suggesting perhaps that he may be using drugs or abusing alcohol."

"Michael likes to have a few beers now and then, but I've never known him to use drugs…of any kind."

Price changed the subject. "Ms. Coletti, how is your father feeling these days?" Startled, Gina pondered the question. *Why is he asking about my father?*

"He's fine. Why do you ask?"

"I understand he suffers from acute heart disease, and I thought I might be able to offer some help."

"Doctor, my father had a severe heart attack that caused extensive damage to the heart muscle. His heart is enlarged and is failing. He is on the most effective medication available. What more could you possibly do fore him?"

"Well, we obviously can't fix his heart muscle, of course…and you're right, he is more than likely on the best maintenance medicine available; medications that make his heart work more efficiently and less laboriously. What we can do, however, is help alleviate what caused his heart attack in the first place. We can greatly reduce the plaque in his arteries, thereby preventing another cardiac event. I don't have to tell you what his having another heart attack would mean. The odds would not be good.

"Now I must tell you, the medication I'm offering has not yet been approved, so you would have to agree to keep this confidential … between us."

"Why are you doing this, Doctor?"

"We want your help in recovering the serum."

"But, Doctor, what can I possibly do to help?"

"You can talk to Mr. Fitzgerald … convince him to return it. You are perhaps the only one he may listen to. If you succeed and he returns the serum within forty-eight hours, we are willing to forget the entire episode ever happened. On the other hand, if Mr. Fitzgerald decides not to return it for whatever reason, not only will he lose his job, Freiz, as well as the clinic, will pursue our legal options. I think that under the circumstances, our offer is more than generous."

Gina stood, realizing the reason for her being there had been accomplished, and replied, "I'll see what I can do."

On the way down in the elevator, Gina thought about the offer to help her father. *Would anything anyone could do really make a difference*, she wondered. Doctor Price was right; in his weakened state, any cardiac event would surely do him in. But, was it worth trying to keep him alive for a while longer, and would he want to be kept alive in his weakened state? She didn't want to lose him, but was she being selfish or would she be acting out of guilt? He was so frail and most of the time uncomfortable. He had told her on more than one occasion that he loved her, but he was tired and was ready to join her mother whenever the good Lord decided. She was confused and conflicted.

As soon as Gina spotted Michael, she gave him a stern

nod. He followed her to the hallway. Gina wasted no time and didn't mince words. "Michael, I'm afraid you are in real trouble. I need to speak with you—and soon. I'll meet you at your room after work."

"But," Michael protested, "I'm supposed to meet a few of the guys after work for a few beers."

"Damn it, Michael, aren't you listening? This is serious. Just be there!" She said before storming back into the office.

Michael was lying on the bed watching TV when Gina arrived. He let her in and plopped back onto the bed. Gina scanned the room, saw a table and two chairs, and took one of them. "Michael, would you please come over here, and turn off that damn TV." Michael reluctantly did as he was told, taking the chair across from Gina. He put his elbows on the table and rested his chin on his hands.

"I know what this is all about," he said nonchalantly.

Gina exploded. "Damn it, Michael! I know you know what this is about. What I want to know is what you are going to do about it. They know you took the serum, Michael."

"How do they know? Did you tell them?"

"Come on Michael, you know better than that. Please Michael, if you return it, nothing will happen to you. If you don't, not only will you be fired, they will press criminal charges against you. Michael, please, think of Arianna and the kids. Give it back."

"Do you believe their crap? How the hell do you know what they'll do? Are you their emissary? Did they send you here, Gina?"

"Michael, stop. I don't want to see you or your family hurt because of your—your compulsive act, as you describe it."

"It was compulsive, but since then I've been doing a lot of thinking. These bastards get away with murder every single day of the year. Every time a man or woman dies of cardiovascular disease that could have been prevented but wasn't because of these greedy SOBs, I say it's murder. Gina, my own mother died of a heart attack when she was fifty-one, barely middle aged. She might be alive today if it wasn't for their avarice and insatiable quest for higher and higher profits."

"Michael, I don't necessarily disagree with you, but there is no law that says they have to bring to market every new drug they develop, no matter how effective it may be. Michael, you are letting your emotions get the best of you. Think about what you are doing. You can't take on the world's largest pharmaceutical company and expect to win.

"Michael, please, I'll ask you one more time: for everyone's sake, please return it. If you give it back within forty-eight hours, they will take no action. Please, Michael," she implored.

"So they *did* send you…forty-eight hours, huh? And what did they promise you for your assistance?' he said snidely.

"You can go to hell! I was only trying to help you, but if you don't give a damn about your job or your family's welfare, why should I," she said as she went for the door.

As she opened it, Michael called out, "Gina, wait." She stopped and turned in his direction. "I'll think about it…I promise, I will." Gina hesitated briefly and then slammed the door behind her.

Michael went over and plopped back onto the bed, but instead of turning on the TV, he placed his hands behind his head and stared at the ceiling.

CHAPTER TWENTY-THREE

FORTY-EIGHT hours had come and gone. In the interim, Gina never mentioned the subject again, and Michael didn't volunteer any information as to whether he returned the serum or not. On Friday, a full seventy-two hours had passed when Gina ran into Michael in the clinic hallway.

"Well?" she asked.

"Well, what?"

"Don't play games with me, Michael, I'm in no mood. Did you return it or not?"

"I'm still not sure what I should do. I'm going to think about it over the weekend. Maybe I'll talk it over with Arianna."

"Michael, I *know* what she'll say and so do you. They gave you forty-eight hours. You already blew that. I think you're making a huge mistake by not taking them seriously."

"Don't worry. I'll decide by Monday, I promise."

"Michael, you just don't get it, do you? You don't have to promise *me* anything." Then she put up her hands in resignation. "I hope you enjoy your weekend," she said and stormed away shaking her head.

On Thursday, Doctor Bauer informed Doctor Monique Rentz that Fitzgerald had not come forward or in some other way returned the serum. Rentz told him to give Fitzgerald the weekend to think it over. Then she called Bitterman and explained the situation. He agreed with her decision, and said he would also work on it from his end.

After hanging up from Rentz, Bitterman picked up the phone again to make the call he had hoped to avoid. In his business, industrial spying was an ongoing problem and as a result his firm's engaging in clandestine operations from time to time was an unfortunate, but necessary part of the job. During his tenure at Freiz, Max Trammel, his head of security, developed the contacts needed to accomplish the assignment at hand. He summoned Trammel to his office. Bitterman briefly explained the situation and what he wanted done.

Max Trammel dialed and waited for "The Facilitator" to answer. He had contacted the man more than a few times throughout the years, but to this day he didn't know the man's name. He thought it odd that he would place his trust in someone he didn't know or had never even met, but that was how this type of business was handled: word of mouth and cash … deniability.

The Facilitator answered and after exchanging a few

code phrases, Trammel explained what he needed. The conversation was short and to the point. The Facilitator accepted the assignment and arrangements were made for prepayment.

The two men accepted their assignment as they always had…through "The Assignor." They never really knew whom they were working for, and they didn't care much either. They were paid in advance and always in cash, and were given just enough information to carry out their mission. They considered themselves professionals, mercenaries in the truest sense of the word. For them, this job seemed like a piece of cake.

After work on Friday, Michael headed home for the weekend. While exiting I-95, he noticed a car that had been behind him for some time exiting as well. He thought it a mere coincidence. He began to worry when he turned down his street and the black sedan with tinted glass followed suit. He pulled into his driveway, stopped the engine and sat in the car. The sedan drove by, slowing markedly as it passed his house, and then it sped up and drove off. Was it an attempt at intimidation or just his imagination? He began to think that Gina might have been right. Maybe he did underestimate how far they would go to get the vial back. It was unnerving, yet, at the same time he realized he had no choice; they needed to be exposed. The world had a right to know that millions of lives could have been saved and millions more would die needlessly because of nothing more than corporate greed.

All weekend he thought about what to do and exactly how to do it. By the time he had to head back to Boston, he still had no answers. Michael did his best to keep his worries from Arianna but he sensed that she could tell that something was wrong, even asking him at one point. He brushed off her concerns, and she didn't pursue it further.

Michael didn't know what to expect on Monday at work. He thought they might call him in and challenge him directly. *Why didn't I just say I dropped one of the vials? Now I have no choice, I'll just have to deny, deny, deny.* To his surprise, no one, not even Gina broached the subject. Although it seemed odd that they would just drop it, he was thankful that the clinic, or Freiz, or even Gina, hadn't challenged him. It all seemed a little surreal. Then on Thursday night on the way back to the hotel after work, things changed. He noticed the black sedan that followed him to his home during the past weekend, at least it looked like the same one, was again behind him. Was it simple paranoia, or were they really following him? He decided to find out.

He floored the gas pedal and pulled away. The sedan followed suit, quickly closing the gap between them. His heart rate quickening, he slammed on the brakes and made a sharp right turn at the next intersection. Looking in his rearview mirror, he watched as the sedan went on, straight through the intersection. He felt a measure of relief and laughed at himself for being foolishly suspicious. Michael's fear returned when he glanced in the mirror again and saw the vehicle backing up to make a turn in his direction. Again he floored it and then slammed on the brakes, slowing enough to fishtail around a corner. He sped toward the interstate and flew up the ramp. He maneuvered past and around the light traffic hoping to attract the attention of a cop. *Where are the cops when you really need them?* His eyes darted back and forth between the windshield and the rearview mirror. There was no sign of the sedan; it appeared that he'd lost them. When Michael was satisfied that he was no longer being tailed, he made his way back to the hotel. He parked the car and kept a weary eye on his surroundings until he entered the building.

Michael heard the phone ringing as he unlocked the door to his room. He hurried to the phone, but was too late. He checked to see if whoever had called had left a message, but found none. He went to the window and scanned the parking lot before drawing the drapes.

He kicked off his shoes and plopped onto the bed. *They are definitely onto me. There's no doubt about it now. Now what the hell am I going to do?*

He was pulled from his thoughts when the phone rang a second time.

"Hello?" he said tentatively.

"You know stealing is a crime. Return what you took and nothing will happen," said the foreboding male voice. "If you don't—" There was a click, then a dial tone.

The call unnerved him. The caller didn't actually threaten him, but the implication was clear: give it back—or else. *What should I do? I can't go to the police because I did steal it. I had to. How many more people have to die? How many more pills do they need to sell and how many needless by-pass surgeries and angioplasties have to be performed for the sake of ever increasing profits? This is corporate greed at its worst and it must be exposed no matter what the consequences.*

Michael wondered how they knew he took the vial. *There are several people who have access to the medication room. It could have been any one of them. How do they know I took it? I know no one saw me and I haven't told anyone about it … except Gina.*

Fruitlessly running these thoughts through his mind was frustrating. *The answers would come in due time, just not tonight.* He peered through the drapes to check the parking lot one last time. Then after engaging the dead bolt and wedging a chair under the doorknob, he went to bed. The adrenalin rushes and stress of the past few hours had taken their toll. He was exhausted, and soon fell into an uneasy sleep.

The ringing phone jolted him awake. He glanced at the clock. It read five thirty. *Who would be calling me at this hour? A phone call this early can't be good.* He snapped up the phone as he sat up, his only response being a cautious, "Hello?" The reply gave him pause. It was the same intimidating male voice.

"You know stealing is a crime. Return what you took and nothing will happen. Do it today. This is your last chance. If you don't—" There was a click; then dial tone returned.

"If I don't *what?*" he yelled into the receiver. *What will they do, come after me or my family?* A cold chill ran up his spine.

He picked up the phone, dialed, and waited. On the third ring a soft, sleepy voice said, "Hello?"

"Hi, honey, it's me," he said trying to sound nonchalant.

"Why are you calling me so early? Is everything all right?"

"Yeah, everything's fine. I just wanted to make sure you and the kids were okay."

"At this hour, you had to find out if we are all right, at a quarter to six in the morning? What's wrong with you?"

"Nothing's wrong with me, I just need to know that you're all right."

"Listen, sweetheart, I know you too well. Now tell me what's going on."

"Honey, I think I might be in a little trouble."

"Trouble, what kind of trouble? And don't beat around the bush, just tell me."

"Okay, Okay, I took something from work and I think—I know—they found out about it."

"Took, you mean stole? What is it—why did you do such a stupid thing? Can't you return it?"

"I can't explain it all to you now, I just can't. All I can tell you is that I didn't take it for my own benefit. Please trust me on this. I'm trying to do the right thing."

"The right thing? How can stealing something from your employer ever be the right thing?" she asked incredulously.

"I'll explain when I come home for the weekend. I'm going to leave right after work. I should be home around seven thirty. Listen, Honey, I'm probably overreacting. Don't worry, everything will be okay. I promise. I'm sorry I woke you. Go back to sleep. I'll see you tonight."

"It's too late for that. I should be getting up anyway. I want to get some things done before the kids wake up." After a brief pause, she added, "Are you sure you're all right?"

"I'm fine, Honey. I'll see you later. Love you," he said and hung up.

His workday seemed to last forever. Although, to his surprise, no one from management had approached him, he had the creepy feeling he was being watched.

When the day finally ended, he wasted no time before heading home. The trip to Waterford was uneventful, although he must have checked his rearview mirror a thousand times during the trip. Maybe his being followed and the phone calls were nothing more than an attempt at intimidation, and an attempt to scare him into returning the vial. At least, that is what he wanted to believe, but he couldn't take any chances. He had to stow the vial somewhere safe, away from his wife and children. He didn't want them involved in any way. He had to think of a place to hide it.

Michael wasn't home for two minutes before his wife demanded to know what was going on. He steadfastly refused to tell her, but tried to reassure her by telling her he would explain it all in due time. Arianna, being a stubborn woman, kept after him until the atmosphere became such that neither spoke to the other except when necessary. *She'll get over it. I have a more urgent matter that needs attention. I need to hide the vial, and I need to do it quickly. After that, I'll figure out my next move.*

He racked his brain trying to think of a safe place to hide the vial. All at once it came to him: a place where he hung out with his friends as a kid. It would be safe there, at least in the short term.

The following morning he arose before dawn. He did his best not to wake his wife. He dressed in the dark and picked up his shoes. As he was tiptoeing toward the bedroom door, his wife called out, "Where are you going at this hour?"

"I couldn't sleep, so I decided to get up." He hated not being able to confide in her; he ached to do so. They had shared everything in their marriage. This, however, was different. He had to protect his family, and the less they knew the better.

"More secrets?" she said sarcastically.

"Please, honey, let's not argue about this anymore." Arianna turned away from him and pulled up the covers sharply to make her point.

After slipping out the back door and getting into his car as quietly as possible, he started the engine, knowing full well Arianna would hear it. There would, no doubt, be more questions and arguing when he returned.

Before leaving his driveway, he looked up and down the street for any suspicious vehicles. Seeing none, he drove out and headed for Ocean Beach. During the short drive to the shore, he checked several times to make sure he wasn't being followed. Satisfied, he pulled into the deserted parking lot. Dawn was breaking; there was just enough light to see his way to the destination. After surveying the parking lot one last time, he grabbed the wooden humidor that housed the vial. He didn't smoke cigars; his grandfather had. Michael kept it as a keepsake after he died. He never imagined it would be used in such a clandestine way. Holding it closely, he headed for the boardwalk.

He descended the few steps to the beach and walked parallel to the boardwalk until he reached its end. He paused for a few seconds to take in a breath of crisp salt air and touch the fine, sugar-white sand that rest beneath his feet. God, did he love the beach when he was a kid. This was the spot where he hung out with his friends; playing cards, girl watching, and soaking up ultraviolet rays in a silent competition for the best tan. The boardwalk was not more than four feet above the sandy beach, providing enough room to crouch, but not stand underneath it. Large creosoted poles buried deep in the sand and rising to the bottom of the boardwalk supported it. There was a space at the top of the poles large enough to accommodate the humidor. He crouched, reached under the boardwalk and placed the humidor on top of a pole. It was hidden from sight. The only way it could be discovered would be for someone to go under the boardwalk and look up at the top; a very unlikely event.

The vial was not a hundred percent safe. However, it would have to do for the time being until he decided what to do with it.

On his way back to the car, he saw no one until he reached the parking lot where a man was walking his dog. "Nice day for a walk," he said to the man.

The man looked quizzically at him and replied, "Yes, it is," and then moved quickly past him.

On the way home, he stopped at a deli and picked up some bagels and rolls. Arianna was sitting at the kitchen table with a cup of coffee when he arrived. He placed the bag on the counter. "I bought some bagels and rolls as a peace offering," he said with a coy smile.

She looked up at him with concern. "I hope you know what you're doing." He poured himself a cup of coffee and thought, *I hope so, too.*

The rest of the weekend he played with the kids and made some repairs around the house. It was otherwise uneventful. He avoided the subject and tried not to dwell on it, and to his surprise, Arianna left it alone.

CHAPTER TWENTY-FOUR

GINA was having breakfast with her father on Friday morning. "Is David coming up for the weekend?" Al asked.

"Yes, we're going to the game on Sunday, it's a double-header."

"It's going to be a tough series. Those damn Yankees are as hot as blazes right now."

"That's what David's hoping for. He loves to razz you about your beloved Red Sox."

"Well, he may be in for a surprise. Our Sox are no pushovers. They are still *our* Sox, aren't they?"

"Don't be silly, of course they are, Daddy. You know I would never betray our BoSox," she said with a loving smile.

Gina turned serious. "Daddy, let me run something by you. I want to get your take on a situation a coworker is in. This coworker of mine thinks she and another coworker have discovered a plot by her employer to keep secret a new medication that could ameliorate or even cure heart disease caused by atherosclerosis. The company, instead, wants to go forward with another newly patented drug that simply treats the disease. The reason seems obvious: there is more money treating a disease than curing it. Anyway, one of the two employees wants to expose Freiz to the public to let them know what they are withholding from the millions of people who could benefit from it, but the other one isn't sure what to do."

"Listen, Gina, this is nothing new. Corporations are in business to make money for their stockholders. That, above all else, is their driving motivation. Sure, they like to polish their public image with grants to charities and the like, but they exist for the sole purpose of making money.

"But wouldn't you think that with something with this kind of potential, they would put the welfare of those in need before profit? I mean, they would still make an enormous amount of money. When is enough, enough?"

"Gina, you are being altruistic and I'm afraid a bit naïve. Think about it. Why would a company go out and cure a disease when they can continue to treat it indefinitely? I'm sure this goes on all the time."

"That's a very cynical attitude, Daddy."

"No, sweetheart, it's being realistic. So what are your coworkers planning to do?"

"I'm not sure, really. One definitely wants to go ahead and make an issue of it, but the other one isn't sure. To make matters worse, the company knows of their discovery and is trying to dissuade them."

"And how are they doing that?"

"Well, one's father has heart disease. The company knows that and is trying to bribe her. In exchange for her silence, they are willing to offer her father the new medication, the one they are not planning to market. She is confused. She wants to do the right thing, but at this point she's not sure what the right thing is."

Al rubbed his chin and thought for a minute before answering. "Well, I'm sure every case is different, but let's use you and me as an example. In my case, it should be an easy choice."

"Why do you say that?"

"Even though my heart attack caused significant damage to my heart muscle, I had triple by-pass surgery, and my arteries are in fairly good shape. This new miracle medicine would be of little value to me. Besides, I wouldn't want it on my conscience regardless, because the benefit, if any, I derived would be at the expense of someone who could have really benefited from it." Gina immediately thought of David. "So, again," Al continued, "using you and me as an example, I would tell you to expose those bastards." Al smiled at Gina and gave her a wink. "And sweetheart, tell your friend to be very careful. I wouldn't want anything to happen to her."

Gina walked over to her father, leaned down and threw her arms around him. "Daddy, are you sure?" She asked with an impassioned look. Al gently pushed her back and held her at arms length.

"Sweetheart, I'm only human. If I thought this medicine could significantly improve my condition, I might be tempted, but you and I know I'm not a candidate for the protocol they're offering. So don't give it another thought. Now let's not discuss it further."

"Daddy, David doesn't know about any of this. I haven't discussed it with him, so please don't mention it to him, okay?"

"Don't worry, sweetheart. It'll be our secret. Just remember what I said about being careful."

"I will, Daddy. I promise." Al hadn't convinced his daughter; she was still undecided. Although he made perfect sense, he was still her father and the thought of extending his life, even for a short period of time, was, for Gina, a powerful incentive. Conversely, she also loved David, and if they were successful in exposing Freiz, perhaps public pressure would force them to market the Sicilia Gene medication. In that case, David could continue the therapy that he so desperately needed.

Gina's thoughts wavered between helping her father or helping David. She felt contempt for Freiz for putting her in this unenviable position.

That night David, Gina, and Al dined on Chinese takeout. They sat at the dining room table for hours. David and Al talked baseball and current events and Gina enjoyed the interaction of the two men in her life, piping in occasionally to defend her Bosox.

On Saturday, after overcoming Al's flimsy objections, David and Gina persuaded Al to go out to lunch with them. After eating, they took Al for a ride, and left the busy city for the lush countryside. Upon their return home, it was obvious to Gina her father had enjoyed himself, and even though it was David's suggestion, she wondered why she hadn't thought of doing this herself. She promised herself she would do this more often.

That night David and Gina went out to eat. Gina suggested they try a seafood restaurant downtown, but David insisted they revisit *Anna's Cucina,* hoping to recapture the magic of their first experience there.

Anna greeted them by giving them both a hug. The genuinely warm greeting gave David the feeling that he had known Anna for longer than he had, and that he had seen her many more times than only the one time before.

After she seated them at their special table by the bay window and brought them a bottle of Chianti, she served them one delicious dish after another. When they had had their fill, they, like the time before, skipped dessert and opted only for cappuccino. It was a repeat of their first dinner date. Everything was perfect; the friendly greeting, the same great table, the good wine, and wonderful food all created the ambiance that David had hoped to experience again. Except, this time something was different. He couldn't put his finger on it, but it didn't have the same feel as the first time. *Maybe some special times in one's life are meant to be experienced only once.* Other special times came to mind that he had tried to replicate, but couldn't. This must be one of those times, he figured. But no, something was different; it was Gina.

Although pleasant and engaging, she seemed to drift off now and again. Then, as if realizing her actions, she would refocus. It was almost imperceptible, yet it was real.

Now that he thought about it, she'd been this way since he arrived, and it was somewhat discomforting.

"Gina, is something bothering you?"

"No. Why do you ask?"

"I don't know. You seem to be preoccupied at times … sort of distant."

"I'm sorry, David. I'm worried about my father."

She hated to lie to David, but she couldn't tell him about what Michael had done, or about the conversation with Doctor Price, or the one with her father. She couldn't draw him into it. Things were going too well in his life. He was feeling better, actually getting better, and their relationship was flourishing. He was on a high and she didn't want to send him into a tailspin.

"Why? He seemed to enjoy himself today."

"I know he did. It's just that he looked so tired and frail when we got home. I'm afraid it was too much for him."

"He probably just needs a little rest. Don't worry, he'll be fine."

"I'm sure you're right. I'll try to be better company," she said as she reached over and took his hand. She hated lying to David, and she felt the pang of guilt for using her father as an excuse.

After dinner they returned home to find Al asleep in his wheelchair. After putting him to bed, David and Gina sat on the porch listening to Johnny Mathis. After their conversation at dinner, Gina was ever conscious of her thoughts and actions. She didn't want David questioning her. Nor did she want him to think something was awry between them. The soft, romantic music was enough of an enticement for Gina to take the lead. She stood, pulled David from the loveseat, and wrapped her arms around his neck. He responded by pulling her close. Instead of dancing, they simply swayed to the music. He nibbled on her neck and then her earlobe. She responded by pushing her hips against his. They kissed passionately as their breathing grew heavy. David slid his hands down to her buttocks and pulled her firmly against him. Then, his hands moved under her blouse and slowly up and down her back. He was about to unsnap her bra when she said in a hushed tone, "No, not here. Let's go inside." She took his hand and led him to her room where she did her best to convince him that everything was good in their world. It was another world that concerned her, the one that included Michael Fitzgerald, the Clinic, and Freiz. A world she felt she was being dragged into.

After the games on Sunday, Gina made a heart-healthy grilled fish dinner. Boston and New York had split the double header, giving both Al and David enough ammunition to hammer one another. Throughout their verbal jousting, thoughts of what Michael had done haunted Gina. She was keen not to let it show as she had before. She looked at the clock. Michael should be back at the hotel by now. She excused herself, citing the need to use the bathroom. She went to her room, closed the door, and reached for the phone. She dialed the hotel and asked to be connected to room 231. It rang until it switched to the electronic message center. Gina hung up without leaving a message. *Damn it, Michael, where are you? I need to talk to you. I need to know what you're going to do.* She couldn't help but wonder what tomorrow held for them. Then, she returned to the dining room and jumped into the conversation to defend her hometown team.

CHAPTER TWENTY-FIVE

On the ride back to Boston, Michael's driving was on automatic pilot. The enormity of his actions had finally settled in. He contemplated what he'd done: stole from his employer. Worse yet, they knew it. He didn't know how they knew, but clearly they knew.

No one saw him take the vial, he was sure of that. Then it hit him. The lab must have been under video surveillance. It made sense. They had security cameras strategically located elsewhere at the clinic, why not in the most secure room in the building? His strength suddenly drained from his body. *I'm dead meat.*

For a fleeting minute, before he had hidden the vial, he thought about returning it. But it was too late for that now. No matter what he did going forward, he knew, at the very least, he was sure to lose his job. And if Freiz went to the police, he may even lose his freedom. He realized it was too late to turn back now. The question remained: What to do with the serum? Who could he turn to? Who could he trust, and what about Arianna and the kids? He had thought of none of this at the adrenalin-fueled moment he took the vial. Arianna had always told him he was impulsive, that someday it would get him in trouble. That someday had arrived.

Lost in his thoughts, he drifted partially into the adjacent lane. The thundering honk of a semi's air horn jolted his consciousness. He jerked the wheel and swerved back into his lane. His heart raced at the realization that his lack of concentration had almost caused an accident. More trouble he didn't need. He had enough on his plate.

He cursed himself for everything he was accused of being: impulsive, reckless, and just plain stupid. He added selfish to the list. Without considering the possible consequences, he'd put the welfare of his family in jeopardy because he thought he could right an injustice. He cursed himself again, this time out loud.

Sometime during the ride, it came to him why the clinic hadn't approached him directly—bad publicity. They wanted to be as discreet as possible so as not to raise any red flags that might draw in the press. The media loved whistle-blowers, and even though what Freiz was doing, or more accurately, not doing, was not in violation of any law, they would be hard pressed to explain why they intended to keep this new, almost miraculous, medication from the market. He tried to imagine what the public outcry would have been if the Salk Vaccine had been shelved and kept from those in need simply due to business considerations.

This convenient rationalization, he figured, gave him the moral high ground. He felt emboldened.

Once the vial's content was revealed to the world, he believed he would be considered a whistle-blower of the highest order; not that he was looking for any notoriety.

First he would have to face some significant, unpleasant encounters both at work and at home.

So consumed by his thoughts, he nearly forgot, except for a few times, to look in his rearview mirror. After all, he had received no more threatening phone calls. Surely they knew where he lived and could have called him at home. *Thank God they didn't. Arianna would have become unhinged.* And he was sure no one was following him now. He had a somewhat reassuring thought. *Maybe they aren't really sure I took it. I'm sure I'll find out one way or another tomorrow at work.*

It was dusk when he arrived back at the hotel. He parked, and before entering the building, he scanned the parking lot for anything suspicious. Seeing nothing, he smiled to himself and headed for his room.

His confidence was shattered by a flush of anxiety when he opened the door to his room and saw that it had been ransacked. *They were here looking for the vial. It's not over. They're not going to give up.*

Frightened, he now realized he needed help; someone to talk to; someone to get advice from. *If they were willing to break into my room, what else might they do?* He ran to the phone, and with his trembling finger, he punched in the number. There was a knock on the door. "Housekeeping," a male voice said. *I didn't call housekeeping … oh shit!* Again there was a knock, "Housekeeping," the man said louder this time. Michael's heart raced as he waited for someone to answer the phone. *Pick up, damn it, pick up!* His heart went into overdrive when he heard the lock being jimmied. *Shit! I forgot to lock the deadbolt.* An answering machine picked up with a canned message: *I'm not available to take your call. Please leave a message at the beep and I'll return your call as soon as possible.* He heard the beep and saw the door swing open at the same time. Panic stricken, he shouted into the phone, "I took the vial. It's where we—" One man, the shorter of the two, yanked the phone from Michael's hand while the other, a large burly man, threw a tight bear hug around him from behind. After placing the phone back in the cradle, the smaller man pulled a plastic bag from his jacket. Michael thrashed about wildly trying to extricate himself from the man's vise-like grip. The smaller man slipped the bag over Michael's head and held it firmly around his neck. Michael gasped for air, but at every try the bag came slamming into his mouth and nose giving them a vacuum seal. In his panic he tried again and again to break free from his captors. His oxygen starved lungs ached as they begged for air. He tried to pierce the bag with his tongue, but to no avail. His resistance weakened as consciousness abandoned him. His last thought was of Arianna and the kids before he became limp and slipped to the floor.

The two men wasted no time. They lifted Michael's unconscious body, dumping it on the bed. One of the men, the smaller of the two, pulled a syringe from his jacket pocket, and after locating a suitable vein in Michael's left forearm, injected a lethal dose of heroin into the limp limb. He then placed an assortment of drug paraphernalia—spoon, matches, and an empty glassine envelope—on the nightstand, and tied a rubber tourniquet loosely around the arm while the other intruder covered the room one last time. When finished, they disappeared as stealthily as they had arrived.

CHAPTER TWENTY-SIX

The White House

THE President of the United States, Jefferson Rayhill, was nearing the end of his regularly scheduled press conference. He was fielding questions regarding the current conflicts in the Middle East. A civil war raged in Iraq and Israel's war with Hezbollah had, after a number of failed ceasefires, spilled over into Syria. Iran, Hezbollah's surrogate, was now threatening to declare war against Israel. The European Union, not uncharacteristically, was reticent to commit troops either under the auspices of the EU or NATO, and the United Nations, it appeared, was collectively wringing their hands.

A reporter asked the president a final question. President Rayhill appeared confused by the question. There was an uneasy silence. The press corps waited for his response. The president looked about the room as if searching for the words. His attempt at speech failed him and he began to stammer. His press secretary immediately recognized something was wrong and quickly stepped up to the lectern, leaned into the microphone and said, "The President has already answered that question. That was the last question. Thank you all for coming." He then, as discreetly as possible, led the president out, leaving a room full of bewildered reporters mumbling amongst themselves.

The scene was replayed on television a thousand times over the next twenty-four hours. While the event itself wasn't very dramatic, it was, by some measure, surreal. It was clear to anyone who saw the incident that something was obviously wrong with the president. He appeared disoriented, confused, and at a loss for words. Speculation was rife with the media and the public at large. Some conjectured that the president had suffered a stroke, while others believed he was either showing early signs of Alzheimer's, or was exhibiting symptoms of exhaustion. Some even suggested he may have been under the influence of medication.

A White House spokesperson assured the media that all was well with the president and that President Rayhill would be addressing the nation the following evening to allay any unfounded concerns the citizens may have.

Brett Bitterman was sitting in Bruce Richards' office when the vice president entered the room. Bitterman jumped to his feet and said, "Bruce, what's the urgency of the meeting, and all of the cloak and dagger antics of your Secret Service people?"

"I'm sorry for all of the drama, Brett, but I needed to get

you here fast, to talk to you before the president addresses the nation."

"Did you ever think of using a telephone? To whisk me off in a jet at government expense seems a bit much, even for you."

Richards smiled. "Brett, in the absence of a secure line, this was my only alternative. Well, first let me thank you for what you've done for me. I cannot remember the last time I felt this good. The medication has worked its magic. You're right; it truly is a miracle drug."

"Bruce, please get to the point. What can I do for you?"

"Tonight the president will explain to the nation that he has experienced a Transient Ischemic Attack, TIA for short."

"Yes, yes, I'm familiar with the terminology."

"Of course you are. At any rate, he has been having these mini strokes for some time, but until yesterday, no one except he and his personal physician knew about it. He has been undergoing tests to determine the cause. The tests revealed he has a clogged carotid artery that requires surgery. He is going to announce to the nation his need for surgery, which is scheduled for tomorrow morning. There will be a temporary transfer of power, beginning at midnight."

"I would offer my congratulations, but under the circumstances, it would be rather tasteless, don't you think?"

"It's only temporary, Brett, but the experience will prove invaluable in my campaign for the permanent job."

"I'm sure it will, but I have to ask you: what does any of this have to do with me?"

"I was afraid that after the incident at the press conference, you might try to contact the president directly. You know, to offer him the same deal you offered me. You see Bitterman; it's not what I *want* you to do, it's want I *don't* want you to do. I know this will sound terrible, but I would appreciate it if you would not offer to help him as you did me."

"I thought he was your college classmate; a close personal friend of the family?"

"He was, and he is. But this isn't about any of that. Politics always trumps friendship. I can say without compunction, if the tables were turned, he would not hesitate to make the same request."

"You don't have to explain yourself, Bruce. You know where my loyalty lies."

"I appreciate your saying that. And I must say, I don't know how I could ever thank you enough for giving me back my health."

"Well, now that you mention it, there is something I could use a little help on."

Richards laughed. "I should have known."

CHAPTER TWENTY-SEVEN

G INA was apprehensive about what Monday would bring. She arrived at the clinic at her normal time and anxiously waited for Michael. When it was time to start work, he had yet to arrive. *Late again.* His lackadaisical attitude drove Gina crazy. She wondered how Arianna put up with it. When he hadn't shown up by break time, she began to worry. In the break room, she approached Doctor Bauer and asked if Michael had called in sick or taken the day off. He gave her an inquisitive look and replied, "No, I haven't heard from him. I was about to ask if you knew why he hasn't reported to work."

"I have no idea why he's not here," she said, shrugging her shoulders.

"By the way, Gina, let me ask you: have any participants in your group complained of chest or leg pain, dizziness, shortness of breath, or headaches?"

"No. Why do you ask?"

"Well, some of our group leaders have reported an increase of these symptoms, and just this morning, I learned a few had to be hospitalized."

"Do you know their condition?"

"No, not yet, but they suspect blood clots may be the cause. Let me know immediately if anyone in your group becomes symptomatic."

Gina assured Doctor Bauer she would, and then she retreated to the hallway. She called the hotel from her cell phone and asked for Michael's room.

No answer.

Gina's concern was now bordering on alarm. She retrieved his home number from her phone and dialed. Arianna answered. "Hi, Arianna, it's Gina. Is Michael there by chance?" She suddenly felt awkward; sorry she'd called. If he wasn't there, it would surely cause Arianna to worry. After all, if he wasn't home, he should be at work. But it was too late. She *had* called.

"Hi, Gina, uh, no he's not here. He left to go back to Boston last evening. Is there something wrong? Are you at work?" Gina could give her no other explanation other than the truth, which she knew would upset her.

"I haven't seen him. I was wondering if he was ill or took the day off." She hoped her inquiry sounded benign.

"Gina, I'm worried. Michael may be impulsive at times, but he is very reliable. It's not like him to just not show up for work. Hold on, let me call his cell phone." *Damn it! Why didn't I think to do that before calling his home?* Arianna returned to the phone and expressed her concern.

"He's not answering." Arianna suddenly broke into a

cold sweat recalling Michael's admission. "Gina, now I'm really worried. He always answers his cell phone. It's our emergency link. We always know we can reach each other. Even when he has to turn it off at the clinic, he checks his messages regularly. I left a message asking him to call me ASAP. I don't know what else to do." She sounded as if she was about to burst into tears.

"Arianna, please calm down. I'm sorry if I upset you. I'm sure he's okay. I'll call you when he shows up."

"Thank you, Gina. I'll do the same."

The rest of the morning, Gina had trouble concentrating on her work. At lunchtime, instead of eating, she drove to the hotel. Her heart leapt to her throat when she arrived and saw two police cars and an ambulance parked at the entrance.

Gina parked and raced to the building. Nothing seemed unusual in the lobby. She went directly to the elevator and pushed two. As soon as she exited the elevator, her worst fears were realized. Outside Michael's door a uniformed policeman stood sentry.

As Gina approached the room, the officer put his arm up. "Sorry ma'am, there's a police investigation in progress."

"Police investigation? What's happened?"

"I'm sorry, ma'am, I'm not at liberty to say. May I inquire as to why you're asking?"

"I work with Michael. He didn't show up for work this morning."

"Hold on, let me get one of the detectives for you."

"Yes, yes, please, I need to speak to someone." The

officer knocked on the door. A mustachioed plain-clothes detective who appeared to be in his mid forties opened the door. Seeing Gina, he stepped out, quickly closing the door behind him.

"Can I help you, ma'am? I'm Detective Morgan."

Gina was near panic. "This is my friend's room. He didn't show up for work today, and no one knows where he is or what happened to him. I spoke to his wife and she doesn't know either—"

"Whoa, whoa, slow down. Take a deep breath and try to calm yourself. Why don't we go down to the café. I'll buy you a cup of coffee. My partner can handle it alone for a few minutes."

"I don't want a cup of coffee. I want to know what's happened to Michael."

"All right, let's go where we can talk." He took her by the arm and led her to the café.

"Oh, God, please tell me he's all right."

Detective Morgan picked a secluded table in the rear of the café. He pulled out a pad from his inside jacket pocket, and asked, "Now, what is your name?"

"Gina Coletti. Now tell me what's going on here, will you?"

"And what is your relationship to Mr. Fitzgerald?"

"Stop it! Just stop it! I'm not answering any more questions until you tell me what's going on here."

"Okay, Ms. Coletti." Morgan paused briefly, took a deep breath and said, "It looks like your friend overdosed on, what appears to be, heroin. I'm sorry, he's dead."

Gina gasped as she clasped her hand to her mouth.

"But that's impossible, Michael doesn't use drugs. Oh my God! Poor Arianna and the children. Oh no, how could this happen?"

"We'll know more when we get the coroner's report."

Again she said as she rubbed her forehead, "Poor Arianna."

"His wife is being contacted as we speak."

Gina's cell phone rang. She looked at the caller ID, excused herself, and walked to the lobby. "David—" He cut her off.

"Gina, I've been trying to get you all morning. When I got home there was a really strange message on my recorder from Michael. He sounded like he was panic stricken, and then right in the middle of his message he was cut off. I tried to call him back on his cell phone, but it went to voice mail. Do you know what's going on?"

"David, Michael is dead," she said and started to cry. Through her tears she explained to him the events that led up to her discovery of this tragedy.

"Michael overdosed on drugs? That's impossible! The Michael I knew wouldn't go near drugs."

"I know." Gina affirmed, "That's what I said to the detective. I just can't believe it."

"This is unbelievable. I'm coming over. I'll catch the next ferry. I should be there late this afternoon. Will you be all right until I get there?"

"Yes, I'll be okay. Come directly to my house. I'm not going back to work. As soon as I finish speaking with Detective Morgan, I'm going home."

Gina met David at the door. By her swollen eyes and red nose, David could see she'd been crying for most of the day. When she saw David, she threw her arms around him and started crying again. He held her until her sobbing ebbed. "If only he had listened to me," she said. "Why didn't he listen to me, damn it!"

Once inside, and after David said hello to Al, Gina took David by the hand and led him to the porch. She didn't want her father to hear any part of their conversation, for it would be sure to upset him.

"Gina, what did you mean when you said, 'If only he had listened to me'? What in God's name is going on here?"

"First, tell me what his message said."

"It was very short. He said, 'I took the vial. It's where we—', and then he was cut off. What vial? What did he mean, 'It's where we'? Gina, do you have any idea what he was talking about?" Upset and exhausted, Gina began to weep as she recalled her conversation with Michael. She lolled on the swing as she gathered her thoughts. She leaned back, closed her eyes, and rested her head on David's shoulder.

"I'm afraid so." Together they quietly rocked to the hypnotic motion of the swing's to and fro as each tried to deal with their own personal loss.

"Remember when we were in the break room and Michael said he was gong to snoop around, and I told him not to? Well, he didn't listen. Oh, God, I wish he had," she said with a deep sigh. "Anyway, he came across a couple of e-mail messages between Rentz and Bitterman. Bitterman is the CEO of Freiz. Rentz informed Bitterman, and this will not be a surprise to you, how effective the Sicilia Gene therapy has been during the trial. Its efficacy went way beyond what anyone expected. It reduced the amount of plaque by an average of ten percent in just a few weeks. Keeping in mind that it takes years for plaque to build up in the arteries, this was an astonishing result."

"That's good news. It validates what I've been saying all along."

"I know. I know, but wait, there's more. In his response to Rentz, Bitterman referred to a contingency plan. He instructed her to start administering placebo to all trial participants."

"Gina, I don't know if I believe that. I don't feel any different since my last injection. In fact I feel even better. Besides, why would Freiz do such a thing? It doesn't make sense. If the drug were even more successful than antici-pated, you would think they would be ecstatic. You'd think they would want to see what the ultimate result would be, wouldn't you? Am I missing something here?"

"I'm beginning to think we both are, or at least, were. Michael believed Freiz intended to sabotage its own trial by replacing the real serum with a placebo. They could then either claim the trial was a moderate success or even declare it a failure."

"But why? It doesn't make sense. You'd think that any pharmaceutical company would kill for such an effective drug."

"David, I'm beginning to believe, in this case, they may have killed to prevent this from being exposed to the world."

"Michael? You think Freiz had something to do with Michael's death?"

"I'm not sure what to think just yet, but Michael's theory is starting to make sense. He believed the Sicilia Gene therapy had the potential to cure coronary artery disease, not just simply to treat it."

"And this would be bad for Freiz?" he asked sounding confused. "I don't get it."

"Michael had a theory that at first, I must admit, I didn't accept. He theorized that if Freiz brought the Sicilia Gene drug to market, it would, in short order, make their cholesterol-lowering drug, Torvistat, obsolete. Think about it. Those who take cholesterol-lowering medication, take it for their entire lifetime. Torvistat is the world's most popular statin medication. It's a cash cow for Freiz. It accounts for over thirteen billion dollars in annual revenue. Now, if the Sicilia Gene medication actually cures coronary artery disease rather than simply managing it, it follows that the need for the Sicilia Gene therapy would be of a temporary nature."

"Wow, Michael's theory is starting to make a lot more sense, but what's this about a vial that he said he took?"

"After he read the e-mails, he impulsively decided to take a vial from the lab, not giving a thought that the most secure room in the clinic would be under the watchful eye of a security camera."

"Oh God, so they have him on tape? Do we know that for sure?"

"Yes. They know Michael and I are friends, so they brought me in and asked me to help them convince Michael to return the vial."

"And you didn't tell me anything about any of this?"

"I didn't want to get you involved." She also left out the part about the offer to help her father. "When I asked them how they knew for sure it was Michael who took it, they told me it wasn't my concern."

"And do you think Freiz had something to do with his death?"

"All I can say for sure is that Michael wasn't a drug user. He hated drugs. He lost a cousin who overdosed some years ago. I don't know if Freiz is involved, but I do know the circumstances around his death are highly suspect."

"The part of his message that got cut off: 'It's where we', must refer to our childhood. Where we—played—fished—hung out?"

"That has to be what he meant. He hid the vial where the two of you used to do … something as kids."

"Gina, we did a lot of things in a lot of different places. It could be anywhere. There are just so many possibilities. I wouldn't know where to start."

"Think, David. Michael wouldn't have said something unless he was confident you would pick up on it. Give it some thought. Maybe you could make a list of places as they come back to you."

"That's not a bad idea. But Gina, what if we get lucky and find the vial? What then? What do we do with it?"

"I'm not sure. All I know is Michael's death should not be in vain."

"Maybe we should go to the police."

"And tell them what? What proof do we have?"

CHAPTER TWENTY-EIGHT

BITTERMAN was livid. He padded Trammel's office while Max Trammel sat listening to his tirade. "Damn it, Max, can you tell me why they felt the need to kill him before finding the vial? Besides, I wanted him to disappear, not be killed in his hotel room. Fitzgerald's death is sure to raise questions. This is exactly what we didn't want. I wanted this matter handled discreetly, kept low key. Now, his suspicious death is sure to garner unwanted attention from several quarters."

"Brett, with all due respect, Fitzgerald was a nobody. His death will hardly be noticed by the public at large. The only loose end we have is the phone call he made at the end. According to the facilitator, the enforcers said he gave a vague clue to someone as to where he hid the vial. The problem is we don't know who he gave the message to."

"Well, I do, Max," Bitterman said in a matter of fact manner.

"You do?"

"Yes, I do. It pays to have friends in high places. At any rate, the call was placed to one David Roy. Interestingly, he is a participant in the Sicilia Gene trial. It appears he is also an old friend of Fitzgerald's."

"This is even more interesting." Trammel walked to his desk and hit a button on a remote control device on his desk. A screen descended from the ceiling.

"Brett, after the vial was stolen, one of the first things you requested was a review of all security videotapes."

"Yes, and I was told they revealed nothing new on Fitzgerald."

"That's correct, but something else of interest appeared on the tape. Take a look," he said pushing another button on the remote control.

A view of the employee parking lot emerged. Two figures, a man and a woman stood, engaging in a lovers embrace. They kissed and then left in separate cars. Trammel hit the pause button. Bitterman looked at Trammel. "What is the significance of that little snippet of voyeurism? I don't recognize either person. Clearly, the man is not Fitzgerald."

"No, he's David Roy...Fitzgerald's last call. The woman is Gina Coletti. She is employed by the clinic and is assigned to the Sicilia trial."

"If all three of them: Fitzgerald, Coletti, and Roy were acting in concert, we have a major problem. We don't know to what extent Coletti and Roy are involved; except that we now know both are aware of the missing vial. They are loose cannons, and we will have to deal with them, but first we must get the vial back. To do that, we must wait for Mr.

Roy to find it. By the content of Fitzgerald's last phone call, he obviously was trying to give Roy a clue as to its location. I want them both under surveillance twenty-four-seven. If and when they find the vial, I want your people to get it from them before the two of them can take any action to hurt Freiz. You see, Max, we don't know what Fitzgerald's motive was for taking the serum in the first place. Did he plan to use it for personal gain, maybe to blackmail Freiz, or did he have a loftier, more altruistic goal? He can't tell us now, but his cohorts may, if they find the vial. Do you think your people can handle this new assignment with a little more finesse?"

"I'll see to it that they do."

"Good. Max, this could not come at a worse time. We have fast-tracked our next potential blockbuster, the next generation of Torvistat, Bi-Torracept-T, and we are ready to launch as soon as we gain approval from the FDA, which should be within the next ten to twelve months. At the same time, we are in the process of shutting down the Sicilia Gene trial."

"How will you justify that to Wall Street and the media? It's been rumored for some time that Freiz has been developing a potential breakthrough in the treatment of coronary artery disease. Most assume it's the Sicilia Gene therapy."

"Yes, I know. I'm confident we can discredit the Sicilia Gene since it has already exhibited some unintended side effects."

"After all the anticipation relating to the Sicilia Gene trial, won't its failure hurt Freiz on Wall Street?"

"It may in the short term. However, if our PR department does its job touting the benefits of Bi-Torracept-T, any dip in stock price should be temporary. And remember, Bi-Torracept is a wonderful drug in its own right. It not only lowers the bad cholesterol, it raises the good. With the right advertising campaign and in the absence of any bad publicity created by the failure of the trial—or our friends, Coletti and Roy—Bi-Torracept-T should prove to be very successful; a worthy successor to Torvistat."

"Max, there is one other item. Doctor Rentz has expressed to me that she has some concern regarding Doctor Bauer's commitment to Freiz. He has made it clear he is not happy with how the trial is being conducted and its inevitable outcome, and we don't know how he's going to react to the death of Fitzgerald. Consequently, I would like you to keep close tabs on him. Monitor his phone and e-mail traffic—you know the drill. If you discover anything that would put his loyalty to the company in question, I want to know about it immediately."

CHAPTER TWENTY-NINE

T HE list, with the heading, "where we ... " had four
sub headings: Played, Fished, Hung-out, and
Miscellaneous. David, while sitting on the porch
at Gina's, started to list the places where he had done
things with Michael when they were kids. Accompanied by
a strong feeling of nostalgia, some locations came to him
immediately: The oil dock, where Michael almost tore his
earlobe off while fishing; their tree house in his back yard,
where countless hours were spent defending the neighborhood from savage Indians and the occasionally inquisitive
girl; and the Mystic Seaport, where, for a quarter they spent
the entire day wandering about the historic whaling community and exploring the old whaling ship, The *Morgan,*
where they would walk the wooden decks and mingle
with the ghosts of the past. Others were more elusive, but
slowly seeped back into his memory: The vast grounds of
Connecticut College's arboretum, where Michael and he

would sled down its long, gently sloped entrance and onto the ice-covered pond below.

David was lost in his recollections when Gina appeared on the porch.

"How's the list coming along?"

"I'm making progress. I haven't thought about most of these places in years. The reminiscing initially brings back fond memories, and then, the reality of what happened to Michael pops back into my head, and I crash. I still can't believe he's dead."

"I know," she said, caressing his cheek. "I just told Daddy what happened. He didn't know Michael, but I could tell he felt genuine sorrow for our loss and for Michael's family's. What's going to happen to them now?"

"I don't really know. Maybe after the funeral when things settle down, we can organize a fundraiser or two to help out. Everyone liked Michael. I'm sure his friends would show their support toward Arianna and the kids."

"I called the funeral home and they told me that Michael is being waked for only one night."

"So why don't we get a room in New London tomorrow night?"

"Makes sense to me," she said and gave him a quick hug. "A fundraiser for Michael's family? Yeah, that's not a bad idea. Not to change the subject, but I didn't make anything for supper. I had planned to, but I just don't feel like cooking. I'll nuke some leftovers for my father, and then we can go out for a bite. "

"Sounds good to me. It will do us both some good to get out."

They decided to go to *Legal Sea Foods* at the Long Wharf for dinner; a restaurant frequented by a robust crowd of diners made up of businessmen, tourists, and as in Gina's case, a good number of locals. As they left the house and walked to David's Jeep, they didn't notice the black sedan parked a half block away.

As they entered the restaurant, they again failed to notice the same black sedan as it parked on the opposite side of the street under a burned-out street lamp

They ate their dinner, but didn't discuss the food. They tried their best to avoid the subject that was hanging over their head like an anvil, but no matter what the topic of conversation, it always came back to Michael. They reiterated to each other their belief that regardless of the circumstances surrounding his death, Michael didn't use drugs, and therefore, could not have done this to himself. The only logical conclusion was that he was murdered. The biggest question, among many, remained: why did the murderer, or murderers, go to the trouble of making it look like Michael's death was self inflicted? Why bother with the elaborate set-up? David and Gina agreed that it had to be related to the taking of the vial, and if so, it followed that Freiz was behind his murder. A chill ran up Gina's spine.

There was no love making that night, instead they lay in bed talking about Michael, Arianna, and their plans for locating the vial. They agreed to wait until after the funeral to begin their search. For now, they would focus on tomorrow, the day they would travel to New London to attend the wake of their friend.

Overnight, a summer storm had moved in. When they

awoke, the wind blown rain was pelting the window like so many pebbles. Under different circumstances, it would have been a good morning to sleep in, to cuddle, or make love in Gina's warm, cozy bed, but today they couldn't afford such a self indulgent luxury.

At breakfast, they decided that due to the inclement weather, David would drive Gina to the clinic, and later pick her up after work when they would leave for New London. David decided to spend the day visiting Al and completing his list of places that could possibly harbor the vial.

The mood at the clinic was grim when Gina arrived. The shock of the news was still raw. Coworkers consoled each other with hugs and tears, before slowly dispersing to attend to their duties.

Sometime around mid morning, it was announced that a mandatory noon meeting of Freiz, the clinic administration, and the staff involved with the Sicilia trial would be held. Speculation was rampant, and the rumor mill went into high gear. The consensus was that Freiz and the clinic were going to make a joint statement regarding Michael's death.

At noon Doctor Rentz, with Doctor Bauer standing at her side, addressed the assemblage. "Ladies and gentleman, we have called this meeting to make a very unfortunate announcement." The group took on the collective look of concern as Rentz continued. "As some of you may already know, several of our trial participants have experienced serious complications within the last week. Three have suffered strokes, two developed thrombophlebitis, two pulmonary embolisms, and one cardiac infarction. All of the events were caused by blood clots, and sadly, two of the afflicted have died. Considering the size of the trial, these numbers are statistically significant and cannot be ignored. Therefore, we are suspending the trial until further notice. However, as a precaution, we will continue to monitor the clotting factor of the remaining trial participants. We are now in the process of informing them of our intentions. We will also issue a press release to inform the public."

An alarm sounded in Gina's head. She had a gut feeling. *Something is very wrong here. Why all of a sudden, did these adverse effects show up? Until last week every one of the participants I had contact with said nothing but good things about how they were feeling. And now this? Something stinks.*

David was waiting when Gina got off work. After getting in the Jeep and giving him a quick kiss hello, she asked him how he was feeling. "I'm feeling great. Why do you ask? Do I look that bad," he kidded.

"No, you look fine." Then she explained what had transpired at the clinic.

"Wow, this sounds serious."

"It is very serious. The really worrisome thing for me is that all of the cases involved blood clots, and I'd bet most of the participants, if not all, were already on a blood thinner of one kind or another. Excessive clotting has never been a consideration in past trials. I admit the prior trials involved much smaller groups, but still, it seems strange to me that this type of side effect would appear all of a sudden in so many subjects. David, I know you are already taking

Coumadin, but I would feel better if you'd also take a baby aspirin a day until you get your blood checked."

"Is that a good idea? I mean, isn't there a danger it could make my blood too thin?"

"Based on what I heard today and what Michael had told me, I think it may be even more dangerous not to. Besides, while I admit it's not the norm, I do know people who take both. And it'll only be until you see the doctor again. You'll be fine, just don't cut yourself shaving." Gina threw him a quick smile.

"Very funny."

David turned serious. "Listen, Gina. Because of what's happened so far with Michael and some of the people in the trial, I think we need to be very cautious and even more skeptical of Freiz and the clinic's motives and actions. I don't trust these people. At this point, who knows what they are capable of?"

"I think you might be over reacting, but if you really believe what you are saying, then you won't be too angry when you hear what I've done. David, I took one of the vials."

David interrupted. "You did *what*? That's when all of Michael's troubles started. Gina, I don't think that was the smartest thing to do."

"Don't worry, no one saw me take it."

"Yeah, that's what Michael thought too."

"Listen, David, what if the vial doesn't contain either the Sicilia Gene serum or a placebo? What if the clotting problem wasn't caused by the serum but by something else?"

"Like?"

"I'm not sure, maybe vitamin K, plasma … who knows. There's more than one way to increase one's clotting factor. That's why I took the vial, to protect you and for proof, if we can ever get it tested."

"And then what?"

"I don't know yet; one thing at a time."

"When did you take it? Aren't you afraid they—"

"David, no one saw me take it, not even you."

"Gina, you lost me. What are you talking about?"

"When I gave you your last injection, I didn't give you their placebo. I injected you with a saline solution I substituted in its place. Then I discarded the empty vial as usual so as not to arouse any suspicion. I have their vial in my pocketbook."

"Hold on a second," David said with a bewildered look. What's this about a placebo?"

"When they saw how dramatic the results of the trial were, they decided to end the trial. We found out, as part of their deception, they began administering placebo to all participants. And God knows what else they added to it."

After riding in silence for a while, David said, "I've pretty much completed my list of possible hiding places. I probably missed a few, but we still have plenty of places to check out."

"It'll be neat; I'm looking forward to seeing where you played as a child."

When they arrived at the funeral home, it was already mobbed. People not only came from his hometown of Waterford, but from New York, the state he had moved to as a young boy. And of course, there were a number of representatives from Freiz and the clinic.

It was a heart-wrenching sight: Arianna, dressed in black, sat in the first row of chairs directly in front of the casket. She sat erect, greeting those paying their respects. Her emotions betrayed her periodically as she intermittently dabbed her eyes with a tissue. Her eyes were swollen from a full day of expressing her deep, immeasurable grief. Her kids sat to her sides looking shell shocked, as if not comprehending what was taking place.

David and Gina approached the casket and knelt to pray. Gina tried her best to swallow the lump in her throat as she viewed Michael's lifeless remains. After a short prayer, they rose together, and turned to meet the new widow. Gina and Arianna embraced and both spewed fresh tears, after which David expressed his sorrow.

In the parking lot following the wake, Gina turned to David, "That was even harder than I thought it would be. This is just terrible. My heart aches for Arianna and her children."

"I know. I know," was all David could say.

Unaware of watchful eyes, David started the Jeep and made his way out of the parking lot and headed for the hotel.

On the other side of the parking lot the black sedan did the same.

CHAPTER THIRTY

THE rain that started the day before had turned to a misty drizzle, adding one more depressing aspect to the already mournful occasion of Michael Fitzgerald's funeral.

At the graveside service, an inconsolable Arianna said goodbye to her husband and best friend. David and Gina, along with approximately thirty other friends and relatives also said their farewells. After the service concluded, the funeral director, acting on Arianna's behalf, invited all of the mourners back to the Fitzgerald house for food and drink, and the commiseration that would follow.

While walking to the Jeep, David and Gina encountered Thomas Price.

"Ah, Ms. Coletti, it's a pleasure to meet you again albeit under such sad circumstances."

Gina was startled by his presence. Even though she knew the clinic would be well represented at the funeral, she certainly didn't expect the head of the clinic, someone who didn't even know Michael, to attend. Gina quickly composed herself. "Hello, Doctor Price." Motioning toward David, she said, "Doctor Price, this is David Roy. David, I want you to meet Thomas Price. He heads the New England Clinic for Cardiac Care."

"Pleased to meet you, Doctor Price," said David as he extended his hand.

"It is a pleasure meeting you, Mister Roy." Price then turned to Gina.

"Ms. Colletti, could I have a moment of your time?"

"Can we talk back at the house?" Gina asked nervously.

"I'm afraid I won't be able to join you there. It will just take a moment," he said as he led her firmly by the elbow just far enough away to insure privacy.

"Ms. Colletti, we know about your improper relationship with Mister Roy, and furthermore, we know that Michael Fitzgerald confided in both of you before his untimely death. Now let me make this perfectly clear, we want the vial back. This is not a request. Do you understand? Let this be the last time we have to discuss the subject. Oh, by the way, if the vial is returned, we will overlook your indiscreet violation of company policy."

"But I don't know where it is. Michael never told me where he kept it. I swear to you, I have no idea where it could possibly be."

"I'm confident you will locate it. I'll be waiting. Now run along with your new beau," he said as he smiled and waved in David's direction.

David looked at Gina who appeared shaken. "What was that all about? Are you all right?"

"Let's just get out of here. I'll tell you in the car."

As they drove away from the cemetery, Gina said, "David, for the first time since all of this has happened, I'm scared."

"Why? What did Price say to you?"

"First of all, he knows about us."

"How'd he find that out?"

"Oh come on, David. We were not always as discreet as we should have been."

"Okay, okay, what else did he say?"

"If you remember, he's the one who pulled me into his office and asked me to help get the vial of serum back. Well, this time he wasn't so nice about it. He basically threatened me."

"He threatened you?"

"Not in so many words, but his meaning was clear."

"What did he say?"

"That he knows that Michael confided in the two of us."

"But he didn't—except for this last phone call. How would they know about that? Unless …"

"Don't even go there. Do you realize what you're saying?"

"Well, it is a possibility."

"I know, but this is getting scary, David. I don't think we should go back there. There's certainly no reason for you to go back. You can be monitored by your personal physician. As for me, there are plenty of jobs out there for someone with my credentials."

"That's all well and good, but what do we do about the vial. We can't just forget about it. They sure as hell aren't going to. They want it back and they think we know where it is. We have to find it. We have no other choice."

"I know we don't. Besides, if we give up now, Michael will have died in vain. We can't let that happen."

"One big question remains: What do we do with the vial if we find it?"

"I'm not sure. I know Doctor Bauer was not at all happy with the way this all went down. I've known him for a long time. He's a good man. Maybe we can confide in him. He may be able to tell us where to go or who to contact."

"That's one option, but before we do anything, we need to locate the vial. When we leave Arianna's, we should have enough daylight left to hit at least a few places on the list."

When David and Gina arrived at Arianna's, people were already milling about with plates and drinks in hand. Some were huddled in small groups outside of Arianna's earshot, discussing, in hushed tones, the improbable circumstances surrounding Michael's death. Most expressed shock, while a much smaller number suspected a far more nefarious reason for his demise. David and Gina avoided any speculative discourse by focusing their conversations on Michael's life. They each shared many anecdotes of their experiences with Michael, both as a child and an adult. The stories, some humorous, some poignant, lifted the spirits of the listeners.

By mid afternoon, the group had thinned considerably. David and Gina were among the last to leave. Before departing, they reiterated their desire to aid Arianna during her bereavement and the long adjustment period that was to follow, and they promised to keep in touch. After a farewell fraught with yet more tears, they left Arianna to deal with her sorrows.

"It's still hard to believe this has happened. It's seems almost surreal—dreamlike." Then as if sequestering these thoughts somewhere deep in the recesses of her mind, Gina changed the subject. "Okay, where do we go first?"

"Well, we're not far from the river, so I figured we'd start at the oil docks. That's where—"

"I know, I know, where Michael hooked your ear with a fishing hook. I've heard the story many times. Michael loved telling it. He always had his audience in stitches."

"Yeah, well, I can laugh about it now, but I can assure you, it wasn't very funny at the time. I spent two hours in the emergency room. Then on top of that, I caught hell from my parents for being down at the docks in the first place."

As they neared the river, David slowed to a crawl, peering through the windshield with a bewildered look. He stopped in front of a condominium complex and turned to Gina. "It's gone. It used to be right here. It looks like the entire area has been redeveloped." Luxury condominiums now lined the waterfront where the oil docks once stood, and a wooden boardwalk ran along the river's edge. "Well, I guess I can cross this one off the list."

"Looks that way. Where to next?"

"C'mon, I'll show you my old neighborhood."

They drove the short distance to where David and Michael had lived as children, but when they arrived their homes were gone, as were the street and the trees that lined the road and shaded their back yards on hot summer days. All were gone, replaced by a maze of concrete ramps that led to a new I-95 bridge that spanned the Thames River.

Again, David stopped the Jeep. He exited the vehicle and stood staring in silence—staring at the concrete roadway and steel guardrail, but seeing his old neighborhood. He visualized Michael and himself in their tree house, a lofty fortress they had constructed the summer before he moved away. He remembered climbing up the rope ladder and pulling it up behind them to ensure their safety and guarantee their solitude. He recalled the time they scared the life out of Mrs. Pappas, when a baseball he had thrown ricocheted off Mikey's glove and crashed through her kitchen window, where she stood peeling potatoes. They had spent weeks collecting and redeeming discarded soda bottles to pay for the damage.

Now, as he looked around at all that was gone—his old neighborhood and his childhood friend—he felt as if life was trying to erase his past. The emotion that David had so successfully suppressed from the time he learned of Mike's death through the funeral now rose in him like a geyser. It overtook him quickly and completely. He put his hands to his face and began to weep. Gina raced to his side and they embraced. They held one another until David regained his composure. When he did, he held her at arm's length and said, "I'm sorry. It all hit me at once." He could see tears had trickled down Gina's face as well. He gently wiped them away with his finger.

"Don't be silly," she said, again pulling him close. "This has been a rough few days. Let's go home. We can look for the vial again tomorrow. I need to check on Daddy, anyway."

Gina took David's hand, drawing him close to her side as they walked back to the Jeep.

CHAPTER THIRTY-ONE

For only the third time in American history, a president of the United States was about to temporarily transfer the power of the presidency to the vice president. The two previous times being when Ronald Reagan was shot on July 13, 1985 and transferred power to Vice President George H. W. Bush, and when President George W. Bush underwent a colonoscopy on June 29, 2002 and Vice President Richard B. Cheney assumed power.

President Jefferson Rayhill called a news conference to inform the American people of his pending surgery the following morning to relieve a clogged carotid artery. He explained that since he would be under general anesthesia, he felt it necessary to transfer power to Vice President Richards until he was again fit to resume his presidential duties.

The President held up a letter that was prepared by the White House counselor invoking Section 3 of the Twenty-fifth Amendment to the Constitution. A copy of the letter would be delivered to the Speaker and president pro tempore of the House of Representatives. The exact time of transfer was not made public for security reasons.

A second letter, declaring himself capable of resuming presidential authority, was prepared and would be signed by President Rayhill upon successful completion of the procedure.

At midnight, President Jefferson Rayhill signed the letter. The Attorney General then faxed copies to the Speaker of the House, the president pro tempore, and Vice President Richards. After confirming the letters were received, he informed the president and vice president that the transfer was complete.

By the stroke of a pen, Vice President Bruce Richards had become Acting President of the United States—and the most powerful man on the planet.

For practical reasons, Richards chose to perform his presidential duties out of the vice president's office. However, he couldn't resist making a short visit to the Oval Office.

Alone in the president's office, Richards sat at the large, carved walnut desk. He scanned the curved walls and eyed the signature rug that every president has custom made to his own liking. He pictured a design for his own. *I should be looking at my rug now—not his. I would be, if the ticket had been reversed, as it should have been. Instead, I acquiesced to the party's wishes and played by the rules. But my time is coming, and this little acting job will serve as a dry run, and will only enhance my odds of winning the privilege of calling this office my own.*

Even though a record was kept of every person who entered the Oval Office, the president had an odd habit of keeping a personal log of his own. Richards picked up the leather-bound log and thumbed through it. The list was comprised of the names of the most influential and generous men in the world. He made mental notes as he flipped the pages. There was one name that stood out: Brett Bitterman. Oddly, his was the only name with a question mark after it. *Was Bitterman here, and if so, why? I specifically asked him not to offer Rayhill help with his medical condition. Is he playing both sides? I intervened on his behalf with his Medicare issue, so he had no need to go to the president for that, and Rayhill is in his second term, so he's not looking for money. What could have been his reason for the visit? It must have been to offer him the serum. But why?* Richards made a note of the date and time of Bitterman's visit with the intention of verifying it with the official White House log, and then returned to his own office.

Richards knew very well that the transfer of power was, except in extraordinary circumstances, mainly for appearance sake. The acting president was not expected to make any meaningful decisions. His job was to keep the seat warm until the president resumed his duties. No matter, he thought. Having held the position even temporarily would elevate his standing among voters and those seeking to reside in the White House.

By the time Richards got to bed, it was one thirty in the morning. At three forty-five he was jarred awake when the bedside phone rang. It was President Rayhill's Chief of Staff, John Codas. "Mr. Vice President, I'm sorry to wake you at this hour. I just got off the phone with the president's physician. The president has suffered a stroke and has been taken to Walter Reed Hospital."

"Do you know how severe? What's his condition?"

"The doctor didn't have time to give me any particulars except to say it was very serious. I am heading to Walter Reed now. I'll call you after I speak with the doctors there."

Acting President Bruce Richards immediately made a call to his chief of staff, and instructed him to arrange for a cabinet meeting in his office at 7:00 a.m.

As Richards was getting dressed, the phone rang again, and again it was John Codas. He sounded somber. "Mr. Vice President, the president is dead. The doctors think a piece of plaque broke off his carotid artery and traveled to his brain causing the stroke. They won't know for sure until they perform an autopsy."

Richards felt a surge of adrenalin course through his body. "That's awful. Has the first lady been notified yet?"

"No. You were my first call; she'll be my next. You will have to address the nation, and arrange to be sworn in by the chief justice. Would you like me to call him?"

"No … no thank you, you have enough on your plate right now. I'll handle it on my end."

Richards called his chief of staff and instructed him to summon Chief Justice John Roberts to the White House for the swearing in at 9:00 a.m. He would hold his cabinet meeting at seven while the American people were being informed of the tragedy. He would then take the oath of office and address the nation as their president.

Richards's next call was to Rayhill's widow, Gloria. He extended his deep condolences to her and her family. Then, he asked her to attend the swearing in, explaining it would give the country a sense of continuity. The same way it did when the grief-stricken Jacqueline Kennedy stood next to Lyndon Johnson on November 22, 1963 when he was sworn in on Air Force One after President John Kennedy's assassination. Gloria Rayhill seemed bewildered and confused at the request, but gave her assent. After hanging up, Richards took a deep breath. *The president is dead. The president is dead. Long live the president.*

CHAPTER THIRTY-TWO

ON the day following Michael's funeral, Gina rose early to fix a special breakfast for her father. She felt badly for having left him alone so much lately and this was just one small way of making it up to him. Unfortunately, it didn't ease the pangs of guilt she felt for having to leave him again so soon. She found Al in the kitchen reading *The Boston Globe* and sipping his morning coffee. As she dug out the iron and prepared the ingredients to make homemade Belgian Waffles, Al's favorite, she brought her father up to speed. She informed him of every detail, except Price's threat. Telling him would serve no purpose, and would only make him worry more for his daughter's safety.

The waffles were almost ready when David joined them in the kitchen.

"Good morning. Boy, something smells good."

"Have a seat, they're just about ready."

"Good morning, David. Gina was filling me in." David grabbed a cup of coffee and took a seat at the table.

After listening to Gina and devouring his waffles, Al sat back, and with a pensive look, said, "This is very serious business you two have involved yourselves in. You are dealing with some very powerful people who have little or no moral fiber. Their only allegiance is to the almighty dollar. No matter how they shape their public image to project a strong social conscience, replete with copious benevolence, in the end however, corporations are all the same; it's only the bottom line that matters. They have vast resources, and will undoubtedly go to great lengths to get that vial back. So you must promise me to be very careful. I'm not telling you this to frighten you, only so you are aware of what you're up against." Turning to David, Al continued, "I don't want anything to happen to my daughter, David. She's all I have."

Digesting what he'd just heard, David responded, "Maybe it would be better if I looked for the vial by myself. After all, I'm the only one who knows the places that Mike might have been referring to." As if surprised by his statement, Gina looked at David with wide eyes.

"No," Al replied, "you and Gina are in this together, and you should see it through together. Two heads are better than one, as the saying goes, and the two of you can watch each other's back. I think that about covers all I have to say." Gina walked over to her father, bent down and hugged him from behind.

Then, kissing him on the cheek, she said, "Thank you, Daddy. I love you so much."

"I know you do, and you don't have to thank me, sweetheart. The way I see it, you'd be constantly preoccupied thinking about how David was doing anyway. Consequently, you'd be miserable and not very good company," Al said with a wink.

After breakfast David and Gina packed enough clothing for three days. They figured if they didn't find the vial by then, they probably weren't going to find it at all.

They arrived back in New London at noon. The muggy low-pressure system that had blanketed the entire northeast for two days had moved out, and was replaced by a fair-weather high that provided blue skies and cool dry air. It was a day more reminiscent of early fall than of mid July. It was a perfect day to begin their search.

The first place on David's list was the pump house at Perry's Pond. Back in the days before pagers and cell phones, it served as a common place where Mike, David, and their other friends would tack notes to let one another know of their whereabouts.

Although in disrepair, David was happy to see the abandoned pump house was still mostly intact. Its roof now sagged slightly and the sides were covered with twining vines that appeared to be consuming the building with their creeping tendrils.

David and Gina walked slowly around the tiny structure looking for signs of human activity, but found none. The door was padlocked and the lone window had been painted shut many years ago. David peered through the window, but could see little. "Doesn't look like anyone's been here in a while. I guess we can scratch this place off the list."

Gina shrugged her shoulders. "Where to next?" David pulled the list from his shirt pocket and studied it. "Let's try the old gristmill over by Winthrop Elementary School."

As they approached the old mill, David could see that, like the pump house, it too had been sorely neglected. "You know, Gina, I can understand how a place like the pump house could be left to die a slow death, but a place like this—you'd think someone would have tried to restore it. It's such a great example of New England heritage. What a shame to see it in this condition. Looks like the historical society missed this one. Actually, it wasn't in the best of shape when we were kids. Well, as long as we're here, let's take a look around."

As they roamed in and around the derelict mill, David told Gina of the times Mike and he had played there. He pointed out where the missing millstones were once located, and speculated that they were now, more than likely, the centerpiece of someone's patio. It didn't take long to realize that the mill, like the pump house, hadn't seen any human activity for a long time.

"This is discouraging. It's like trying to find a needle in a haystack, and we can't even find the haystack."

"I know, David, but we knew it wasn't going to be easy. We can only do our best and then, whatever happens, happens."

"You're such a fatalist. I wish that I could be more like you in that regard."

"In that regard? Just in that regard? Is that my only redeeming quality?" She said, poking him in his stomach.

"Well, not you're only one," he said raising his eyebrows.

Gina gave him a playful punch in the arm. "You men are all alike. Let's go."

They visited several other locations before they decided they'd had enough for one day and drove back to the hotel.

At dinner, Gina did her best to bolster David's sagging spirits, but she too was becoming discouraged. There were only a handful of places left on the list to explore, and if they didn't locate the vial at one of them, it was back to square one. To make matters worse, David believed they had already been to the most likely places where Michael would have hidden the vial.

That night, as he lay next to Gina, he tried to remember locations he may have overlooked. Tired from the stressful events of the past week, Gina had fallen asleep almost immediately. David suddenly realized the two of them hadn't made love since Michael had died. Not for any particular reason, maybe just as a result of stress and fatigue, their healthy libidos had temporarily gone dormant. Whatever the reason, it didn't cause him any concern. What did worry him was his apparent lack of energy. In the past few days, he noticed he was more fatigued than he'd been just the week before. Did something he was given at the clinic cause him to regress, or was he simply emotionally drained? These thoughts competed in his mind until he fell into an uneasy sleep.

They started out early the next morning. It was another beautiful day, and it gave them a renewed sense of hope.

They visited the historic Hempstead House. Built in 1678 by Joshua Hempstead, it was one of the oldest wood-framed houses in North America.

"Of course, as kids, we weren't very much interested in its historical significance; we just liked playing on the grounds." As they walked around the outside, David was hoping something would jar his memory, perhaps a long-forgotten detail of their playing here would pop into his head, but nothing came to mind.

From the Hempstead House they traveled across the Thames River to Groton where Fort Griswold, a Revolutionary War era stone fortress sat high above the river and looked back across to New London.

"David, if you weren't allowed to go to the oil docks, I can't believe you were allowed to cross the river to this place."

"You're right, we weren't, and when we dared to come here, it was a real adventure. To us, it was almost like being in a foreign land. And look at this place, with all of the stone walls and canons, there must be a thousand places to hide something, but nothing registers. I don't know, Gina, I'm beginning to think this is an exercise in futility."

Disappointed and dejected, they drove back to New London. Gina, the eternal optimist, said, "David, we can't give up. It'll come to you. We just have to keep looking. Even though Michael said very little in his message, he seemed sure you'd know where to find the vial."

"It looks like his confidence may have been misplaced because right now, I don't have a clue, and there's only two places left on the list."

"It's near lunchtime. Why don't we take a break? Do you know somewhere we can grab a sandwich?"

"There used to be a family-owned restaurant not far from where my old house is, or I should say, was. If it's still there, we can get something there."

To David's surprise, with all that had changed in his hometown, Mr. G's was still there, and even more surprisingly, under the same family name.

After they bought their lunch, David said, "C'mon, let's go down by the beach and eat there. We might as well take advantage of this gorgeous weather. Besides, it's one of the last places on the list. We can kill two birds with one stone."

"David, you see that black car over there? I swear I saw that very same car at Fort Griswold. Maybe it's not or maybe it's just a coincidence…or maybe we're being followed."

"There's one way to find out." David pulled away from the curb. Instead of driving to Ocean Beach, he took a different, serpentine route through the city. He drove at normal speeds so as not to alert those in the black sedan. He made one turn after another. If they were being followed, it would soon become obvious. David checked his rearview mirror before each turn. Sure enough, the black sedan was behind them. The many short turns made it difficult for the sedan to keep an inconspicuous distance between them. "Looks like you're right, Gina. They must have been tailing us all along, waiting for us to locate the vial."

"What do we do now?"

"Go to the beach and have our lunch."

"What! We're being followed by God knows who, and you want to have a picnic?"

"Listen, Gina. I could lose them in a New York minute, but what good would that do. First of all, they will know we are on to them. Secondly, they surely must know where we're staying. I think it's better to play dumb for the time being. I don't think they'll try anything until they think we have the vial."

"I guess you're right. It just scares me to think what they might do if we ever do find the damn thing."

"At the rate we're going, we might not have to worry about that."

"David, what do you think they'll do if we never find it? At what point will they leave us alone. And what will they do to my father?"

"Let's just take it one step at a time."

David made his way to Ocean Beach and parked in one of the few empty spaces. They sat there for a few minutes waiting for the black sedan to show up, but it didn't. "Where are they?" Gina asked rhetorically.

"Maybe they think we're on to them, and they're trying to be more discreet. Whatever the case, let's try to forget about them for a while. C'mon, let's eat at one of the picnic benches over there," David said pointing to a shaded area that lay beyond a huge concrete whale that was the center piece of the park's miniature golf course.

"David, why did they name this park Ocean Beach when it's on Long Island Sound, and what's with the whale?"

"Good question." David laughed. "It's funny. As kids, we never questioned the name, and that's the only whale

I've ever seen in the sound," he said pointing to the huge likeness. I can't tell you how many times I looked at that stupid tail while playing cards with Michael on the beach.

After they finished the grinder they had split, Gina asked if they could take a walk on the beach. She was removing her shoes as she spoke. David wasn't in the mood, but went along without protesting.

They walked down the soft, sandy beach, hand in hand, at the waters edge, while the gentle wave action lapped at their feet. David was reminiscing about the many times he spent here as a kid, when he stopped suddenly. Gina looked back, "What's the matter?"

"I don't know why I didn't think of this earlier." He resumed walking, this time at a much faster pace. Gina fought to keep up.

"What's the rush?"

"I want to check something out. You see this board-walk," he said as he motioned to the wooden boardwalk that ran parallel to the beach, "Well, down at the end, we used to hang out, and one of the things we did was to play cards, you know, Poker and Pitch."

"Yeah, so?"

"We used to keep a deck of cards hidden on top of one of the spiles."

He now headed away from the water and toward the end of the boardwalk. A few feet from his destination, he let go of Gina's hand. Then he hunched down and went under the boardwalk. His heart raced as he looked up to see a wooden humidor where a deck of cards once sat. He removed it from its perch, sat back in the sand, and opened the box like a child might open a treasure chest. "Well, I'll be damned! We've found it. I can't believe I didn't think of this place earlier."

Gina was now kneeling next to him. She threw her arms around him and they shared a few quick kisses before settling down to examine the contents. Inside, they found the vial wrapped in bubble-wrap and two pieces of paper lying, neatly folded, beneath it. After examining the two sheets of paper, David said, "These are e-mails between Doctor Rentz and Brett Bitterman. Wow, you've got to read these." He passed them to Gina. After reading them, she passed them back. "Pretty incriminating, huh?"

"Well, up to this point, we knew what they've done was just plain unethical, immoral, and wrong. But now we can prove it's illegal, and sure to result in indictments that will create a firestorm of bad publicity for Freiz as well as the clinic, if it gets out."

"You mean *when* it gets out."

He wanted to say, unless they get to us before we can expose them, but he thought better of it, and simply said, "Yes, when it gets out. Gina, do you have the vial that you took? I'd like to keep everything in one spot."

"It's in my pocketbook at the hotel."

"You left your pocketbook in the room?"

"Don't worry; I put it in the safe."

"Okay, let's leave the humidor here for now. I don't want to carry this stuff around any more than necessary in case those guys following us decide to get more aggressive. We'll get the other vial and come back later for this one."

As they exited the park and headed for the hotel, they

failed to notice the black car that was parked on a side street.

CHAPTER THIRTY-THREE

ONCE back in the hotel room, Gina retrieved her pocketbook from the safe. She fished out the vial and gave it to David. "How are we going to keep track of which vial is which? They look the same," David said, as he regarded the vials.

"I cut a notch in the rubber stopper on the one I took."

"Okay, good. Now listen, Gina, we have to go back and get the other vial. In order to do that, we will have to lose our tail. Once we do, they will definitely know we are onto them. At that point, anything can happen. They have laid low until now, but I'm afraid that's about to change."

"If you're trying to scare me, you've succeeded."

"I'm not trying to scare you. It's just that you need to be aware that things could get a little dicey from here on out."

"Well, the way I see it is, we don't have much of a choice,

so let's just do it." Gina looked at her watch. "Doctor Bauer should still be at the clinic. I think we should call him to get his advice."

"Are you're sure you can trust him?"

"Right now, I'm not sure who we can trust, but he seems to be our best bet. At least it's a starting point." Gina picked up the phone and dialed the clinic. The receptionist connected her to Doctor Bauer's extension. The phone rang six times, and Gina was about to hang up when he answered.

"Hello. Doctor Bauer here."

"Doctor, it's Gina Coletti. If you've got a minute, I need to talk to you."

"Gina, how are you? I saw that you called in sick yesterday. Are you all right?"

"Yes, I'm fine. Doctor Bauer, I found the vial of serum that Michael took. I don't know where to go with it, and I thought you might be able to help."

"You have it in your possession?"

"No, but I know where it's located."

"Gina, I would be remiss if I didn't first advise you to return it to the clinic. You know how upset management is about this."

"I'm sorry doctor, I can't. Michael died because he was determined to expose Freiz. In doing so, he believed enough public pressure would be brought to bare that Freiz would have to bring the Sicilia Gene to market. I would feel like I was betraying him if I did so.

"Doctor, I know you also are upset with their decision

to end the trial. You saw first hand how positive the results were."

"Yes, I can't say I disagree with anything you've said so far, except you can't discount the negative side affects that have occurred lately."

"Yes, I know, and I have some thoughts on that as well. Doctor, don't you think it rather odd that so many participants experienced similar side effects at the same time? Look, I'm asking for your help. If you can't give it to me, I'll try elsewhere."

There was a short pause as Gina anxiously awaited Bauer's response.

"I don't know how much help I can offer but … okay. I'll try to help your cause. However, I don't think we should be discussing this on the telephone … especially this one. Can you meet me at the Patriot Diner this evening at 6:00 p.m.?"

"Yes, we'll be there. Thank you so much Doctor. I really appreciate it. I knew I could count on you."

"I'll see you then. Oh, and Gina, to whom were you referring when you say 'we?' "

"David Roy. We're working together on this."

"The same David Roy who is a participant in the trial?"

"Yes." There was a short pause.

"I see. All right then, I'll see you at six."

Max Trammel picked up the phone on his desk and called Brett Bitterman. "Brett, can I see you in your office? I have something we need to discuss."

"Max, I've got a full calendar today. Can it wait?"

"No, it's imperative I see you right away. I have something you need to hear."

"All right, be in my office in fifteen minutes. I'll squeeze you in between appointments."

When Trammel entered Bitterman's office, he was carrying a small handheld recorder. He placed it on Bitterman's desk and, after greeting each other, Trammel hit the play button. They both listened in silence. And when the taped telephone call between Gina and Doctor Bauer ended, Bitterman stood and walked to the window. Speaking with his back to Trammel, he said, "Max, Doctor Rentz warned me Bauer would be trouble. At least we know they have located the serum … and what their noble intentions are," he added with sarcasm.

"Max, we don't need Bauer complicating things. I want you to take care of him. I want him out of the picture, and soon. I don't want him giving those two any of his sage advice. And Max, I want that serum back."

"I'll take care of it."

After Trammel left Bitterman's office, Bitterman sat at his desk and again listened to the taped message. When it ended, he raised his fist and brought it down hard, smashing the recorder.

After checking out, David and Gina left the hotel and walked as nonchalantly as possible to his Jeep. This time he wanted to be followed so he could lose them in the maze of city streets that he knew so well. After that, they would go back to the beach and collect the contents of the humidor.

They stopped in their tracks when they spotted the black sedan parked next to David's Jeep. They quickly retreated to the hotel lobby.

"Now what do we do?" asked Gina with a concerned look. David took her by the hand and ran through the dining room and into the kitchen. He approached the first person he encountered. When he realized the man didn't speak English, he yelled in desperation, "Is there anyone here who speaks English?" A tall, rotund man appeared from an adjoining office.

"Is there something I can help you with, sir?"

"Yes, I need someone to go to the parking lot and bring me my vehicle," he said as he fumbled through his wallet. He extracted a twenty-dollar bill and waved it in the big man's direction. "Please, it will only take two minutes of your time." The man looked outside to see if it was raining. Then he turned his attention back to David with a confused look.

"Look, I haven't got time to explain. If you won't do it, I'll find someone else who will." The man shrugged and took David's keys. David described the Jeep and its location, and he instructed the man to drive it to the kitchen door located in the rear of the hotel.

In the parking lot, the men in the black sedan waited. They didn't pay much attention to the burly man dressed in white until he entered David's Jeep. Puzzled, they looked at each other. The Jeep then turned toward the hotel. They weren't too concerned because the only way off hotel property went past them.

David and Gina were waiting outside when the chef

pulled up. The man no sooner got out when David and Gina jumped in. David quickly thanked the man and took off as the man stood watching with a bewildered look on his pudgy face.

"Here we go," David said, as he accelerated. "Hold on. This is going to be a wild ride." Gina snapped her seat buckle and grabbed the armrest in anticipation of what loomed ahead.

David raced to the exit. He slowed, but did not stop at the stop sign. The black sedan, its tires screeching, left a black trail of burned rubber behind it, as it followed in hot pursuit. A frightened Gina said, "David, why don't you drive straight to the police station? They wouldn't dare do anything there."

"And then what? We can't stay there forever. It wouldn't end there. These people are on a mission … and so are we. Gina, this is my hometown. I know these streets like the back of my hand. Trust me; I'll lose them."

"Like the back of your hand? David, you haven't lived here in years. Look what happened when we went to see your old house."

"Gina, please, I need to concentrate on my driving." David slammed on the brakes, yanked the wheel hard and fishtailed around a corner. The sedan did the same. David made a few more sudden maneuvers, but still failed to shake their pursuers. He made his way to I-95 and flew across the bridge to the Groton side of the river. He weaved in and out of heavy traffic. After luring them into the left lane, he waited until the timing was right, then he pulled the wheel hard to the right. He crossed two lanes of traffic and just made the exit ramp, leaving his pursuers heading east on the interstate.

David got back on the highway going west and returned to New London.

"Oh, my God! I thought you were going to get us killed! But I have to admit, that was a fine bit of driving. It would've made Jeff Gordon proud."

David looked over and winked. "I told you I could lose them. Now we have to move fast. They won't stay lost forever. Let's pick up the vial and get back to Boston."

They headed for Ocean Beach. Once there, David surveyed the area making sure they hadn't been followed. "Let's go," he said, and they both headed for the boardwalk. When they reached a vantage point at which the parking lot and the end of the boardwalk could be seen, David said, "You stay here. If you see anything, give me a yell. I'll be back in a minute," he said, and trotted off.

David's plan was to remove the vial and e-mails from the humidor and put them in the plastic wastebasket liner he had taken from the hotel, and then put the bag in his pocket. He had just about finished shuffling through the contents when he heard Gina scream, "It's them! They're back! C'mon! Hurry!" David had to think fast. *What do I do now?* He made a few quick moves, then grabbed the humidor and ran to meet Gina. Together they dashed to the Jeep. The sedan was weaving between the many rows of vehicles when they spotted David and Gina. David peeled out and sped toward the parking lot exit. As he did, he hurled the empty humidor out the window, hoping to distract his pursuers. To his dismay, the wooden humidor shattered on impact revealing its lack of contents.

Oh, no, here we go again, thought Gina.

To her surprise, David drove directly to the New London police station.

"I thought you said this wasn't a good idea."

"It wasn't then, because, at the time, they could have waited for us to return to the hotel to pick up our tail."

"If I can convince someone inside to give us an escort to I-95, we'll be on our way back to Boston." The sedan drove slowly by and rounded the corner.

Inside the police station, so as not to have to explain the real reason for needing their help, David told the duty officer that they were being harassed by a bunch of unruly teenagers who appeared to have been drinking. Because they had tried to run them off the road, he asked to be escorted to the interstate. The officer reluctantly agreed.

As they left the station, Gina whispered to David, "Why don't we just show him what we have?"

David discreetly shook his head and whispered back, "Because we don't know who we can trust in this town."

Once safely on the highway, Gina said, "That was a lot better than that Grand Prix ride you took me on the last time."

"I thought you said you liked it."

"No, I said you did a good job. There's a difference. I was scared to death the whole time."

"Now, let's hope we can get to the right people and hand off the ball to them. Hopefully, Doctor Bauer will be able to point us in the right direction."

"I sure hope so."

CHAPTER THIRTY-FOUR

Doctor Charles Bauer left the clinic for his meeting with David and Gina. He knew full well the risk he was taking in agreeing to meet with them. If Freiz or the clinic knew of the meeting, his career at the clinic would surely be over. However, he also knew the significance of what David and Gina were attempting to do. It wasn't simply to expose and embarrass the largest pharmaceutical company in the world; ultimately, it was to save the million lives a year lost to cardiovascular disease. He had to take the risk. He had no other choice. He wouldn't be able to live with himself if he felt he could have helped them but didn't.

Doctor Bauer arrived at the Patriot Diner at five forty-five. He pulled into a parking space and was walking to the diner when a scruffy looking man with a beard approached him. Before Bauer could react, the man pulled a metal pipe from his belt and swung it hard, hitting the doctor on the side of the head. Dazed and bleeding, he staggered forward, holding his hand to his head. The assailant struck him again and Bauer fell to the pavement. He gave him two more solid blows to the head. His scull shattered, Bauer lay dying. The murderer stripped him of his wallet and watch before fleeing the scene.

When David and Gina arrived at the diner, they encountered a beehive of activity. There were two police cars and an ambulance, all with their lights flashing. A crowd of onlookers had gathered and was kept at bay by yellow police tape. Two policemen were standing next to what looked like a body covered with a gray blanket.

Gina recognized Doctor Bauer's car and felt a surge of adrenaline shoot through her body. She grabbed David's arm. "Oh, God, David, I'm afraid that's Doctor Bauer. That's his car," she said pointing to a silver Mercedes.

David also felt a wave of anxiety. He cautiously scanned the crowd before reassuring Gina. "Don't jump to conclusions. Let me check out the diner to see if he's inside. I'll be right back."

David returned shaking his head. "He's not in there."

They made their way through the curious crowd and when they reached the yellow tape, they summoned one of the two officers who were interviewing an eyewitness to the crime. The officer seemed annoyed that he was interrupted, but met them at the tape.

"Officer, do you know the identity of the victim? We were supposed to meet someone, Doctor Charles Bauer, but he's not here. That's his car over there," she said, again pointing to the Mercedes.

"I'm sorry ma'am; we don't have a positive ID on the victim yet. His wallet is missing. It looks like the motive was robbery."

While they were talking, the forensic unit arrived. After consulting with the other officers on the scene, a detective approached David and Gina and introduced himself as Detective O'Malley. "Officer Moore tells me you were supposed to meet someone here. We ran the plate on the car you ID'd, and it belongs to a Doctor Charles Bauer. Would you be able to recognize him?"

"Of course I would, I work with the man."

The detective lifted the yellow tape and Gina and David ducked under it. He led them to the covered body. Gina squeezed David's hand like a vice.

"I want to warn you, ma'am, it's a pretty grizzly scene." Gina's heart pounded in her chest as the detective lifted the blanket, exposing Doctor Bauer's crushed skull lying in a large pool of blood. Gina quickly turned away and buried her face in her hands. David wrapped his arms around her and tried to consol her. While holding Gina, David nodded to Detective O'Malley. "That's him...that's Doctor Bauer. Do you know what happened?"

"No, not yet, but there was an eyewitness. He's being questioned as we speak, but from what I see, it looks like a mugging."

After Gina regained her composure, Detective O'Malley took her personal information. Then David took

Gina by the hand and led her away from the gory scene and into the diner.

David requested a booth that shielded them from the activities in the parking lot. He ordered a glass of wine for Gina and a beer for himself.

"Drink it, sweetheart. It'll calm your nerves."

"Poor Doctor Bauer. If I didn't get him involved, he'd still be alive. It's my fault he's dead."

"Gina, you can't take the blame for his murder. He knew exactly what he was doing. He was a good man, and he was trying to do the right thing."

Gina took a deep breath and exhaled as if trying to expel the guilt she felt. "He didn't deserve this, David."

In an effort to divert her attention, David asked, "Did you hear what the eyewitness said about the murderer?"

"No, not really. I was preoccupied with thoughts of Doctor Bauer. All I remember the cop saying was that the motive was robbery."

"Yeah, that's right, and the witness said the guy looked like a bum. He also said he was wearing what looked like a glove on the hand that held the pipe. I don't believe that a bum looking for a quick score would go to the trouble, or even think of wearing a glove so as not to leave any finger-prints. No, he was no bum. I'd bet my house on it."

"David, we could be next. What are we going to do?"

"I don't think they would try to get us as long as we stay in the public eye. The question is: who do we go to now that Doctor Bauer can't help us?"

Emotionally spent, Gina replied, "I don't know. Right now, I just want to get some rest." Just then her cell phone rang. She looked at the phone; the caller's number was blocked. She quickly put the phone to her ear and apprehensively said, "Hello?"

"Have you spoken to your father today?" was the reply.

"Who is this?" Gina demanded. There was no response; the caller had hung up. Gina punched in her father's phone number as fast as her fingers would allow and waited. Each unanswered ring seemed an eternity and further dampened her spirits. Gina turned to David with a look of fear on her face. "David, we have to get to my house now! I think they've got my father."

During the ride they spoke very little. Gina leaned her head against the window and stared blindly at the passing scenery.

It was dark when they arrived at the Coletti household, and Gina could see no light emanating from the house. My father goes to bed early, but not this early," she said frantically as she raced to the house. She was about to insert her key when she saw the door was ajar. Hysterical now, she ran to his room, flicking on the lights as she went.

"Daddy?" she called out. "Daddy!" When she reached his room, she threw on the light. When she saw that he wasn't there, she raced to the bathroom and then the kitchen. There was no sign of her father. A wave of anxiety hit her like a lightning bolt when she saw her father's wheelchair lying on its side near the back door. "David!" She screamed. "David, something's happened to my father. He's not here."

David rushed into the kitchen and saw the overturned wheelchair.

"Let's check the rest of the house. I'll cover upstairs."

"David, he wouldn't go upstairs. He couldn't go upstairs. Something terrible has happened to him. I just know it. Do you think they took him to get to us?"

"I don't know. Don't panic. Maybe he hurt himself and called for help. I'll call the police station and ask if they got an emergency call from this number. While I'm doing that, find me the number of the nearest hospital."

Gina did as requested while David spoke with Boston Police Emergency Dispatch. Gina found the hospital's number, and then she stood next to David gnawing on a fingernail. David said, "Thank you," and hung up.

"They have no record of a call from your father. Let's try the hospital."

"Something terrible has happened to him. I just know it," she said and started to cry. David took the number from Gina and called the hospital. No one by the name of Alphonso Coletti had been admitted or treated at the facility.

"No good, he isn't there either. Is there anyone—a friend, or relative that he might be with?"

"No, and even it there were, how do you explain *that*?" she said pointing to his wheelchair.

Gina walked over to the wheelchair and was about to upright it when David shouted, "Don't touch it!" Gina flinched back. "Just in case it needs to be checked for fingerprints."

"See, you think something's happened to him too. Oh, David, what are we going to do?"

I don't know yet. We should call the police and report

him missing, but first I'm going to run upstairs and look around. Just to cover all of our bases." He ran up the stairs two steps at a time. When he reached the top he became dizzy and somewhat winded, and he felt what he believed was the beginning signs of angina. He stood in place for a minute and the feeling left him. *It must be my imagination,* he thought, and passed it off. He returned to the kitchen and shook his head. "You were right, but I felt I needed to make certain. Let's call the police."

Before David could pick up the phone, it started ringing. Gina put her hand to her mouth, then, looking at David with fear in her eyes, she picked up.

"Hello?"

"Ms. Coletti, we know you have located the vial, and the owner wants it back. We have your father. If you want to see him again, return the vial."

Horrified at what she'd heard, she blurted out, "They have Daddy!" She then directed her attention to the caller. "How do I know he's all right? Let me speak with him," she demanded.

There was a rustling sound on the other end. "Gina, it's Dad. I'm okay. Don't listen to these bastards, and don't worry about me. Remember what we talked about. You're doing the right th—"

"Ms. Coletti, this is one time when it would be wise to disobey your father. That is, if you want to see him again. Return the vial. Once it has been tested, he will be released."

"Don't you dare hurt my father! Do you hear me?" She screamed in a panic. She heard a click and they were gone.

"David, what are we going to do? They said I'll never see my father again if we don't return the vial. Things seem like they're spiraling out of control. My poor father," she said, and began sobbing. David held her, but offered no answers.

After Gina calmed down, she fixed them tea, and they moved to the kitchen table. "David, what am I going to do? I don't want anything to happen to my father, but I also have to think about Michael and Doctor Bauer and the million or so people like you who die every year from cardiovascular disease. But, who's to say the Sicilia Gene will indeed prove to be a miracle drug, and I don't want to lose my father for nothing. I don't know what to do. I'm so confused."

"Gina, I know what I would do, but this is something you're going to have to figure out on your own. I could never recommend going forward, because if I did and something happened to your father, I think it would always be an issue between us."

"Oh, but it's okay for *me* to make such a decision?"

"Unfortunately, yes. He's your father, not mine. I know that sounds cold, but try to understand my position."

Gina sat pensively for a moment. "I guess I do understand, but it doesn't make my decision any easier."

"What did your father say to you on the phone?"

"He said 'I'm okay. Don't give in to these bastards, and don't worry about me.' Then he said to remember what we had talked about, and he said I was doing the right thing. At that point, they took the phone away from him."

"Well, I'm not trying to influence you one way or another, but you know what your father wants you to do."

"I know. I know. Let me think on it overnight," she said rubbing her temples.

"Sure…and Gina, I'll be okay with whatever you decide. And if you decide to follow through with this, then I think that tomorrow we should go to my place on the island. I think we'll be safer there. And I don't think it's wise to stay here tonight. We can get a room, and leave for Greenport in the morning." Gina agreed and, after packing a few things, they left the empty house.

Before stopping at a Holiday Inn, David checked to see if they were being followed. Not seeing anyone, he proceeded to the hotel. He was checking in when Gina burst into the lobby and shouted, "David, there here! What do we do now?"

David grabbed his credit card from the counter, took Gina's hand, and ran for the exit.

"C'mon, get back in the car. Let's get the hell out of here."

The black sedan spotted them speeding for the exit and gave chase.

David weaved in and out of traffic on the service road like a serpent chasing a mouse. He had almost reached the entrance ramp when he saw the red and blue flashing lights behind him. He braked and pulled up to the curb. He was fishing in his wallet for his license and registration when the officer appeared at his door. As he was handing them to the policeman, the black sedan drove by and disappeared into the night.

"What's your hurry, Mr. Roy? Changing lanes like you were doing constitutes reckless driving."

Gina leaned over to address the officer. "It's my fault, officer. My father has been ill, and when he didn't answer his phone. I became worried. We were in a rush to get to his house. I'm sorry, officer. We—"

"Sit tight, I'll be back in a minute." David watched in his side-view mirror as the policeman returned to his car.

"That was a stroke of good luck. I never thought I'd say that about being pulled over by a cop." David could see him talking on his radio. When he was finished, he returned. "Okay, listen up. I'm going to let you go with a warning. Just remember, you can't put others in danger because of your own concerns." He handed David his license and registration. Then he tipped his hat in Gina's direction. "Ma'am, I hope your father is okay."

"Thank you, officer."

David pulled away and after locating a brightly lit gas station, he turned in and parked. Gina looked at him. "What are you stopping here for?"

"I want to check for something," he said as he reached under the seat for a flashlight. "It'll only take me a minute." Gina sat in the Jeep while David looked at the undercarriage of the vehicle. He started in the front and worked his way around. When he got to the rear of the Jeep, he found what he was looking for. He got back in the Jeep holding a black metal box about the size of a pack of cigarettes. Attached to it were magnets and a battery pack. Its red LCD was blinking steadily.

"What is *that?*"

"It's a GPS tracking unit. I was wondering how they found us so quickly at the beach, and then at the hotel. And now I know." David found the switch and turned it off, and said, "Let's go find another hotel. Now we can rest easy—at least for the time being."

As he pulled away, David made sure they hadn't picked up a tail before heading to another hotel.

CHAPTER THIRTY-FIVE

ETWEEN worrying about her father and wrestling with the decision she had to make, Gina's mind was too active to allow for sleep.

She knew from the moment she heard what her father had said on the phone what her decision would ultimately be. She just needed to find a way to reconcile the decision—to somehow rationalize that what she was about to do was the right thing. It was a classic battle of the mind—one between emotion and reason. She would make her decision, but living with the possible consequences would be another matter.

When David stirred at five-thirty the following morning, Gina was lying next to him, staring at the ceiling. David hunched up on an elbow and looked at the clock. Gina turned to him. "Did you sleep well?" she asked.

"Not too bad, how about you?"

"I dozed off a few times, but for the most part I didn't

sleep. Since we're both awake, why don't we get an early start for the ferry?"

"Sounds good to me. We can catch the first trip of the day."

Before leaving the hotel grounds, David cruised the predawn parking lot. When he saw a moving van with Florida plates, he pulled up to it, blocking the rear of the vehicle with his own. He reached into the back seat and grabbed the GPS unit. He turned it on, and after scanning the area to make sure there was no one else around, he quickly got out of the Jeep, and ran around the rear of his vehicle to the back of the moving van. He knelt down and attached the unit to the undercarriage; its powerful magnet held it firmly in place. He positioned the antenna alongside the muffler, after which, he took one last look under the vehicle to make sure the red light was blinking. Satisfied, he returned to the Jeep. "That ought to keep them busy for a while. I wonder how far south they'll get before they realize they've been had."

"No matter how far it is, it won't be far enough."

On the way to Greenport from the ferry, they had stopped at the Hellenic snack bar in East Marion and picked up gyros and homemade lemonade for lunch. They arrived at David's just before noon.

As a precaution, David parked on a side street, and entered the house from the rear. He peeked through the blinds, but saw nothing suspicious on the street.

The two sat on David's deck overlooking the bay. The intense rays of the sun were mitigated by the cool bay breeze. Under normal circumstances this idyllic setting would have provided the perfect venue for a romantic lunch, but not today. Not with so much on their plate, and certainly not with her father being held against his will.

Gina aimlessly picked at her gyro while she was herself consumed by thoughts of her father and what he might be going through. David could see the concern she wore on her face and placed his hand over hers. Gina looked up. "David, I'm so worried about my father. Do you think they are mistreating him? He's on several medications, and I doubt they took the time to see that he had them when he was abducted. What if I never see him again?" Her eyes welled up and her mouth twitched as she tried to stifle yet another crying session. David squeezed her hand and with his other hand, he wiped a tear that had escaped through the corner of her eye.

"Listen, sweetheart, they have absolutely no reason to hurt your father. It would serve no purpose. It's us they want. You know, to lead them to the vial. They are just using him as leverage. They would be fools not to attend to his needs."

"Oh, David, I pray you're right."

"We have to figure out who to get the serum to. The sooner we do, the sooner they will release your father. They'll no longer have any motive for keeping him."

"Do you really believe that?" Gina said, doubtfully.

"Yes, I absolutely do," he said confidently. *God I hope I'm right.*

"What about your personal cardiologist? I'm sure you can trust him."

"I thought of him, and if we had time, he would be

one of the people I'd go to, but he would only have to take it somewhere else. He would be acting as a middleman. It would take too much time. And right now time is of the essence. No, we need to get directly to a source. We need to find someone we can trust to expose these bastards."

"Can we go to a large university that does medical research? Surely, they would do the right thing."

"Don't be so sure. A lot of their research funding comes from federal grants. I'm certain they would consult with their benefactors before going public. And once the government figures out that hundreds of thousands of people will be added each year to the Medicare and Social Security rolls, and the significant impact that will have on the federal budget, I don't think they'll be in any rush to expose Freiz. There may be a few congressmen and senators who could be trusted, but I don't know who they are, and once again, we don't have enough time to research it. We need to find an organization or individual that is beyond reproach. One that is not only honest, and credible, but also has the horsepower to make things happen."

Gina piped in. "How about the Centers for Disease Control and Prevention in Atlanta? Certainly they would have an interest in saving an additional million or so lives every year, and that's in this country alone. After all, saving lives and improving health is the sole reason for their existence."

"I know. I thought of the CDC myself. The problem I have with them is they're a government agency. And as I just said, because of the monetary burden a cure for coronary artery disease would place on Medicare and Social Security,

I don't think we should trust any government agency. They have as much of an incentive to see that the Sicilia Gene is kept under wraps as does Freiz."

"Then how about the World Health Organization?"

"WHO? They are a United Nations organization. Based on how successful the UN is in almost every other endeavor they engage in, I don't think we should consider them."

"Well, David, I'm about out of suggestions. Do you have any other possibilities?"

"We need an organization or some individual that is not connected to government or the medical industry in any way; someone with absolutely no motive to prevent the deployment of the Sicilia Gene." David went silent as he searched his mind for an answer. "Wait a second. Why didn't I think of him earlier?"

"Who?" Gina asked impatiently.

"Alfred Danar, the consumer advocate. He has the credibility and muscle to get it done. He'll know how to proceed."

"Are you sure he'll take this on, especially after we tell him what's happened to Michael and Doctor Bauer?"

"Gina, think about it. If Freiz had developed the Sicilia Gene as soon as it acquired Expharmica, think of how many lives could have been saved. We're talking about millions of people who would still be alive if not for corporate greed. This is a major scandal in the making.

"I'm sure Freiz will spin the information in order to defend themselves. But when the truth gets out, they will be hard pressed to stop stifling its development. The pressure from the general public would be just too much.

"Danar has a history for taking on the big boys and winning. I'm sure he'll jump at the chance to go after the world's largest pharmaceutical company. This is what this guy lives for. He's been doing it for—I don't know—thirty years or more. He's proven to be incorruptible, and I'd bet he's been offered many bribes from those he's investigated over the years. Gina, the more I think of it, the more convinced I am that he's our man. In fact, I know he's our man."

"I think you're right. The next question is: how do we contact him?"

"Let's start by Googling him." David went to his computer and typed in Alfred Danar as Gina looked on. Several hits popped up. David clicked on each one, looking for a way to contact him or his organization. All the sites chronicled his life and his noble pursuits: how he fought for automobile safety, championed workplace safety, and his current crusade of taking on the drug companies in an effort to have them stop using mercury-based thimerosal as a preservative in children's vaccines, arguing it was the cause of the current Autism epidemic. But oddly, none provided a way to contact him or his organization. The closest he could get was his organization's Washington D.C. address.

While David continued searching the Internet, Gina dialed Directory Assistance trying to obtain a phone number, only to be told it was non-published. In frustration Gina said, "Wouldn't you think a consumer advocate would make it a little easier for a consumer to contact him? This is ridiculous."

"Gina, Danar has to choose his causes carefully. Can you imagine how many calls his office would take if his number was readily available? But don't worry, we'll find a way to contact him, or at least his organization. If we have to, we'll go to D.C. and show up at his office. Even if he's not there, I'm sure we can get to talk to someone.

"All we need is a chance to explain the issue and present the evidence. Once he understands the magnitude of what they've done, and what they haven't done, I don't think any further convincing will be necessary."

"But David, the evidence was obtained illegally."

"Yes, and Michael paid for it with his life. Danar nor anyone in his organization had anything to do with that."

"But we did. We are accomplices to the crime?"

"I'm well aware of that, and I'm sure we will have to deal with that at some point. Look, Gina, let me try to make an analogy. Do you remember learning about the leaking of the Pentagon Papers during the Nixon administration?"

"Vaguely. History was never my strong suit, but obviously, it was yours."

"Well, in the sixties and early seventies, a guy named Daniel Ellsberg worked as a military analyst at the Pentagon. He had access to recommendations and plans put forth by the Joint Chiefs for escalating the war in Vietnam. Even though Nixon was telling the American people that the war was nearing its end, he was planning a major escalation. Ellsberg had spent two years in Vietnam as a civilian, and had come to the conclusion that the war was un-winnable.

This view was even shared by Nixon himself. However, Nixon was unable to admit defeat and intended to press on, no matter how high the human cost.

"Ellsberg decided to leak the classified papers to *The New York Times* who then printed all seven thousand pages in installments. The Nixon administration tried to stop the publication. The fight went all the way to the Supreme Court. The Court ruled in favor of the *Times*.

"Daniel Ellsberg was charged with a twelve-count indictment that included charges of theft, conspiracy, and espionage. He could have spent the rest of his life in prison. Eventually, all the charges were dropped because the Court decided that the administration had engaged in gross governmental misconduct and the citizens had a right to know. It was the beginning of the end for Nixon."

"I thought it was Watergate that brought him down?"

"Yes, but it all started with the Pentagon papers. Nixon tried to discredit Ellsberg. He even ordered "The Plumbers" led by G. Gordon Liddy to break into Ellsberg's psychiatrist's office in an attempt to find something incriminating, but they didn't find anything. These were the same guys that subsequently broke into the Democratic Campaign headquarters at the Watergate.

"In my opinion, Ellsberg had a hand in ending the Vietnam War and preventing the loss of God knows how many more GIs."

"I see the parallel between what Ellsberg did and what we're trying to do, but, David, do you think the analogy is pure enough?"

"I don't know. One thing I do believe, if we ever get

before a jury, I'm confident their sympathy will lie with us, and not with a cold, calculating pharmaceutical giant like Freiz. But let's not put the cart before the horse. We've got a lot to do before we have to think about that."

David continued searching the net while talking to Gina. There were pages of websites devoted to Alfred Danar, but none offering what they were looking for: a phone number. Finally, he found one that provided an e-mail address: alfreddanar@consumeradvocate.org.

"This is better than nothing," David said, as he started typing furiously while Gina looked over his shoulder.

Dear Mr. Danar:

I, along with two corporate insiders have uncovered a conspiracy by a major pharmaceutical company. One of us, along with another employee, has already been murdered, and we are being pursued. We believe we can prove that an amazing new treatment for coronary artery disease is being kept under wraps by Freiz pharmaceuticals in order to protect its best selling cholesterol drug, Torvistat. We urgently need your help. Please respond to this e-mail ASAP, as we are in danger and cannot stay here much longer.

PLEASE HELP US!

David Roy and Gina Coletti

David hit the send key, sat back, and turned to Gina. "That's all we can do for now." He looked at his watch. "Wow, it's almost five o'clock. Why don't we go out for a bite to eat? Hopefully, by the time we get back, we'll have an answer. If not, I think we should leave. I don't think it's going to be safe here for much longer anyway. These guys aren't stupid; they're going to catch on to my little deflection ploy sooner or later, and I'm guessing it's going to be sooner rather than later. The longer we stay here, the less safe I feel."

"I agree it's the prudent thing to do. Where do you suggest we go?"

"I hear the nation's capitol is nice this time of year."

CHAPTER THIRTY-SIX

D AVID and Gina's entrée had just been delivered when David spotted the black sedan enter the parking lot. After circling the lot and locating David's Jeep, the sedan parked in a position which enabled it to block the exit. "David, what are you staring at?"

"It's them. They're back. C'mon, we have to get out of here." David summoned the waitress and asked her to call a cab. He gave the excuse that Gina wasn't feeling well, and needed to go home.

"I'm sorry, sir, I'm not really allowed to do that, but I'll ask the hostess to call one. Is there anything else I can do?"

"Just the cab will be fine, thank you, and I think you'd better hurry, if you don't want my companion vomiting all over your fine restaurant." The waitress hurried off to make the call.

Fortunately, the restaurant entrance faced Main Street,

and the parking lot was on the side of the building, enabling them to leave without being seen.

The ten minutes it took for the taxi to show up seemed like an eternity. They waited impatiently in the small vestibule in the front of the restaurant where the hostess greeted the patrons, peering through the window every few seconds until Gina spotted the cab. They exited the restaurant and quickly walked north, hailing the cab as they moved away from the restaurant. The cab pulled over and they jumped in. "Where to folks?"

"Take us to the corner of Front and Fourth Street. And could you do me a favor and not turn around in the parking lot. My ex-wife just pulled in and I'd like to avoid a confrontation. I'm sure you understand."

"Sure, buddy, got me one of those too. I know exactly what you mean." The street was narrow, but the cabbie maneuvered a skillful U-turn and left their stalkers behind.

As per David's request, they were dropped off two blocks from his house. Standing on the corner, Gina looked up at David. "Now what?"

"I didn't want to take the cab all the way home just in case they have someone there too. We can take the backyards. If we can get to the house without running into trouble, I'll grab the keys to the boat. Once we're out on the water, they won't be able to follow us. When we feel it's safe, we can take the boat to the restaurant dock, get the Jeep, and get the hell out of town."

They made their way to the house through the manicured backyards that faced the bay. Most of the houses were summer or weekend homes, so many were vacant. They cautiously approached the house. David held his hand out to signal Gina to wait where she was. He tiptoed onto the deck and peered through the kitchen window. Seeing nothing unusual, he moved to the sliding glass doors that led to the living room. Again, he saw nothing to arouse his fear. He moved back to the kitchen door. After unlocking it with as little noise as possible, he slid into the house. He kept the keys to his boat on a hook on the pantry door. As he reached for the doorknob, the door flew open with such force that he was knocked to the floor. Surprised and dazed, he clumsily tried to get to his feet. Before David realized what had happened, his assailant caught him in a chokehold from behind. David thrashed about trying to free himself, but to no avail. The attacker squeezed harder, cutting off all oxygen. David began to blackout. Gina, hearing the commotion, ran up the steps to the deck. Aghast at the scene before her, she picked up an antique ceramic liquor jug that sat next to the door and without hesitation smashed it over the head of the assailant. Unconscious, the intruder fell to the floor.

David was on all fours gasping for air when Gina ran to his side.

"David! Are you all right?"

"I'm okay. I just need to catch my breath." He didn't mention the sharp pain emanating from the center of his chest. Gina helped him to his feet and sat him at the kitchen table. "Gina, we have to get out of here now."

"I know. Just drink this first," she said, handing him a glass of water. "David, I don't like the way you look. Your color is gone and you're sweating profusely. I'm calling 911." Ignoring his protest, she dialed the number.

Just then David heard the unmistakable sound of a vehicle entering his gravel driveway. "Quick, let's go," he said as he snatched the boat keys. He grabbed Gina's arm, and they ran for the boat. The phone was left dangling in the kitchen.

Their pursuers spotted them and gave chase. They were on the dock, halfway to the boat when the pain in his chest intensified and traveled down his left arm and up to his jaw. There was no mistaking what was happening. He needed to act quickly. He stopped running and turned to face his pursuers. Surprised by his unexpected move, they also stopped. He reached into his pocket and produced the vial. His voice was weak and he teetered as he spoke. "Is this what you've come for?" he said holding it up for them to see. Suddenly, he fell to his knees. He tried to break his fall with his hands, but in doing so the vial was smashed in the process, its contents spilling down between the dock's deck boards and into the water.

Gina rushed to his side. Although the men had not retrieved the vial, they had attained the next best thing—its destruction. Now they just had to take care of loose ends. "We'll take the girl with us," said one of the pursuers. Sirens wailed in the distance, drawing the attention of the neighbors on both sides. "She can't hurt us now. She's a nobody. Let's get the hell out of here," responded his partner. Seeing there was nothing else they could do, they fled the scene.

"David! David!" Gina screamed. David was barely conscious now. His breathing was shallow and it was clear she had to act if she was to save him. She laid him flat on his back and was about to begin CPR when he tried to speak. She stopped and leaned in close. His voice was now so weak he could barely be heard. "I … love you. Tell—tell." David began to lose consciousness.

"Oh David, I love you too. Say it again, I couldn't hear you."

"What do you want me to tell?" Gina couldn't make out what he was saying and couldn't waste anymore time. He was fading away. She administered mouth-to-mouth resuscitation while kneeling beside him. She placed one hand on top of the other and interlocked her fingers, pushing down hard on his chest with the palms of hands trying to jar to life his dying heart. "C'mon, David! Oh, God, Please don't let him die."

When Gina heard the ambulance arrive, she yelled, "Help! He's had a heart attack. Hurry, he's not breathing! Oh, God, please don't let him die!" Gina continued pumping even after the EMTs and paramedics arrived. They quickly set up a defibrillator while Gina tore open his shirt. One of the EMTs pulled Gina away from David as the other placed the pads on his chest and fired the jolt of current. David didn't respond. A second jolt failed as well. "Oh, God, please!" Gina was frantic. The EMT embraced her and tried to turn her away from his partner's futile efforts, but she jerked herself free and returned to David's side just as the paramedic was injecting a syringe of adrenalin directly into his heart. He then administered another shock, and again David didn't respond. The paramedic looked up at his partner and shook his head. Gina embraced David's lifeless body and wept uncontrollably. One of the EMTs tried to console her as he continued working on David while the other went for the gurney.

The EMT continued to work on David during the ride to the hospital as Gina stood next to him, praying for what she knew would now have to be a miracle.

Upon their arrival at the emergency room, David was whisked away. Gina was escorted to the waiting room where she sat, dazed and numb, with a blank look of despair, waiting for the inevitable.

Nearly an hour passed before a doctor took Gina aside to tell her what she already knew.

The next three days were a blur for Gina. She was on automatic pilot. The day after David died she received a call on her cell phone from her father's abductors telling her that her father would be returned unharmed within the next few days as long as she didn't go to the authorities. Gina readily agreed and felt a measure of relief during these harrowing days.

Arianna stayed with her at David's house until the day following the funeral. She helped Gina with the arrangements and was her rock at the heavily attended wake and funeral service. Gina couldn't get used to hearing David being referred to in the past tense, and at every expression of sorrow, she felt a renewed sense of emptiness and longing. Gina had known David for only a few months, but he was her first true love, and she couldn't imagine living without him.

Gina thanked Arianna for being there for her. Arianna

promised to keep in touch. Their losses still fresh, they vowed to support each other through the very difficult months that lay ahead.

Arianna had an early reservation for the ferry back to New London. Gina was leaving the next morning. She needed to close up the house, which now felt so empty, and she wanted some time alone to try and come to grips with the events of the past few days. She was straightening up around the house when she came across the white, plastic bag containing David's personal effects given to her at the hospital. She sat on David's bed and spilled the contents onto the bed: his clothes, a wallet, a comb, the keys to his boat and Jeep, a money clip with cash, and some loose change. Gina picked up his plaid shirt, the one that she had once worn herself, and held it to her face, taking in his scent. She closed her eyes and held the shirt to her heart. Just when she thought she was cried out, a flood of emotion arose in her like a volcano and she again began to quietly sob. When the crying subsided, she felt drained, both physically and emotionally. She lay down to rest and soon her weary mind and body drifted off to sleep.

When she awoke, she was still clutching David's shirt. She sat up and looked at David's personal effects strewn across the bedspread, and then it hit her: *where's the other vial and the e-mails?* As far as she knew, David was in possession of them when he died. *What could have happened to them? Did someone at the hospital take them?* One thing was certain, they were missing. Without them, their quest—her quest to expose Freiz was over, and three innocent lives would have been lost. And all for nothing. Suddenly, Gina felt nauseated. She went out to the backyard for some fresh air. She took in several deep breaths of the cool bay air as she strolled down the dock to the spot where she had lost her lover.

She was reliving the traumatic event when she saw the cap of the broken vial wedged between two deck boards. She bent down and carefully removed it. It was the cap she had notched when she took the vial containing the placebo. The realization set in: David broke the vial that contained the placebo; the vial with the Sicilia Gene serum still exits. But where could it be, and what happened to the e-mails? She didn't know where to begin to look.

Gina thoroughly searched the Jeep and the house. She was determined to see that David' death would not be in vain. But she came up empty.

The following morning, Gina finished closing up the house and headed for the ferry. She had a reservation on the ten o'clock boat. During the drive to Orient Point, she replayed her last moments with David. She was happy that he had said he loved her and that she had a chance to tell him she loved him, but he was trying to say something else. She couldn't make it out. He had repeated it twice. It sounded like, "Tell." *Tell what? Tell who? What was he trying to say?*

CHAPTER THIRTY-SEVEN

T HE ferry ride across Long Island Sound seemed agonizingly long. It was Gina's first trip across the Sound without David. And as she stood on the top deck with the wind blowing through her hair, as she had in the past, she could almost feel his warm embrace; his tender touch; things she would never again experience with David. She missed him so much. Along with the unbearable sense of loss—the anguish caused her physical pain—her heart literally ached.

Gina stood at the railing looking down at the frothy, white wake that was created by the ferry being pushed through the water by its huge twin screws.

Visions of David collapsing repeatedly flashed through her head. She tried to push them aside by recalling happier times. She even managed a smile when reflecting on their relationship's testy beginning at the clinic. She tried to replay in her mind every detail of their courtship as it progressed. She remembered their walks on the beach at Sixty-Seven Steps. How enthusiastic and encouraged he was with his improving health. She recalled, fondly, the romantic candlelit dinners and their erotic lovemaking. *How fast things changed.* In a flash, her life had changed forever. Her hopes and dreams of a life together disintegrated before her eyes. Again the vision of David falling to his knees on the dock forced its way back into her mind. She thought of his defiance toward their pursuers, and wondered if he had intentionally confronted and taunted them with the vial. Had he purposely smashed it on the dock, thereby destroying any further reason for their pursuit, possibly saving her life? Was this his last, valiant act before dying? At least Gina chose to think so.

These thoughts again reminded her of the missing vial containing the Sicilia Gene and the two e-mails. *What could have happened to them? Where were they? And what was David trying to tell me before he died?*

Gina was shaken from her thoughts when her cell phone rang. She looked at the screen on her phone. It was her home number. She quickly answered it. "Hello?" she said anxiously.

"Gina, it's Dad."

"Daddy!" She yelled, drawing the attention of other passengers. "Are you all right?"

"I'm fine. A taxi picked me up, and now I'm at home. The taxi driver helped me into the house."

"Oh, thank God! When did you get home?"

"Just now, honey, I wanted to call you right away because

I knew you'd be worried, and I was also worried sick about you. Are you two okay?"

Gina didn't want to tell her father what happened to David over the phone. "I'm okay, Daddy. I'm on the ferry. We're almost to New London. I should be home in a few hours, and we'll talk then." Al sensed something was not right, but chose not to push it. Whatever it was could wait until Gina got home.

Gina changed the subject. "Daddy, how did they treat you? Did they hurt you?"

"No, sweetheart. Actually, except for being kept blind-folded, they treated me quite well. They even saw to it that I took my medications, and was fed three times a day. It tasted like fast food take-out, but it could have been worse."

"Thank God for that. When I saw the wheelchair was knocked over, I thought the worst."

"Well, I did try to resist. This old bird still has some fight left in him, but not nearly enough to ward off two strapping men in, I would guess, their late twenties or early thirties. I couldn't tell for sure because they were wearing ski masks. They told me from the start that they weren't going to hurt me, and thank God they didn't. I was kept in a room with a TV that was tuned to CNN. I have to say, listening to the news did help pass the time. They never said why they abducted me, and then without a word, they released me. They sat me blindfolded on a park bench, and told me to count to twenty slowly before removing the blindfold. They said a cab would be by shortly to take me home. And here I am in one piece, talking to you."

"What a relief. I was beside myself with worry. Thank God you're okay."

"As I said, I'm fine. So don't rush; take your time coming home. I don't want you having an accident because you're in such a hurry to see me."

"I'll be careful. I'll see you in a few hours. I love you, Daddy."

"I love you too, sweetheart."

Gina took a deep breath and exhaled forcefully, purging herself of all the pent up worry that had accrued since her father's abduction.

With the relief of knowing her father was okay, her thoughts turned back to David. She was wracked with ambivalent emotions: the elation she felt when she heard her father's reassuring voice was colliding with her overwhelming grief. She was in an emotional no-man's land.

Shortly after hanging up, the ferry docked and passengers scurried to their vehicles. Gina made her way down the long steel staircase to David's Jeep. She sat waiting for her turn to disembark when a flashback of the scene on the dock again popped into her head. And again, she tried to make sense of what David was trying to say to her before he died. He had said that he loved her. She heard that plainly, but what he said after that was slurred and barely audible. It sounded like *tell, tell. What was he trying to tell me?* Gina was driving off the ramp when it hit her.

Instead of making a right turn toward Boston, Gina turned left and made her way to Ocean Beach. *He was trying to say the tail! The tail of the big concrete whale at the miniature golf course in the park. Why didn't I think of that sooner?*

If he chose those as his last words, they could only have meant one thing.

Gina pulled into the parking lot, parked and headed for the boardwalk. The beach was filling up, but not yet crowded. She made her way down the beach, walking parallel to the boardwalk until she reached the end. This section of the beach was empty except for a teenage couple who obviously were looking for a little privacy. They were lying on a blanket facing each other. The guy had his arm around his girlfriend and they were kissing. They heard Gina passing and looked up briefly before resuming their necking.

Gina walked directly to the spot where they had hidden the vial. She crouched down and went under the boardwalk. She placed her hand up on the top of the post and felt around. *Nothing!* Then she remembered David taking the plastic trashcan liner from the hotel room. She knelt in the soft sand and began pushing it away with her hands. She dug deeper and deeper. The more she dug the more discouraged she became. She was sure she would have found what she was looking for by now—if it was here. She was about to give up when she felt the plastic bag. A surge of adrenalin shot through her body as she quickly unearthed the bag and shook off the sand. She could feel the vial and copies of the e-mails inside. "Thank God," she said out loud.

After filling in the hole, Gina emerged from under the boardwalk with the plastic bag in hand. The couple that was lying on the blanket were now sitting and staring at Gina as if she just retrieved a stash of drugs or some other contraband. Gina smiled as she passed them. They just sat with their mouths open, not knowing what to make of what they had just witnessed.

Back in the Jeep, Gina removed the vial and e-mails from the bag. She held the vial containing the Sicilia Gene to her chest and closed her eyes. *Thank you, David. I promise I will not let you down.* She opened her eyes and read the e-mails. The first was from Monique Rentz. *Brett, as you can see from the figures provided by Doctor Bauer, the results of the preliminary tests are nothing short of astounding. The average lessening of occlusion in the group receiving the Sicilia Gene is 10%. While that may not seem significant to the average person, it should be noted that what took years to form on the artery walls was removed in a few short weeks. Unfortunately, I believe we may have discovered the magic bullet. I trust you will use this information to best serve the interest of our Freiz shareholders. Monique*

These bastards knew exactly what they had discovered. *There was no mistake*, she thought. She grabbed the second e-mail and read on.

Monique, after evaluating the data in your preliminary report sent via e-mail, I agree, the results are incredibly impressive. I have decided to immediately implement the first course of action of the contingency plan we discussed with Price. So go with the placebo for all immediately. If this fails to produce the desired effects, we will meet to discuss a more aggressive course of action to bring the trial to an end. Also, submit your formal report as soon as practicable. Brett

The e-mails alone were incriminating enough, but along with the vial Gina knew she had all of the evidence she needed to expose Freiz for what it was: a ruthless and hypocritical corporate giant whose only interest was the bottom line. And although she had no proof, she believed they were murderers as well.

Gina was determined to get the evidence to someone who would know what to do with it. One was Alfred Danar, and perhaps there were others. *I'll figure all that out after I get home. First things first, right now I need to see Daddy.*

CHAPTER THIRTY-EIGHT

GINA couldn't wait to get home to see her father. After all that had happened in the last few days, she needed to see him and be near him; to feel his comforting embrace and hear his reassuring words; to hold him and to be held.

Gina pulled up to her father's house. Eager to see her father, she ran to the door. The second she was inside she called out, "Daddy! Daddy!"

"I'm in the kitchen." Gina found him sitting at the kitchen table with the *Globe's* sports pages spread across the table; a familiar scene that she'd seen hundreds of times, but now it brought new meaning.

Gina rushed to her father's side. She collapsed to her knees and with her head on her father's lap, she broke down and sobbed uncontrollably. Al stroked her hair and when the crying abated, he said, "Gina, I know you were worried sick about me, but honestly, I'm fine."

Gina looked up at her father and through a few hitches, caused by the intense crying, she said, "Daddy...David, he's dead."

"My God, what happened?"

"He had a heart attack. We were being chased. We found the vial and some incriminating e-mails. We were running for our lives, trying to reach his boat. He fell on the dock and smashed the vial—"

"Whoa, slow down." Gina was now shaking uncontrollably. Her father leaned over and embraced her. "Calm down, sweetheart, calm down. You've been through a lot. You look exhausted. Why don't you go lie down for a while? We can talk about all of this after you get some rest." Gina didn't protest. She felt like she had been put through a ringer. She was beyond tired—she was spent. After kissing her father on his forehead, she made her way to her room, where she collapsed onto her bed.

Gina's cell phone rang, waking her from a sound sleep. She didn't know how long she was asleep, but it must have been quite awhile because looking out her bedroom window, she could see it was starting to get dark.

She looked at the display screen on her phone. There was no number, just the words: Private Caller. "Hello?"

The male voice said in a calm manner, "This is just a friendly reminder. If you go to the authorities regarding any of the events of the past few days, you will hear from us again. Trust me, you don't want that. If you remain quiet, you will not hear from us again. The choice is yours." There was a click and the caller was gone.

Gina entered the kitchen and found her father sound

asleep at the kitchen table. Trying not to wake him, she maneuvered gingerly around the kitchen. Still feeling sluggish, she decided to make some tea. She put a pot of water on the stove and went into the bathroom to freshen up. When she heard the teapot whistling, she ran into the kitchen and pulled it off the stove. It was too late. Al sat up straight and looked in the direction of the stove. He yawned, stretched, and said, "I guess you weren't the only one who was tired."

"Sorry, Daddy. I thought I could get back before it started to whistle."

"That's okay, sweetheart. If I slept much longer, I wouldn't be able to sleep tonight."

"Would you like some tea?"

"Yes, that will hit the spot." Gina made up two cups then sat at the table with Al. "Why don't you tell me what's happened?"

"I don't know where to start." She took a deep breath and exhaled slowly. "I guess I should start with the call that I received on my cell phone a few minutes ago. I think it was from one of the men who took you—at least it sounded like the same person who called before."

"What in God's name do they want now?"

"He threatened me—"

"Damn them! That's enough, we're calling the police."

"Hold it, Daddy, let me tell you what he said first."

Al put up his hands and cocked his head in assent. "All right, all right, a lawyer should know to listen first. Go on."

"He said that if I go to the authorities, they would come

back for us, and if we kept quiet, we'd never hear from them again."

"I'll reserve comment until I hear what else has happened. Now tell me about David."

Gina recounted the events that led up to the fatal incident on David's dock. Al listened intently, interrupting occasionally for clarification. When she was finished, Al sat there rubbing his chin momentarily before he spoke.

"All right, the way I see it is, there are two issues: the vial is one and my abduction is the other. You have no proof on anything else that has happened, so as far as I'm concerned that part is moot.

"As I already told you, I was treated humanely, even courteously. I personally don't see, for the time being, the need to provoke them any further on that issue. We don't need to be looking over our shoulders. Besides, we have no material proof that it happened. All we have is our word. That's simply not enough. No jury would ever convict on that alone. I don't believe we could even get them charged—if we knew who they were. So, my advice is to comply with their request, and concentrate on the second, more important issue: the vial and e-mails, and what to do with them. Have you given any thought to just how you might use them to expose Freiz?"

"The day David died we spent the entire afternoon trying to figure out where to go with this. We ruled out every organization and each individual for one reason or another, except one. We finally decided to try to bring it to the attention of Alfred Danar."

"Right to the major league, huh?"

"Well, we're dealing with one of the most powerful corporations in the country...if not the world. The problem is, we are having a difficult time trying to contact him. We seemingly checked hundreds of web sites trying to locate a telephone number. We came up with zip. David did find a web site for his organization that provided an e-mail address. Before we left for the restaurant, David e-mailed him. He briefly explained our objective and our plight. We had hoped to get a response before we left Greenport, but then all hell broke loose, and you know the rest," she said, her voice trailing off. She got hold of herself and said, "So, I don't know if anyone answered our e-mail, but I intend to send another, and if I don't get an answer, I'm going to do what David had planned."

"Which is?"

"I'm going to visit his office and stay there until someone hears my story. All of this sacrifice by Michael, Doctor Bauer, and David will not be in vain. Not if I can help it."

Al could see she was getting worked up. "All right, I understand. I still know some attorneys in D.C. I can't promise you, but I might be able to help. Let me see what I can do."

CHAPTER THIRTY-NINE

BRETT Bitterman arrived at his office at seven a.m., as usual. As always, copies of *The New York Times* and *The Wall Street Journal* sat neatly on his desk. He was scanning the headlines and sipping coffee when his secretary announced that Max Trammel was in the office and needed a few minutes of his time.

Eager to hear the latest on the missing vial, Bitterman welcomed Trammel into his office. After exchanging pleasantries, Bitterman wasted no time.

"Max, I hope you have some good news for me."

"Well, yes and no." Trammel recounted the incident that took place on the dock at David Roy's place on Long Island. "So you see, Brett, although we didn't recover the vial, it no longer exits and is no longer a threat to Freiz."

"Good work Max. Did you tie-up all lose ends?"

"Well, not exactly."

"What do you mean, 'not exactly'?"

"Well, they tried to grab the girl so we could get rid of her and her father at the same time. That way it would appear that Roy died of natural causes. But the sirens drew the attention of the neighbors, and they had to flee the scene. Since they were unable to get the girl, I had no choice but to release her father."

"Can anything be traced back to Freiz?"

"No, we don't believe so. Ms. Coletti, as far as we can ascertain, is the only conspirator left, but without the serum, she can't prove a thing."

"So you don't believe she will pursue this matter any further?"

"We've made it abundantly clear to her that it would not be in her best interest to do so. However, we'll monitor her closely for the next few weeks or so, to be certain she doesn't have a change of heart."

"Max, you know I don't like loose ends, and now I have two because you released her father. Max, I want you to call off your watchdogs so as not to draw any unwanted attention, but let me know immediately if anything unexpected develops. And when things calm down in a week or two, I want them taken care of."

"I understand. I'll take care of it."

Bitterman opened his desk drawer and produced an envelope. He offered it to Max. "Here's a little something extra for your efforts. I believe success and loyalty should be rewarded." Trammel thanked his boss and left.

Bitterman, feeling good about Trammel's report, went back to his newspaper. Something had caught his eye before he was interrupted by Trammel's visit. *Speculation Grows in*

China. President Zhou Ming has not been seen in public for over three weeks, fueling speculation regarding his health…

After Bitterman finished the article he placed a call to the White House. He was privileged to have been given the personal cell-phone number to the president's Chief of Staff, Randy Decker.

"Decker here."

"Mr. Decker, this is Brett Bitterman, CEO of Freiz Pharmaceuticals. I would like to speak with the president on a personal matter at his earliest convenience."

"He has a full schedule today, sir. I don't think—"

"I just need a few minutes of his time."

"He's just finishing up his morning intel meeting. Uh…hold on, Mr. Bitterman, let me check with the President."

Bitterman heard some muffled speech and then, "Brett, how are you? I wanted to thank you for your message of congratulations, but I've been busy cleaning up the mess that Rayhill left me."

"I'm fine, Mr. President, and you're very welcome. How does it feel to be the most powerful person on the face of the earth?"

"Well, Brett, it's too early to tell. As I said, Rayhill left his desk a mess. Do you know he kept a personal visitation log on his desk, and personally logged in every visitor to the Oval Office? That's a little idiosyncratic, don't you think, Brett?"

"Yes, it was." Richards sensed Bitterman knew he was referring to seeing his name on Rayhill's log, and even though it no longer mattered, he had made his point.

"So Brett, what's the reason for the call?"

"I read an article in the *Times* about China's Zhou Ming. What can you tell me about him?" Bitterman heard the president laugh. "What's so funny, Bruce?"

"Boy, you don't miss a trick."

"That's why I'm a CEO and you're just the president of the United States." This time they both laughed.

"Yes, I suppose so." Richards asked Decker for privacy, and waited for him to leave the room before continuing.

"Listen, Brett, what I am about to tell you is classified, so you must not repeat it. Do you understand?"

"Of course. Of course."

"According to a CIA intelligence report, Ming has suffered a heart attack. The CIA has known for years that Ming has been on Zimstan."

"How in the world do they know that?"

"You'd be amazed at what we know."

"I'm sure. Well, that's what he gets for cutting a deal with our main competitor. If he was on Torvistat, it may not have happened. What kind of shape is he in?"

"It was fairly severe, but he is expected to return to work when he finishes his cardiac rehab. We guess it'll be another few weeks before he returns. So why are you so interested in President Ming's condition, as if I didn't know?"

"I would like to offer President Ming another opportunity to forge a business relationship with Freiz."

"And would he become one of *the chosen few*?"

"Of course, that's my ace in the hole. But I need you to arrange a meeting so I can meet with him or one of his closest advisors."

"That's a tall order, especially given the fact that we're not even supposed to know about his condition. You know how tightly the Chinese government controls the information stream."

"Bruce, you're a diplomat. I know you can find a way to broach the subject. You could refer to the article in the *Times*."

"You mean the one we leaked to the press?"

"I should have known." Again, they laughed. "And Bruce, a little push by you would help give me some additional credibility, because I'm sure they, as you did, will have their doubts."

"Okay, let me see what I can do. You should hear something by the end of the day."

"Thanks, Bruce, and as always, I will show my appreciation in the usual manner."

After hanging up, Bitterman put his feet on the desk, crossed at his ankles. He sat back with his hands behind his head and smiled. In the past he had missed an opportunity to gain a foothold in China; an emerging giant with potentially the largest market in the world.

Now, he would get a second chance.

Life is good.

CHAPTER FORTY

GINA sat patiently in the waiting room, but with a measure of apprehension. She was a full fifteen minutes early for her nine o'clock appointment. After a brief phone conversation with Doctor Howard, David's cardiologist, they had agreed to meet in his office. He said he would squeeze her in between appointments.

As she sat waiting, Gina thought about what she would tell him and what she wouldn't. She decided to inform him about their discovery how Freiz sabotaged the trial, and nothing more. She wouldn't mention anything about the murders. She couldn't prove anything anyway and it might scare him off. Hopefully, that would be enough to get him to help her, and if he didn't want to get personally involved, surely, he would know where to direct her.

Doctor Howard appeared from his office door. After introducing himself, he motioned for Gina to enter his office and take a seat. He closed the door to ensure their privacy, and then took a seat behind his desk.

"First, let me say how saddened I was to hear of David's death. He was a patient of mine for quite some time and I got to know him fairly well. He was a good man. If there were more people like him, the world would be a much better place. You have my deepest condolences."

"Thank you, Doctor."

"You're very welcome. Now, what is so important that you felt it imperative to see me right away?"

"Well, Doctor, as you are fully aware, David was participating in a double blind study for Freiz that was being conducted by The New England Clinic for Cardiac Care, located in Boston."

"Yes, I'm familiar with the clinic."

"Well, just two weeks into the trial, participants were saying how much better they felt."

"That in itself is not unusual; the perceived results could be psychosomatic. That often happens in these kinds of tests. That's one reason why placebo is given to half of the participants."

"I agree, but this time the improvement was real—and dramatic. I witnessed them first hand, and if you would have had a chance to examine David, I think you would have been amazed at the change in his physical condition."

"Okay, I'll accept that. Go on."

"Well, one of the clinicians working on the trial came across two e-mails." She produced a manila envelope from her bag, and pulled out the two e-mail copies and handed them to him. "Doctor, please read these."

Doctor Howard carefully read them in the order in which they were given. When he was finished, he removed his glasses and put one of the temples in his mouth, as if buying time to form a response.

"So Doctor, what do you think now?"

"I'm at a loss for words. These are remarkable—and I might add—incriminating," he said, holding up the e-mails. "What do you intend to do with these?"

As he was handing them back to Gina, she put up her hand, "No, Doctor, You can keep them; I made those copies for you.

"Doctor Howard, I came to you because I didn't know where else to go. What they've done is unconscionable. They have the ability to save millions and millions of lives, but are willing to let people die in order to protect their profits. It's hard for me to comprehend that Freiz would do this."

"Well, young lady, I'm afraid you are being somewhat naïve. That's not to say that what they are doing is justifiable. It certainly is not. But I would guess this type of deplorable corporate behavior goes on more often than you think. Sure, most probably are not life and death issues like the one we have here, but I'm sure their motives are the same. Take the auto industry—don't you think they could produce cars that are far more fuel-efficient than the ones they are currently producing? Don't you think big oil companies would develop an alternate fuel like hydrogen if it were in their best interest? The same goes for finding a cure for cancer. All of these industries that I just mentioned and a good number of others have a strong motive not to do what we believe should be done to best serve the public. Think about it, what would happen to EXXON-Mobil if someone figured out a way to efficiently produce hydrogen fuel from seawater? The answer is obvious. The same goes for the pharmaceutical industry. Finding a cure for a particular disease, cardiovascular in this case, could have a disastrous effect on a drug company's bottom line."

"Doctor, I understand all of that. What I need to know is, are you willing to help me expose Freiz?"

"Well, Ms. Coletti, I'm not sure how much help I can be, but let me think it over. I'd like an opportunity to look into it a bit more. Leave me your contact information, and I'll get back to you. And again, I'm sorry for your loss."

"Thank you so much, Doctor. At last I feel the ball is rolling."

After Gina left, Howard sat at his desk and repeated in his mind what he had said to Gina. He hadn't mentioned it, but his field of medicine could be just as adversely affected as the ones he had referred to. If cardiovascular disease were eradicated, he would loose the vast majority of his patients. Hospitals and clinics, which rely heavily on the revenue from cardiac bypass surgery, would suffer such massive loss of revenue that they may not be able to remain solvent.

Hundreds of local people could lose their jobs. And this was just in his little world. Magnified throughout the country, it could be an economic calamity.

Doctor Howard pondered these scenarios for a few minutes. He turned to the pictures on the wall of his wife and two children, a boy and a girl. They were both in high school, his son, a senior and his daughter a sophomore.

College was approaching fast, and both were aiming for Ivy League schools. His son had already been accepted at Princeton and his daughter was shooting for Cornell. They were great schools with tuitions to match. And then there would be graduate school, and maybe even medical school.

And how would he be viewed by his colleagues and family for attacking the very industry that helped provide such a lucrative medical practice? He would become a pariah among his peers.

He looked at his bronzed, framed copy of the Hippocratic Oath that hung from the wall opposite his desk. He thought of his youthful days when idealism governed his every action. He had always prayed for such an opportunity that would enable him to make a difference that would benefit mankind. Now he had the opportunity to realize his childhood dream, the one that inspired him to become a doctor in the first place; a healer, a saver of lives. But this was before he had the ski chalet in Vermont and a four thousand square foot mansion on the bay, before he had a wife and two children, a huge mortgage, three cars and a boat, and colleagues who admired his success and status within the community. He again glanced at his oath that had always been his guiding light.

That afternoon after seeing his last patient, Doctor Howard sat at his desk for nearly an hour contemplating the ramifications of his involvement. Suddenly, he picked up the e-mails and walked toward the copying machine. He stopped and turned to look at the family pictures one last time. Then he changed his direction away from the copying machine and toward the shredder. He turned it on and hesitated for a minute. Then he took a deep breath and ran them through.

He turned out the lights and left for home.

CHAPTER FORTY-ONE

G INA sat nervously, waiting for the meeting she never thought she'd get.

She had all but given up when Doctor Howard failed to call her, and calls to his office were not returned. She was further discouraged by her unsuccessful attempts to contact Alfred Danar's organization. Her e-mails were answered in a form-letter format, which stated that only information regarding his current campaign against the neurotoxin Thimerisal would be welcomed. Unsolicited correspondences were not currently being accepted. So, she was shocked when she received a phone call from Danar's office to set up a face-to-face meeting with the man himself.

Gina replayed the moment while she waited. She remembered being awestruck and calling out to her father. "Daddy!" she yelled as she ran for the kitchen. "You're not going to believe who just called." She didn't give him time to respond. "Alfred Danar's office. He's going to meet with me—himself—in person—next Tuesday. Can you believe it?"

"I'm happy I was able to help," he said smugly.

"Whatta ya mean? What did you do? You never said anything to me."

"I didn't want to get your hopes up in case I couldn't pull it off. It's been a long time. I was afraid Danar wouldn't remember me."

"You know him?"

"I worked with him when he was just starting out. He and his Washington attorneys were working on an asbestos case here in Boston, and they needed a lawyer who was a member of the Massachusetts bar. They hired me, and that's how we met."

"You never told me that."

"Why would I? Until recently, his name never came up."

Gina was deep in thought when she heard her name.

"Ms. Coletti, Mr. Danar will see you now."

Gina picked up her brief case and headed for the door that was held open by the receptionist. She thanked her as she passed and thought, *here I go.*

Gina entered an inner office with two secretaries situated on either side of a large oak door. One of the secretaries looked up and motioned toward the door. "You may go right in, Ms. Coletti." Gina felt her stomach tighten. This was the opportunity she had been waiting for, but suddenly she didn't feel as confident as she had only moments before. She took a deep breath and entered Danar's office.

Alfred Danar stood and walked from behind his desk to greet Gina. Extending his hand he said, "So you're Al Coletti's daughter. I'm very pleased to meet you."

Gina shook his hand. "Mr. Danar, it's an honor to meet you."

"Please, have a seat." Gina sat in one of the two leather chairs that faced Danar's large walnut desk. "It was a pleasant surprise to hear from your father. We worked on a case together many years ago, as I'm sure he's told you. He is a capable attorney and a good man. I was dismayed to hear of his failing health."

"Thank you for your kind words." Gina felt awkward and didn't quite know where to start. Sensing her unease, Danar led her to the reason for her being there. "So, Ms. Coletti, how can I help you? Your father informed me regarding a conspiracy involving Freiz Pharmaceuticals. When I discussed the issue with my staff, one of them produced an e-mail from you and David Roy and apologized for not bringing it to my attention sooner. Okay, tell me what you have."

"Well, I work, or I should say did work, for the New England Clinic for Cardiac Care in Boston. They were in the process of conducting a phase three, double blind trial on a new Freiz medication to treat atherosclerosis. The trial was going along fine. Many of the participants reported they were feeling better, and it appeared that they actually were. A good number were able to increase the intensity of their physical activity."

"I assume they kept a record of each participant's performance."

"Yes, they did, and in one particular case the improvement was dramatic."

Danar interrupted, "How do you know that to be so?"

"I became very close to one of them, David Roy. Contrary to clinic rules, we developed a close personal relationship."

"And where is he now?"

Gina's eyes suddenly welled up and she swallowed hard. "He died a little more than a week ago—from a heart attack." Her voice cracked as she spoke. Danar came around from his desk and sat in the chair beside her.

"I'm so sorry," he said. Then he poured her a glass of water from the carafe that sat on the table between the two chairs.

Gina took a deep breath and continued. "David was very sick when he entered the trial. Several years ago he suffered a debilitating heart attack. Since then he had undergone several angioplasties, and a by-pass surgery. David had severe physical limitations. He could barely climb a flight of stairs without becoming fatigued, and he often suffered from bouts of severe angina. Not more than two or three weeks into the trial he started to feel better."

"That soon? What exactly were the participants given?"

"Half of the group was given a synthetic gene serum derived from the apoA-1 Sicilia Gene, the history of which is an amazing story in itself. Anyway, when David told me he was feeling better so soon, at first I thought it was a psychosomatic response. That often happens in these trials, you know, the participant wants so badly to get well—"

"Yes, I understand the placebo effect. Please, go on."

"Well, David was very methodical regarding how he measured his progress, and without going into detail, let me just say that he convinced me that he was indeed getting better. Many of the other participants were making the claim as well.

"Then, out of the clear blue sky, the clinic abruptly stopped the trial, citing an alarmingly high instance of serious side effects."

"Well, were there?"

"Yes, but—"

"Wouldn't that be the prudent thing to do?"

"Normally, yes, but another coworker, Michael Fitzgerald, came across two e-mails between Brett Bitterman, the CEO of Freiz and Monique Rentz, his liaison with the clinic." Gina snapped open her brief case and pulled out a manila envelope. She extracted copies of the two e-mails and handed them across the desk to Danar.

Alfred Danar took the e-mails. His brow furrowed as he read.

"That's not all; Michael took a vial of the serum from the lab."

"You mean he stole it?"

"Yes, he felt it important enough to take it … he felt he had no other choice. Freiz found out about it and by one means or another attempted to get it back. When that didn't work, David and I believed Freiz had him killed. He was found dead in his hotel room with a needle sticking out of his arm. His death was ruled an overdose."

"And you think otherwise?"

"Mr. Danar, I worked with Michael for many years, and at no time did I or anyone else who knew him, suspect he was using drugs … and I still don't believe it."

"I see. But of course you would have a difficult time proving otherwise. Do you know if Freiz recovered the vial?"

"No, they didn't. Michael had hidden it, but he left us a clue as to its location. David and I eventually found it along with the e-mails."

Gina again reached into her briefcase and produced the vial. "This is the vial containing the Sicilia Gene serum," she said handing it to him. Danar held it up to the light and examined it.

"This is very interesting."

"There's more. We convinced the doctor who was administering the trial to help us expose Freiz. We had arranged a meeting, but he never made it. He was mugged and murdered in the parking lot just outside the place we were to meet."

"And you think Freiz had a hand in that also, I assume?"

"Yes, I believe so, and again I can't prove it, but I think you can see a pattern."

"So, the only concrete evidence we really have are these e-mails and the vial."

"And the fact that they kidnapped my father and threatened David and me. The night he died they were after us, and we were desperately trying to get away from them. They had been following us for days, and they had finally decided to make their move when they realized we had the vial in our possession."

"But you can't prove any of this. Did you at least report it to the police?"

"No, we didn't. We were afraid we wouldn't be believed and possibly be detained as co-conspirators—for aiding and abetting Michael. We needed to get to someone we could trust first … and that's why I'm here."

Danar thought for a moment before he spoke. "And what exactly were the side effects that caused them to stop the trial?"

"Several trial participants suffered heart attacks and strokes. A few even died."

"Not being a medical person, maybe you can help me understand this. The participants were given a drug to reduce the plaque buildup in their arteries, and by all accounts it seemed to be working. Am I right so far?"

"Yes."

"Okay, then inexplicably, a number of them experienced heart attacks and strokes. Normally, I wouldn't think that to be so strange. After all, they did suffer from cardiovascular disease. Except for the fact that they appeared to be getting better and significantly so, and then experienced an abrupt reversal." Danar rubbed his chin. "It doesn't add up. What's your take on it?"

"Well, based on the content of the e-mails you just read, and the dramatic change for the worse in a number of participants, David and I believed the participants were not only given a placebo, but one that contained another substance, possibly a blood clotting factor, like vitamin K for example, that caused the adverse reactions, thus, giving Freiz an excuse to immediately shut down the trial. Perhaps a reexamination of the deceased is in order."

"Well, Ms. Coletti, this is a first. I've heard of pharmaceutical companies that tried to alter trial data to hide adverse side effects, but never have I heard of one that manipulated the data to intentionally discredit their own product. Do you have a sample of the placebo that we can have analyzed?"

"We did, but it broke when David fell on the dock. When he had his heart attack." Gina lowered her head.

"Again, Ms. Coletti, I'm sorry for your loss."

Gina raised her head and forced a thin smile. "Thank you."

Danar stood. "I think you're onto something here. We'll have to move fast before they can completely cover their tracks... if they haven't already. But first, I must practice due diligence. One does not accuse or attack the largest drug company in the world without doing one's homework.

"There is one other matter," Danar said, looking concerned. "I don't want to scare you; however, this is serious business. As you are well aware, you are dealing with very powerful and determined people and nothing is beyond these corporate criminals. So, I'd like to move you and your father to a safe house... just until all of this is made public. After that happens, coming after you would be pointless."

"You don't have to convince me. I've seen them in action."

"Very well then." Danar picked up the phone and dialed the intercom. He instructed his secretary to make the necessary arrangements. Then, he stood and offered her his hand. "Good luck, Ms. Coletti. My office will be in contact with you with further instructions. If you have any questions or concerns, please feel free to call my office. Give my best to your father. And Gina, good luck… and be careful."

Gina thanked him and left feeling confident that Alfred Danar would see to it that Freiz was finally going to be held accountable for their criminal actions and for not developing and deploying the most effective medication for treating cardiovascular disease ever discovered.

CHAPTER FORTY-TWO

GINA and Al Coletti were moved to a chalet-style lodge in the White Mountains of New Hampshire. The home was used by Danar primarily for skiing vacations, but was mostly vacant for the rest of the year.

The chalet was equipped with all of the modern conveniences, including a large gas-fueled fieldstone fireplace, cable TV, and high-speed Internet service. Gina and Al were advised to avoid contact with anyone they knew while there, and to keep their cell phones turned off for the duration of their stay. There was a landline in the chalet for their use. Before leaving home, they had their mail held by the Post Office. To eliminate the possibility of being tracked down through their personal credit card records, they were given a corporate credit card for the purchase of gas, food, and anything else they might need while sequestered in the mountains. For transportation, a rental vehicle was provided.

Gina walked over to one of the three large picture windows that looked out over the verdant valley below. It had been almost a week since her meeting with Danar, and she hadn't heard a word. He had said he needed to act fast. *Was there a problem? Did he run into some sort of legal snag or other complication? Was he having difficulty getting the cooperation and verification he needed from various sources?*

Gina was tempted to call his office, but Al Coletti, while expressing his understanding of her impatience, invoked the wisdom of age and convinced her it would be counterproductive to pester the people in Danar's office. Although Gina didn't see it as pestering or nagging, but simply inquiring, she followed his advice.

She was standing at the window when the wall phone rang. It was the first call they had received since coming to the lodge. Gina glanced at her father, and then ran for the phone. "Hello?"

It was a representative from Danar's organization. "Hello, Ms. Coletti?"

"Yes, this is she."

"Ms. Coletti, Mr. Danar wanted me to call and tell you to tune in at six o'clock this evening to one of the all-news stations, CNN, MSNBC, or Fox News."

"Did he say why?"

"No, but he was emphatic that I give you the message, so please watch."

"Okay, thank you. We will."

At six o'clock, Gina and Al sat in front of the TV tuned

to CNN. Lou Dobbs was opening the broadcast with the headlines of the day and his usual tirade on illegal immigration and the plight of the middle class. The two watched and wondered what exactly they were waiting for. Suddenly, across the screen appeared: BREAKING NEWS. The screen was split to show Freiz's headquarters and the New England Clinic for Cardiac Care. Strategically placed TV cameras showed law enforcement officers coming out of each building carrying what appeared to be boxes of records of one type or another. Two policemen escorted by an agent from the Food and Drug Administration wheeled out a refrigerator from the clinic.

Gina and Al sat on the edge of their chairs with their mouths agape.

A reporter at the scene gave commentary: "At exactly six o'clock this evening local, state, and federal law enforcement officials, acting on information regarding alleged illegal activity, and armed with search warrants, simultaneously entered the offices of Freiz Corporation and the New England Clinic for Cardiac Care. As you can see behind me, corporate files and clinic records and other potential evidence are being removed by authorities. Speaking with the condition of anonymity, sources tell CNN the investigation started with information provided to consumer advocate Alfred Danar by a former employee of the clinic. Requests for a response from both Freiz and the clinic have been denied. We will keep you updated on this dramatic story as it unfolds and new information is received. A joint press conference will be held by all of the agencies involved at seven o'clock tonight. We will bring you that live. Stay tuned."

Gina jumped off the chair, and gave her father a high-five. Al walked to the fully stocked wet bar and poured them each a glass of cognac. After touching glasses, Al raised his and said, "To my gallant daughter."

Gina smiled. "And to David," she said raising her glass again. After taking another sip, she raised her glass once more. "And, to Michael and Doctor Bauer."

"Here, here," Al replied.

They sat and sipped their cognac while reminiscing about her childhood. They talked about Gina's mother, Al's loving wife, the woman they both so terribly missed. Gina told Al of the guilt she carried all those years pertaining to the night she left in anger—the night he had his heart attack. But she was interrupted by Al's warm embrace.

"Sweetheart, it wasn't your fault. I was a heart attack waiting to happen." They talked for nearly an hour before Al decided to retire for the evening.

Gina walked over to the large stone fireplace whose fluttering flames cast life-like shadows that seemed to command a presence of their own. Tears ran down her cheeks and over her smile as she thought of David and Michael and how the giant shadows these men cast had enabled her to initiate an investigation with the potential to topple a titan of corporate America, as well as the largest clinic for cardiac care. She sipped the last of her cognac, and turned off the gas. As Gina watched the flames retreat and burn out, she couldn't help but think of how the lives of both her lover and her close friend had been snuffed out at their brightest moment. *What a waste. So many lives lost and changed—and all for the almighty dollar.*

AUTHOR'S NOTE

ALTHOUGH *The Chosen Few* is a work of fiction, the premise for the plot was derived from a series of actual events that occurred decades ago.

In 1979, Valerio Dagnoli, a middle-aged man from the mountain village of Limone sul Garda in the Italian Lakes Region, was diagnosed with very high triglycerides (fat in the blood). He also possessed low levels of high-density lipoprotein or HDL, commonly referred to as the good cholesterol. Because of these two risk factors, Mr. Dagnoli was sent to the University of Milan's Lipid Center for further testing.

What doctors discovered confounded them. Although Dagnoli had high triglyceride levels and low levels of HDL, his arteries were clear—totally free from any signs of coronary artery disease. It was exactly opposite of the expected.

Researchers decided to test the entire population of the

village. Of the one thousand inhabitants tested, forty individuals had the same blood anomaly.

Through birth records maintained by the local church, it was discovered that these forty people had common ancestors dating back to 1780. All of the ancestors lived to a ripe old age, many reaching the century mark.

Further research led to the discovery that all forty individuals had a genetic mutation in the gene that makes a protein called apo A-1. This protein, apo A-1, becomes part of the HDL cholesterol particle. It is now referred to as apo A-1 Milano.

In simple terms, this mutant gene supercharged the HDL, enabling the small amount of HDL to keep their arteries plaque free.

The apo A-1 gene was synthesized by biochemist Doctor Roger Newton at Esperion Therapeutics. Doctor P.K. Shah and his colleagues at Cedars-Sinai Medical Center conducted further tests. The tests were conducted on laboratory animals that were fed a high cholesterol diet.

Doctor Shah's tests proved that after five weeks of injections, not only had the progression of plaque buildup been halted, but existing plaque began to regress. In one test, a single, large dose of apo A-1 Milano removed cholesterol and reduced inflammation within 48 hours.

Based on the body of evidence provided by this study, and others conducted by Doctor Cesare Sitori in Milan, Esperion Therapeutics initiated human trials. The results were nothing short of amazing. Tests showed existing plaque was substantially reduced. The Cleveland Clinic, under the direction of Doctor Steven E. Nissen, conducted additional tests yielding similar results. Nissen was surprised by the results. "It is unprecedented. Nobody has this kind of plaque regression. It really is an epiphany."

The drug apo A-1 Milano has been dubbed, 'Roto-rooter for the arteries,' 'Arterial Drano,' and 'The Magic Bullet.'

In 2003, Esperion Therapeutics was purchased by Pfizer, Incorporated, the world's largest pharmaceutical company, and maker of the most popular statin drug, Lipitor, with annual sales exceeding thirteen billion dollars.

Currently, several drug makers are working on dozens of new medications to treat coronary artery disease. Hopefully, one will fulfill the promise of the fictitious Sicilia Gene. The millions of people who suffer from cardiovascular disease, their families, and loved ones deserve no less.

Sources: U.S. Department of Energy Research News, Office of Science, May 2002; Journal of the American Medical Association, Nov. 3, 2003; Dr. Steven Nissen, The Cleveland Clinic; Cedars-Sinai Heart Center.

ABOUT THE AUTHOR

AUTHOR Joseph DiLalla worked in the communications industry for thirty-three years, the last fifteen years of which were as vice president of a local union of The Communications Workers of America. His primary responsibilities were as chairman of the grievance and arbitration procedures and collective bargaining. This experience also afforded him the opportunity to work on political campaigns at every level of government. Beyond writing articles for the locals' newsletter, his busy career left little time to devote to his passion—writing. He retired from his advocacy and now writes full time. His first novel, *Bloodlines*, was published in October 2006. He resides in Naples, Florida, where he is working on his third novel.

ABOUT THE AUTHOR

AUTHOR Roy Eaton, a graduate of New York Military Academy, earned a Bachelor of Science degree from Pennsylvania Military College, an M.A.T. from Connecticut College, and a commission in the U.S. Army Reserve Officers Corps. Roy taught mathematics and wrestling at St. Bernard High School in Uncasville, Connecticut, and was recently inducted into their Athletic Hall of Fame. He has been included in the publication "Who's Who Among America's Teachers," and was elected by his faculty to the school's Board of Trustees. He was selected as the first team coach by the Connecticut Freestyle Wrestling Federation, and his high school team has been cited by the state's Governor and Legislature for their outstanding performance. In June of 2006, at the National Sports Achievement Dinner held on Marco Island, Eaton was awarded the lifetime achievement award in wrestling, and in June of 2007, he delivered the commencement address at New York Military Academy. Eaton's recently published autobiography, *Soldier Boy*, has been endorsed by Donald J. Trump.